After her marriage ends in betrayal, Eleanora Howard finds herself struggling to navigate the dating scene as a thirty-one-year-old divorcee. But feeling undesirable, and living alone in the house she once shared with her ex, is hardly the recipe for finding new love—until she meets Rob. He's just the kind of charming, old-fashioned guy she needs—but he's also eager for intimacy…

After serving in the Air Force and getting a well-paid civilian career, Rob Vanderhoff planned to settle down with the right woman and raise a family. But at thirty-six, he's still single and searching—until he meets Eleanora. She's everything he wants. All he has to do is draw her out of her shell. Soon he's taking her on high school-style dates, fanning the flames of her desire—and helping Nora re-discover the sexy, adventurous woman they both know she really is…

Visit us at www.kensingtonbooks.com

Books by M.Q. Barber

Neighborly Affection Series
Playing the Game, Book One
Crossing the Lines, Book Two
Healing the Wounds, Book Three
Becoming His Master, Book Four

Her Shirtless Gentleman

Published by Kensington Publishing Corporation

Her Shirtless Gentleman

M.Q. Barber

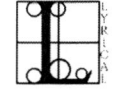

LYRICAL PRESS
Kensington Publishing Corp.
www.kensingtonbooks.com

Lyrical Press books are published by
Kensington Publishing Corp. 119 West 40th Street New York, NY 10018

All Kensington titles, imprints, and distributed lines are available at special quantity discounts for bulk purchases for sales promotion, premiums, fund-raising, and educational or institutional use.

Special book excerpts or customized printings can also be created to fit specific needs. For details, write or phone the office of the Kensington Special Sales Manager:
Kensington Publishing Corp.
119 West 40th Street
New York, NY 10018
Attn. Special Sales Department. Phone: 1-800-221-2647.

First Electronic Edition: August 2015
eISBN-13: 978-1-61650-703-9
eISBN-10: 1-61650-703-9

First Print Edition: August 2015
ISBN-13: 978-1-60183-546-8
ISBN-10: 1-60183-546-9

Printed in the United States of America

Chapter 1

Dead last. Again.

The four of them went out after work every Friday, and every Friday Eleanora sat and smiled while guys bought drinks for Sharilyn. Hit the dance floor with Amber. Chatted up Chelsea's breasts.

Even the sidekicks—wingmen, whatever guys called themselves—refused to give her a second glance. She couldn't blame their lack of interest on the ring. She'd taken off the meaningless metal circle before the divorce had been finalized.

But to the endless crowd of broad-smile bar-hoppers, she rated five seconds of stilted conversation between texting or checking sports scores or playing Angry Birds. The highlight of four hours of boredom. Single life almost matched the worst tedium of married life.

That's what she got for saddling herself with David and galloping through her twenties with his ring on her finger. He'd been her first. Her only.

Now she performed rotating roles as babysitter, chaperone, and charity case. She didn't belong at a too-small table packed alongside tight-skinned and perky-breasted girls who flashed their IDs with the affected nonchalance of twenty-two-year-olds.

She downed the final sip of her third beer of the night. She didn't dare hop in her car and head home yet. Given her luck, she'd end up pulled over and facing a drunk-driving charge. David would love any excuse to point out her idiocy. Hiring a lawyer without him finding out would be impossible in this town. She'd never live down the humiliation.

"—and it's deep, too."

Chelsea laughed along with what's-his-name. Dog Collar Dude. Not attractive, but he had deep pockets. Probably thought he'd be getting in deep with Chelsea tonight, payment in exchange for buying round after round of drinks. God knew he hadn't taken his eyes off her breasts.

Laughter came dangerously close to making Chelsea spill out of her silky, sleeveless v-cut. Eleanora's closet didn't hold a shirt anywhere near so revealing. Boring and staid, as much an accountant in her fashion picks as in her career choices. And in her bedroom habits.

She tilted her brown bottle. All gone. No magical extra swallows remained to knock David's voice from her head.

"Whoa." An unknown quantity stumbled to a halt beside her chair. "Your friend's hot."

Fantastic. The newest Mr. Drunk-and-Horny leaned in close and drenched her nose with the scent of teen body spray. Probably the same disgusting brand he'd used in high school. Probably lived in the same bedroom, too.

"Oh? Which one?" She'd come to this lousy bar with three friends—well, acquaintances—and he didn't have a chance with any of them.

The skinny blond kid blinked as he scanned their table. Jesus. He looked barely old enough to buy the three beers he held, and she'd celebrated thirty-one six months ago.

Sooner or later she'd have to inform her coworkers she wasn't going out with them anymore. They were twenty-four, twenty-five, and poaching college boys was fine for them. For her, the whole scene smacked of desperation. Three months of this bullshit added up to quite enough.

"Uh, all of 'em?" He presented a dopey smile.

"Damn, Ellie. Picking 'em young tonight, aren't you?" Sharilyn swung her martini glass upward, sloshing vodka over the rim. "Good for you."

"Yeah, no, I'm not—"

The kid wobbled into her chair. "I don't feel—"

Vomit splattered her shoulder and rolled down her chest. Ugh. Should've dodged faster. She shoved him back.

Stumbling over his own feet, he landed on his ass, spilled his three beers all over himself, and retched. The acrid stench of puke replaced the flood of body spray in her nose. A toss-up, really.

She laughed over the chorus of oh-my-gods from the rest of the table. At least the night wasn't boring anymore.

* * * *

"Oh, fuck."

Rob swallowed the last of his beer. Lucas had better hurry up with the refills. "What now?"

They'd hit a handful of bars already. Brian had found trouble with every damned one. With Lucas staying at his place for the summer, he'd been playing mother hen for the last three weeks.

"I think my baby brother's puking his guts out."

"Take him home. Happy beer-buying birthday and all, but he's done for the night." He'd celebrated his own twenty-first on base with a pack of fellow tech geeks. Good guys, including Brian. How had fifteen years gone by so fast? "Pour him into bed."

"Yeah." Brian grimaced. "Soon as I figure out what to say to the woman with puke running down her shirt."

"Try an apology." He shoved his chair back and stood, scanning the tables for Lucas's god-awful sea-green pullover. "Where is he?"

He spotted the vomit-splattered woman about the same time Brian answered, "Your four o'clock."

Shit. Lucas had spewed at a full table, and he couldn't get eyes on him. Man down. Threat?

No punches thrown, so far as he could tell. A circle of horrified and disgusted faces clustered to one side, their owners staring at the floor. One guy held his phone up. On the far side of the table sat a laughing woman with a beautiful smile and a stained shirt. Damn. He hadn't taken a woman home in almost four months, and Lucas had party-fouled the first to catch his eye. "C'mon, let's go rescue Lucas and get out of here."

Looked like tonight wouldn't be the night to break his sexless streak.

* * * *

"Oh my God, Ellie, seriously, how can you laugh about this?" Light glinted off glitter-speckled fingernails. Amber pushed back from the table. "Yuck. Danny, take me dancing." She dragged her boy of the night away with a theatrical flounce.

"You do kinda reek, Ellie." Sharilyn wrinkled her nose. "Not your fault, but eww."

Waving in front of her face, Chelsea nodded.

Dog Collar Dude flipped through his phone. "Fuck, I missed the kid's first splash. You think he could upchuck again? The visual'd make the video so much better."

Eleanora glanced down with care. The regurgitated beer soaking into her shirt quickly lost its amusement value. The kid had added a puddle beside her chair. He barked out coughs like a hoarse dog.

"No, I don't think he's got anything else in his stomach." She poked his knee with her foot. "Kid? You all right? You got somebody we can call for you?"

No answer, unless she counted more retching. Between the sound and the smell, her stomach started to turn.

A second man with the same pale hair as the first dropped to the floor beside the kid and laid a hand on his back. "Shit, Lucas, I thought you might've passed out."

"Are you all right, miss?"

Sex on a stick. Thick thighs encased in denim inches from her eyes. She launched her head back and her chin skyward. Eyes up. Ohhh, bad idea. The stranger loomed over her with his strong jaw and his short, dark hair and his no-nonsense eyes.

"No, of course you aren't." His aborted hand movement stopped short of her shoulder. "Ugh, he did a number on your shirt. Let me give you a hand."

He slipped around the other side of her seat. Cupping her elbow in one hand and pressing against her back with the other, he coaxed her to her feet. Large hands. Warm hands.

Her body jangled like a change jar spilling on tile.

"Look, he's really sorry, or he will be when he's sober." The stranger glanced down, shaking his head. "He's twenty-one today."

She nodded. The blond guy picked the younger one off the floor. First legal drinking day. Okay. She filed the data under *don't care* and waited for details about Mr. Tall, Dark and Handsome.

"You can't wear that home."

Her chest had snared more attention in the last five minutes than in three months of flaunting herself at bars. She'd found the secret of dating. When introversion and modest assets failed, distress attracted the good guys. Not how she'd hoped to find someone.

The man with large hands squeezed and let her go. Peeling off his shirt, he revealed a to-die-for body. Solid, toned muscles from top to bottom. Too bad his jeans came almost to his waist. Denim blocked the enticing slope heading into his pants. God, David had never reached such nonchalant bare-chested perfection.

Her rescuer held out his shirt and gestured her toward the back of the bar. "Here, let me give you mine for tonight."

No fucking way. This guy couldn't be for real. She stumbled over her chair.

He steadied her with a quick hand on her clean shoulder.

"Thanks." Oh, hallelujah. She'd started thinking she'd never find her voice. "That's, umm, I appreciate it."

"Least I can do, miss." He guided her in front of him past the line for the ladies' room and stopped at the door.

"Yo, man, you gotta put your shirt on." A beefy guy in a black shirt with the bar's logo over his chest held out an arm. "Carrying it don't count. You can't be shirtless, not in here."

She disagreed with strenuous, silent objections. Her gentleman deserved to go shirtless wherever he liked.

"You wanna run around half-naked, you gotta head down the street to the Lazy Eight."

Making that man put his shirt back on would be a crime. Her skin heated at the slow slide of excitement between her legs. Thirty minutes of fantasizing and foreplay with David left her dry as a desert compared to three minutes of standing next to Shirtless Gentleman. The longer she lingered in his orbit, the harder her lungs worked to serve up oxygen.

Lust walloped her with embarrassing swiftness. She lacked the looks and flirty attitude to pull a guy without adding a vomit-soaked shell to the mix. Riding off into the sunset with Shirtless Gentleman glinted so far out of the picture the location didn't exist on her map.

"Yeah, I get that." Shirtless Gentleman raised a hand. "You can toss me out in a minute. Right now, this pretty girl's got someone else's puke on her clothes, and I'm going to make sure she's safe while she's changing."

Gripping his shirt, she ducked into the ladies' room past the line of pissed-off, well-beyond-buzzed women. Shirtless Gentleman's presence seemed to deflect any cursing about cutting the line.

"No, ma'am," he rumbled over the din of music and chatter. "I don't wax and you may not touch."

Ma'am. Polite. Mannered.

She stuffed her shirt in the trash and grabbed a handful of paper towels.

Fit. Chivalrous.

The damp paper towels scraped her neck under her hardy scrubbing. At least the kid hadn't destroyed her bra. The practical white soft-cup would serve.

Was Shirtless Gentleman military?

Tucking in the shirt didn't give her the fitted look it had given him, but she managed to minimize her resemblance to a child swimming in her father's clothes. Squinting hard almost made the outfit look intentional. A style choice to wear a black wide-neck tee with exposed white bra straps.

Yeah, almost.

She slipped into the hall, her skin electric. His bare chest greeted her from two feet away, his arms crossed and his feet planted in a wide, easy stance. A few hoots and drunken catcalls rose from the women waiting in line.

Shoving aside her embarrassment, she tipped her head back and met his eyes. "Thank you."

His attention stayed centered on her. The unsmiling bulk of a man sported solid pecs and a penetrating stare.

"Again." She fumbled for a classy conversation starter. "Your shirt's really soft."

Your shirt's really soft. What the fuck. Her brains had gone soft. Complete mush. Mashed potatoes held the edge in outthinking her.

His mouth twitched. "Must match your skin."

"Sorry?" She'd heard him wrong. No way had he complimented her skin. Men didn't say those things to her. "I didn't catch that."

He shook his head and dropped his arms. "Shirt looks better on you than it ever did on me, miss. Let me walk you back."

Turning, he swept his hand behind her and landed with a light touch. Five points of pressure, a half circle of fingertips keeping in contact as they returned to the table. More than a few whistles followed them.

"It doesn't bother you? Being"—she waved at the crowded tables—"stared at? Graded? Like you're on display?"

Stupid question. Of course, the attention wouldn't bother him. He had cool, calm confidence perfected. Anyone with his godlike body would want to show off.

"I got over any fear of public grading in basic training."

Military. Nailed it.

Not yet, you haven't.

Her face flamed.

"A'course, the opinions of a bunch of yappy drunks aren't worth all that much, positive or not." Shrugging, he tapped her back. "Being on display for the one woman who matters, well now, that's a whole other thing. That'll make a man nervous, sure enough, however cool he plays it."

Great. He had a woman who mattered. Smooth, too, about sliding the revelation into the conversation. No ring, but an empty finger didn't mean much these days.

"I think you've got cool down." Months of going out with the girls from work had taught her how to categorize the bar crowd. The unholy chaos broke into three groups, all ring-free, with the singular difference whether they were ring-free but committed, ring-free and open or cheating, or ring-free and actually unattached. Limiting herself to the third group hadn't done her any favors. "I hope your woman who matters sees through the facade and tells you what a great catch she's made."

He paused his tapping. “Oh, I don’t—”

“Woo, I didn’t know you were that kind of girl.” Sharilyn slapped her hand on the table. “Swapping clothes in a stall?” Her nosy, flamboyant attitude owed nothing to the drinks she’d downed. She came by her perky personality naturally. “What else did he get on you, Ellie?”

Ugh. She smiled through her irritation. Eleanora was bad enough, thanks to her mother’s obsession with family history. Every girl wanted to be named for the great-grandmother she’d never met.

Shortening her name to Ellie might as well transform her into a cow. Get along now, Bessie, Daisy, Ellie.

Sharilyn made her sound like a cow giving the milk away for free with a man she’d met ten minutes ago.

“I’m—we weren’t—”

* * * *

Christ. Her little friend produced as much bile as Lucas had, and the bitter sting seemed to hit her harder. The woman who’d laughed over a ruined shirt faced her sniping girlfriend with hunched shoulders, stammering a response somewhere roundabout her shoes.

“I’ll overlook that because you’re young and drunk, but you might wanna think on what you’re saying about your friend.” He’d dropped into his gruff tone, a favorite for his square-your-shit speech. A touch of gravel worked great for rattling the nerves.

The bile-producer dropped her mouth open, amazingly without the rim of a drink glass attached. The modest beauty wearing his shirt lifted her head.

“I’m not the sort of man to take a beautiful woman in a bar bathroom for an audience.” Not on the first date, at least, and not unless he’d be fulfilling a fantasy for her. “And she seems like a fine lady who deserves a better class of friends.”

“Did he just—who the hell are you to say what—”

Lordy, Miss Martini could screech. The woman beside him stood silent, watching him with narrowed eyes. Not angry, so far as he could tell. Assessing, like she’d spotted something new. Good. She might spare more than a thought for something new, if he got the chance to correct her misunderstanding about his relationship status.

“Shar, be chill.” The curvy blonde beside the screecher leaned forward.

He averted his eyes from her gaping shirt. His daddy’d taught him to be polite. Daddy’d also taught his sisters to have more respect for themselves than these girls possessed.

"Hey, rescue dude, your buddy took the spew monkey outside for some air or whatever. Said they'd wait for you out there."

Fuck. He'd offered to drive tonight so Brian could get smashed with his brother.

"Right. Thanks for the message." He turned to the woman in his shirt, torn between handing her down to her chair the way a gentleman ought to and asking if she'd care to go for a drive.

He should've bought the extended cab. Nothing romantic about sitting four across in the pickup with a boy sick as a dog hanging his head out the window.

Of course, he'd have the lovely lady beside him, her thigh pressed alongside his. Maybe the tickle of her honey brown hair on his shoulder. His cock twitched, eager as a teenager's for a shot at action.

"I'll walk you out," she blurted. "In case the staff gives you any more trouble. About the shirt, I mean."

Holy hell. He might have a better-than-nothing chance of getting her number yet. "My heroine. That's right kind of you, miss."

She linked her arm around his, sweet as you please, and tugged him away from the table.

"Yeah!" Stemware drained, martini girl slung the empty glass with loud, obnoxious, sloppy encouragement. "You're halfway there, girl."

At sixteen, he'd begged every night in his dreams for that type of rowdy girl. At thirty-six, he had other ideas.

"Take him out and ride him home, Ellie." The girl's shout followed them. "You deserve it!"

The one who mattered tightened her hand around his arm, and her steps quickened. She'd already been taking the better part of two to his one. Five-five, he estimated.

The top of her head came to his lips. The perfect height for tucking under his chin or dropping a kiss on. Or picking up and pressing to a wall to deliver a real kiss. Get those curvy legs wrapped around his hips.

He cleared his throat in a vain bid to distract his cock. "So your name's Ellie?"

She scrunched her nose. Cute, but not a happy scrunch. "It's Eleanora, actually."

Hell, he had experience with disliking his name. Points in common melted ice faster than taking a chisel to the deep freeze.

"Eleanora." Nodding, he held open the door. A classy name. Old-fashioned. No wonder she didn't appreciate her friends' butchery.

The July heat slapped his face. Same as the inside of the bar, with all its sweaty bodies, but with added humidity.

Eleanora released his arm.

Loathe to let her slip away so soon, he extended his hand.

"I'm Rob." Leaning close, he kept her hand clasped in his. "My mama named me Robin, but don't be letting that get around, all right? It's another one of those things that'll make a man nervous."

Had as a boy, more like. Calling him Robin constituted grounds for schoolyard fights. Though he damn well wouldn't share how the guys in basic had settled on Sherwood, or that Brian had joked later his nickname ought to be "Sure Wood" for the string of ladies he'd taken to bed.

"You don't have anything to be nervous about." Her smile held a trembling hint of shyness at the corners. "I know how to keep my lips sealed."

He hoped not. It'd be a crying shame not to taste her sweetness. "Good to know." He spotted Brian over her shoulder, leaning against the truck with a shit-eating grin. "Lucas will pay for the damage when he sobers up. You can text me the cost."

"Oh—that's—he doesn't have to."

He resisted the urge to drop his head and kiss away her frown.

"But, I should probably get your number anyway." Blinking like she'd startled herself, she pulled her hand free and dug in her pocket. "So I can return your shirt."

He didn't give a damn about the lost shirt, but he rattled off his number when she produced her phone. A smidge skittish, a mite shy, and hanging with a crowd unsuited to her reserve. His Eleanora must've ended a long-term relationship not so long ago. She didn't seem keen to hop on a rebound train.

Good. Neither was he. Take things slow, help her build up her dating confidence, and with any luck she'd see the potential in him he saw in her.

He walked her to her car, said a polite goodnight, and closed the door for her. Crossing the lot back to his truck, he waved off Brian's laugh.

"Lost your shirt to the newest Maid Marian, eh, Sherwood?" Brian opened the passenger door and swung into the middle seat, leaving the window for a green-around-the-gills Lucas. "Hope you got a little something in return."

Lucas groaned as he hoisted himself up. "Man, tell me I didn't puke all over that MILF."

Rob turned over the engine. Christ. Drunk or not, twenty-one-year-olds were blind stupid about women. Anyone past twenty-five probably registered ancient-to-prehistoric on the Lucas scale.

"Sorry, man, you did, and I didn't." The chance for something more, maybe, if she—

His phone sounded with a text alert. Yanking the digital leash from his back pocket, he jammed his arm against the seat.

The message originated from a caller unknown to his address book.

Just checking. I hear people give out fake numbers sometimes, and I'd hate to leave my shirtless gentleman without his shirt for long.

Well now. That was promising. Bolder in text than in person, was she?

He typed a quick response.

Brian craned his neck. "Still got nothing?"

Lousy snoop. He threw an elbow at Brian's ribs and tucked his phone away. "Maybe a little something."

* * * *

The living room curtains glowed cheery yellow as Eleanora pulled her secondhand Civic into the driveway a skosh after eleven. The security timer would've shut off the light between eleven-thirty and midnight if she hadn't made it home.

One of the many things she'd gotten accustomed to remembering since David had moved out. A woman living alone couldn't be too careful.

Of course, in the two years since their trial separation started and the three months since they'd finally signed the damned papers, she'd never not come home for the night. And she still hadn't brought anyone with her.

Tonight, though. "Temptation, thy name is Rob."

The dashboard didn't reply.

She parked in the garage and navigated the dark kitchen with ease. Five years since they'd bought the place by the grace of a falling housing market and down payment help from David's parents. Now she wished he'd taken the house in the settlement or they'd sold the rotten thing. Living here entombed her in a mausoleum of their dead marriage.

She hadn't been able to make herself sleep in the master bedroom, not one more night after David had left. Flipping the mattress hadn't helped. Dousing it and the sheets with lawn mower fuel had brought by a crew of very polite volunteer firefighters in their wailing truck. They'd explained the open burning ordinances while she'd raged and sobbed beside the mound of flames in the backyard.

The spare bedroom she'd taken for her own bore the neutral tones of an inoffensive motel. Off-white rug, off-white walls, dainty floral wallpaper border near the ceiling. No reason for a makeover—no one else saw the place. No money, either. The plain double bed had been intended for family visits, the empty room across the hall for a nursery someday. Scant chance of children now, when she spent her Friday nights in pathetic attempts to attract attention at student-heavy bars.

Not like she had much choice. David's hometown didn't contain all that many options. Cruising the classier places ran the risk of encountering David's legal buddies. The dives held the dregs of boozehounds, the guys her age and older who hadn't grown out of college binge-drinking weekends and never would. If she stopped tagging along with Chelsea and the girls at the places they preferred to shop for men, she'd be going alone. Hell no.

Jeans shucked and tossed aside, she slipped her bra out from under her borrowed shirt. She shambled into the bathroom to brush her teeth and chug a glass of water. Beer mouth, that cottony, swollen tongue and stale taste, wasn't a joy to wake to.

Not like Rob would be. His tongue, in the morning, on her—

Choking, she spat toothpaste into the sink.

Thirty-one had to be too young for hot flashes.

She abbreviated her bedtime routine and scurried to the thermostat. Boosting the air conditioning would end this foolish heat chasing her. Life would return to normal by morning. The air kicked on. She sprawled under the thin top sheet, snug in his t-shirt and her panties.

She'd been so unlike herself at the bar. Asking Shirtless Gentleman for his number. Calling him by that name in her text message. She hadn't dated since college. Ten years. David had walked into her life, and she'd been head over heels.

Not like tonight. With David, she'd experienced a girlish fluttering in her stomach. With Rob, the quaking in her body danced closer to…heels over head?

Dragging the sheet over her face, she groaned. Hiding from a nonexistent audience solved nothing. She flung the sheet back.

Spreading her legs failed to ease the ache. Closing them triggered the dim memory of adolescent explorations. Back when she'd still listened to her own body and chased pleasure by herself, for herself. Before David's wounded act the one time he'd walked in on her, and oh, how she'd believed him.

"Is this where your love goes, Eleanora? To yourself? I give you everything you need, and you don't want it. Not the jewelry or the lace negligees or those perfumed bath scents to make you feel like the wife you're supposed to be." Sagging to the bed, he sold his performance with his bowed head and his lips against the ring on his left hand. "You're betraying our marriage vows, touching yourself when you should be touching me. No wonder our bed is so cold."

She'd stopped. A lifetime ago. Those pleasures belonged to them as a couple. Going after pleasure herself was no better than trawling bars for strangers to excite her. David said so, and he only wanted the best for her because he loved her.

Lies. Every word from his mouth, a lie.

Hand drifting across her belly, she rubbed the soft, soothing cotton. Such an undemanding cloth, accepting her strokes without quibbling over speed or direction.

Rob's dark brown hair might be soft. She'd have to touch to find out. As she dragged his shirt up, the bottom roughed her fingertips. Maybe his super-short hair would be more like the hem, all bristle-brush and tingly.

He had a handsome face. Kind, with quiet strength and gold-flecked hazel eyes that had never seemed to leave her. Whenever she'd looked at him, he'd been looking back at her.

She dipped her fingers inside her panties and yanked them back. Wetness, thick and slippery. Her rare brushes with desire since David's reprimand had always produced far less evidence. Even headed down the road to divorce, she'd obeyed his edict. In the months since they'd signed the papers, her furtive, aborted attempts ended in numbness or sobbing—rewards not worth the hassle.

Burying her face in her shoulder, she breathed in an earthy warmth, the freshness of a garden in spring as the spade turned over the old soil and exposed the new. Rob's scent. So unfamiliar, untainted by the rank stench of fail-sweat and unshed tears. A cocoon rather than a grave. Snuggly and humid and sparking with life, warming under—her fingers. Moving with purpose between her legs. He hadn't handed over his shirt for this.

But he'd never know how she fisted his shirt in one hand and succumbed to her body's compulsion with the other. She'd launder the cozy cotton before she gave his shirt back to him. Another meeting, returning his unexpected generosity, would present a second chance to appreciate his strong grip. To imagine more places he might lay his hands.

Squeezing her eyes shut, she blocked out the bland bedroom where she lived like a guest in her own home. This body belonged to her. The wetness, hers. The spreading heat, hers. The musk mingling with Rob's earthy embrace, hers. She pushed herself faster, her fingers controlling the knots tightening her muscles, making them dance and shake from one central point. When her breath stuttered, his voice delivered the words of his reply to her text.

I'd rather see my shirt go home with you than me.

And I promise you there won't be anything fake between us.

—Your Shirtless Gentleman

Pleasure shot through her in shuddering waves. God, how had she forgotten the thrill of this peak and the stealthy contentment creeping in after? Embarrassed and giddy, she wiped her fingers on the bottom of his shirt.

G'night, Rob.

* * * *

He dropped Brian and a healthier-looking Lucas at Brian's apartment with the promise to meet them Saturday afternoon for the game. "Swear you'll keep Lucas outta the beer cooler. He throws up while tagging a runner out at second, and we'll have a brawl instead of a ballgame."

"Yeah, yeah." Brian flipped him a friendly bird. "Go meet up with your damsel in distress. Don't get so much action that you're sluggish running the bases tomorrow."

No chance of that.

He pointed the truck for home and cruised on autopilot, every turn one he'd made a thousand times before. Sometimes with a woman, but less and less so in the last year.

One place he and Brian disagreed. They'd marked the same number of years on the planet, but Brian wasn't looking to settle down and probably never would. He lived for short-term romance. Rob craved the family life.

He'd bought this old farmhouse five years ago with the hope of having a wife and a toddler or two to fill the place by now. The sort of family he'd grown up in, with laughing siblings and loving folks and room to run. Between his older brother and his two baby sisters, his folks had eight grandkids to spoil already.

So far, he had a yard to mow and an upstairs full of empty rooms.

The shine wore off every relationship. The girls crawling the bars dreamt of luxurious suburban mansions or penthouse apartments in distant cities. Their ambition didn't extend farther than a man's wallet. Fun for a night or three, but not interested in or interesting enough for more.

Desire ate at him for a real woman, one with the ability to stand on her own two feet. One who chose to lean on him when he made her weak in the knees. One worth protecting and cherishing for the rest of his life.

One like the woman at the bar tonight.

Eleanora.

Made of stern stuff. Able to laugh off a disaster. Compassionate, too—covered in sick up and still asking Lucas if he needed help. Fuck, she had good mom instincts, and humor, and brains, and blue-gray eyes stirring as a summer storm and honey brown hair robust as dark lager. He prayed for the opportunity to drink deep.

Standing at the kitchen sink downing a glass of ice water to stave off dehydration, he unzipped his fly and eased the pressure on his hardening cock. He set the glass down and pulled himself free, hissing at the chill of condensation from his fingertips. Mixed with his heated thoughts, the slick pleasure promised steam.

Out the window, beyond the empty clothesline, the tall grass waved in the moonlight. The lone bur oak in the lawn proper waited with leafy arms for a tree house. He had plans aplenty. What he lacked was the right woman to share them.

"How about it, honey girl?"

Her shy smile mesmerized him. Fuck, the sight of her in his shirt. He stroked his cock with a loose grip. He'd claimed her in front of the whole bar tonight, whether she'd recognized the move or not. Scoped out his target and draped his shirt over her in a warning to any idiot who thought he had a shot.

He stretched his jaw, tension building at the idea of any other laying a hand on her.

She was the one.

His mind and body united in that truth. His thoughts on her ran in directions no other woman had matched. Oh sure enough, he wanted her in his bed. Wished he'd be seeing her still in his shirt in the morning as she rolled on top of him and he teased the fabric off to feast on her flesh.

His grip tightened. His motion quickened. Icy chill forgotten, he imagined her soft heat cradled him.

But he wanted her in the yard, too. Hanging sheets on the line together and dancing between them. Chasing her through the billowing fabric and bringing her to the grass. Fingers fumbling at buttons and zippers, her laughter turning to moans that soared on the wind the half-mile to the neighbors' place.

"That's right, let the whole world know I'm loving you. Deep as I can go." He splayed his left hand on the counter, grunting at the rush pooling in his balls. "Gonna make you mine. My Nora."

Tension and relief climbed up his cock and sprayed the window over the sink, blurring his vision with milky white streaks. Bedsheets, waving in the wind.

Sleep tight, honey girl.

Chapter 2

Monday morning. Eleanora's favorite point in the week, the point farthest from the struggle to fill up the long, lonely weekend hours.

I can't believe you.

Her ex-husband seemed determined to ruin her mood with annoying texts.

What the hell were you thinking?

She shoved her phone beyond the mess of paperwork cluttering her desk.

Answer me, Eleanora. Eight blocks away, in his holier-than-thou office, he probably bent the nearest ear with a martyr's tirade.

Her phone buzzed a fourth time.

With her coffee mug emptied and a two-finger forehead massage doing jack-all for the growing pressure behind her eyes, she snatched her phone off her desk.

Shirtless Gentleman here. I'm having this crazy problem where my stomach growls and I can't seem to stop it. Any chance you know a cure?

Mr. Friday Night. The thrill zipped down to her toes, a high stronger than caffeine. Shit, and she'd almost ignored him. He deserved a personalized chime.

Have you tried lunch? It's nearly noon.

Damn. Too standoffish. She should've wandered over to the teller counter and asked Chelsea what to say. No customers in line except at the ATM. Idiots, waiting outside in the heat for a machine to spit money when they could walk inside and get air-conditioned teller service in under a minute. Two tellers, no waiting.

What's this thing you call "lunch"? I need a personal guide. Are you available?

The divorce papers and the ring she'd yanked off her finger months ago declared her on the market. But the girls swore by the whole playing hard-to-get thing. She'd forgotten how many times they insisted she had to say no before she could say yes. Unless their standards didn't apply until after the first date.

Ugh. She'd been married too long. Singlehood came with an exhausting, bizarre web of rules. So much confusing nonsense required a spreadsheet to track.

Time to ask Chelsea and Sharilyn for advice. She pushed back her chair, stood, and stretched. Hunched over projections for a consignment shop expansion loan for the last hour, she'd spawned a kink in her back. Her stomach growled.

Yes.

Oh God. Impulsive fingers. Why didn't phones include an un-send button? Lunch with a sexy stranger outstripped her dating readiness level.

New text chime. Too late. He'd suggested an upscale place far from the bank. No clue how he made his living, but her job didn't accommodate whole afternoons off. She countered with the café down the street. Jackpot.

She locked out her desktop and dropped her phone in her purse. "Hey, Chelsea, I'm heading out to grab lunch." The loan department would be closed while she stepped out. Department. Ha. A one-woman team. "Back in a few."

"Can you bring me a salad and a diet orange iced tea?" Chelsea bridged her hands beneath her chin and pouted. "I'm trying to limit my sun exposure."

Trying to…okay, whatever. No time to get trapped in a beauty regimen discussion. "Sure, but I'm not sure how long the wait'll be. I'm meeting someone."

"Ooooh, another client lunch? I wish I could expense my meals the way you can."

"No, it's not—I'm paying—" Well, maybe not. Lunch date. Rob might be buying. Another one of those dating uncertainties impossible to calculate in advance. "There's no client. He's—"

"Ohmigod, are you going on a date?" Chelsea's squeal bounced off the glass.

Ow, ow, ow. She resisted the desire to slap her hands over her ears—or her coworker's mouth.

"Is it a nooner? I love nooners." Sharilyn sighed and stretched her arms across the counter, fingers interlaced. "They're all fast and rough, and you don't have to waste time tossing the guy after because you're not at home." She tapped her nails. "You should hike up your skirt and undo a button on your blouse. You gotta get the guy all worked up before the main event. The sex'll be hotter."

Exactly the advice she didn't need. Fabulous moment for a bank robbery. She shot mental pleas toward the ATM line. Bonus bills for anyone who popped inside and redirected the conversation.

"Please. Ellie doesn't have enough skank in her tank for your style, Shar." Chelsea giggled. "I can't believe she even met a—waaait a minute. Is this the guy from the bar? Did he give you more than his shirt?"

Yes, if more encompassed half a dozen orgasms from frantic fingering while wearing his shirt at home in bed alone. If her vivid, uncomfortable dreams starring his bare chest and muscled forearms counted.

"Ohmigod, it is, look how red her face is." Baby-pink lips pulled back in a grin, Chelsea drummed her palms on the counter. "Holy shit, Ellie's got a man on the hook."

"So, umm, going to lunch now." She edged toward the door. "Not having sex. Just lunch."

"Wuss," Sharilyn shouted. "Undo the button."

Escape. The wall of heat slammed into her face with soothing relief. Sweaty, sticky, late-July-humid relief. So much better than the atmosphere inside.

* * * *

Rob planted himself facing the door at the cozy cross between "hey we make mochaccinos" and "I know, those people, right? Get the Reuben with the heaping side of fries." She'd rejected his suggestion of a more frou-frou place. No telling what her choice meant yet. If she didn't go in for showy shit, fantastic. If she didn't want to waste her time and his money because she wasn't interested, fuck-all.

She'd taken an awful long minute to say yes.

The door opened, and he snapped to his feet.

Eleanora shimmered like a heat-wave mirage. A serious woman pulled away from her desk, not a hair out of place. Her sedate blouse promised no nonsense, and her narrow skirt hugged a line above her knees.

His cock twitched. Half thrill for those gorgeous hidden curves. Half disappointment she hadn't kept his shirt on three days straight. Stepping around the table, he pulled back a chair. "May I offer the lady a seat?"

"Thank you, that's—" A phone buzzed from her purse, and she jerked. "Thank you."

"Short drive, I hope?" He retook his seat and canted his menu as if he cared about the contents. No sense scaring her off with a heavy stare.

"Oh, no, I walked." Waving over her shoulder with one hand, she snatched up her own menu in the other. "I work at the bank up the street."

"You like what you do?" Proximity made a good reason for the change in lunch venue, but her answer offered no clue about her interest in him.

"I love my job." Her smile lightened her face and lifted her neck. She chatted some while she scanned the choices, serving him a sampler platter of the eager entrepreneurs she helped. More she talked about other folks, more the slope of her shoulders relaxed and her voice warmed.

The server came by with brisk pleasantries and a hard-set gaze. "What can I put in for you?"

With the waitress hovering beside her and her phone going off again, Eleanora tightened up. The menu wobbled in her hand. She glanced across at him, her brows raised and her blue-gray eyes wide. "Um."

"You want more time?" Tricky, if her lunch break had strict limits, but he'd sit all afternoon and listen to her talk. Intelligence gathering never hurt a man. "Tough decision, plenty to think about."

"Well—I don't usually—" She split her focus, shifting from him to the menu and back. "You could pick."

Worried about his wallet, maybe. He tapped the back of her menu. "No can do. Get whatever you like. My treat for not making me face these hunger pangs alone."

She rattled off her order in a heartbeat, her grin broad and beautiful—and unexpected. No trouble deciding. She must've been waiting on permission.

He added his selection, and the server went on her way. His date's phone buzzed twice more while they talked, but she ignored the insistent pest.

When the food came, she tucked into her turkey club with a side of chips and plain black coffee. Not too fancy, not too expensive, and not one of those tee-hee-I'm-always-on-a-diet salad monstrosities. Her bland, inoffensive choice matched her surface, a woman coated with a protective, shiny sealant.

She wiped mayo off her finger and cleared her throat. "I'm sorry I don't have your shirt with me. I didn't think to bring it to work." Dropping her gaze, she resettled her napkin.

Meant to say more but wouldn't? His shirt hardly seemed a cache for secrets. The code-cracker in him begged for a shot at getting under her smooth shield. "Consider it on extended loan." To use however she liked. Practicality suggested his shirt lay atop her washing machine, gathering enough partners to take a spin. Fantasy had her sprawled across her bed waiting for him to come along and nose up the hem.

"I didn't think you'd be texting me today." Her shy little smile said she didn't mind, though. "Or inviting me to lunch."

Her phone buzzed.

"You're in high demand." Business clients or her nosy girlfriends from Friday night, maybe. A practical woman like her might've set up a mayday system. "Sure you don't wanna get that?"

She flashed the face of a kid offered liver and broccoli for supper. "I'd rather pretend I didn't hear it. If I don't answer, I can't get trapped in an argument."

Well, that was blunt. Good. A woman bent on honesty and chucking foolish games suited him. He couldn't abide secrets in relationships anyhow. Work had enough of them. "Nuisance caller?"

Laughter brightened her cheeks and relaxed the slopes of her shoulders. "That's probably the most accurate description. This morning, at least. I don't know what's gotten into him."

Him. Shit. "Unhappy boss?"

"He seems to think so," she muttered.

Boyfriend rolled 'round in his head, a ball bearing popped loose from its cradle. He didn't poach. If she said boyfriend, the connection he felt for her didn't mean squat. "You tell him different?"

"I—" Her eyes went distant, tracking a line as if she followed a heads-up display. "I should." She dug into her purse. "My ex."

Ex-not-current. Hallelujah.

"You don't mind?"

"Not a bit." Mind if she told off the guy trying to take back the woman he wanted? Hell no. Tell him off a thousand ways to Sunday. He raised the check on a dented plastic tray. "It'll give me a minute to do some math."

She paused her digging and sighed. "I love math."

Beautiful and brilliant. Sure as hell wasn't gonna lean over the table and pin her to her chair with a kiss to bring down the roof. Foolhardy move. Didn't stop him from wanting to, though. Or his dick from reminding him it and his brain converged on the same page. "Who doesn't?"

* * * *

She scrolled through three cryptic messages from David. More of his nagging nonsense.

Why are you having lunch with him?

Her blood surged, his fourth message the starter's pistol and her pulse a sprinter off the mark. His law office resided less than a mile from the café. More than enough time had elapsed to allow David to cruise past if he wanted to spy on her.

Rob laid a crisp twenty on the check tray. Was he an ATM-in-the-heat man or a come-inside-and-chat man?

The big front window revealed no David lurking outside. Ridiculous speculation aside, he wouldn't know where to find her. Except he shouldn't know she'd stepped out for lunch, either. No one in the café paid the least attention to her paranoia.

Multimedia arrived attached to his next text.

Her.

In the bar.

Her breasts, anyway, her bra straps peeking out from under Rob's shirt as the camera shot widened. The jerky image swung wild, unfocused, and re-centered with her face in view.

"I told you someone was doing it in the bathroom. She had a totally different shirt on five minutes ago. What a slut." Snorting laughter accompanied an unfamiliar woman's voice. "Guess the whore couldn't wait to get him home."

Oh God. Who—why—shame stung hotter than a sunburn.

Answer your phone, Eleanora.

Alanis Morissette blared. *Did you forget about me, Mr. Duplicity?* David's ringtone, her post-separation rebellion. The song cut short as she clutched her phone to her ear.

"Finally. My time is valuable, Eleanora, and so is my reputation."

Not hers, though. Never hers.

"Don't ignore me again. I had to call your office and speak to those girls you work with. They fell all over themselves to tell me about your lunchtime dalliance."

Not watching her. Relief took at least a nickel off the armored-truck-sized weight stifling her breath.

"Do you know where I got this video, Eleanora? The Internet." He seethed, his voice the rapid staccato of every time he'd pulled her aside in front of his business partners and potential clients and delivered a devastating reprimand through a brilliant, unfaltering smile. "A bar association contact sent me the link through his son's Facebook page."

Five chips remained on her plate. Four good. One soggy. Soaking up the juice from the pickle spear had converted bold strength into a bitter, mushy mess.

"People know we were married, Els. You can't behave like a slut in this town."

As if he hadn't. Was she supposed to pretend he'd been better, fucking his paralegal in the same sheets where he'd slept beside her night after night for years?

"Nothing to say? You're doing this deliberately. I won't let your public indiscretions taint my practice."

Sure, because keeping affairs at home made everything fine. With a woman who'd sat at their table and made small talk with her during business dinners dozens of times. How many of those times had that woman's smile been a giddy *I'm fucking your husband* grin?

"Did you take this stranger home and fuck him in our bed or was the bar—"

She stabbed the screen and silenced him. Her stomach rolled in uneasy waves. People making accusations and assumptions about things she'd never done. Never would do. "When I take him home and fuck him in *my* bed, I'll at least have the courtesy to change the goddamned sheets." The right words to fling at David never appeared until the moment for them had passed.

Talking to her gynecologist about disease testing had been unbearably embarrassing. She handled the woman's loan account, for chrissake.

Silence. The clatter of plastic cups and the clinking of soupspoons and salad forks no longer added their voices to the diner's lunchtime symphony.

A furious blush crossed her cheeks and heated her neck as she raised her head. Stares and sidelong glances galore, and an intensity in Rob's eyes she couldn't read at all.

Oh shit.

* * * *

When.

She'd said so plain as day, the sun in a cloudless sky. The words had flowed from her mouth as sweetly as he hoped honey flowed from her sex.

She'd given thought to taking him home with her. If he focused hard enough, maybe he could peek inside her head and reveal her fantasies. The minute she showed him her dreams, he'd devote himself to bringing them to life.

Her red-cheeked face and tight lips didn't bode well for his chances. Best fix the unwanted drama, or she'd resist seeing him again. Bad things came in threes, and now he'd played witness to two of her uncomfortable moments. "Bravo, darlin'." Standing, he clapped with zeal. Eyes intent on her turned to him. "How about a hand, folks? If she puts that much passion into the audition, she'll get the part for sure."

The two white-haired women in the corner booth actually applauded. The other seven patrons put their attention back on their own meals where it belonged. He dropped into his seat.

Eleanora snorted. "You didn't have to do that, but thank you."

"I didn't figure offering my shirt would help this time."

Her receding blush gave way to a half-smile and soft, dream-spiced eyes. "Might've."

She kept her thought train on that track, and he and his honey girl'd arrive at the station together. He grabbed the back of his collar and started hauling. "Working yet?"

"Joking! I was joking." She thrust her hands up in a sure command to stop. "You'll get yourself banned from every beverage-serving place in town."

A quick shake resettled his shirt. "Guess we'll start going to the next town over." Discretion might not be a bad idea in any case. A ninety-minute drive would be worth the trouble if the distance upped her comfort. Kept her ex from hearing about their date and hassling her. "We don't have to wait until the places here ban me. I'll take you to Ames for dinner. All the way to Des Moines if you want."

She glanced away, smiling, and sipped her coffee. "So I passed your audition, huh? What's the role?"

Leading lady, by his side, hands down. Or under him. Or over him. He'd spread those legs, bury his face between her thighs, and savor her satisfaction with all his senses. And then he'd take her hand and offer her a—"Ring." Fuck. Too fast. He best ease up, else he'd scare her off. "Ringer. Can you shoot pool?"

"Not well."

"Bowl?"

She shook her head. "Also not well."

"Then I suppose it'll take a slew of nights out before you can be the ringer." He shrugged and leaned back in his seat. Women liked confidence on a man. He'd put his desires on the table no matter how his heart quailed. "Good thing my schedule's clear."

"What if mine's not?"

He caught and held her gaze, his voice low and steady. "I'll keep asking until it is."

Her eyes widened. Her nostrils flared. The sharp intake of her breath sent blood rushing to his cock. He pined for her just so, naked and squirming and pouring sounds in his ears.

"I—" She broke their stare and released a bitter-edged laugh. "I'm sorry. I don't know how to do this. I'm not—I'm sure you date women who know what they want and say all the right things and flirt intelligently, for god's sake. But I…"

He waited in stillness, but she didn't seem inclined to finish her thought. Sliding his hand across the table, he risked brushing her fingers. "But you what, Eleanora?"

She grimaced. "I was barely old enough to drink when I started dating David. We married young, and…" She sagged like a windsock on a calm day, listless and empty. Way her husband had made her feel, maybe.

"Been a while since you've been in the dating market." He'd envy her the freedom from the chase, if her marriage hadn't turned out to be such a botch job. He'd have rather washed his hands of the whole dating scene and settled down a good six or eight years ago himself.

"Ten years." Sighing, she stared at their hands.

He risked a second touch, rubbing his thumb over her knuckles.

"Bars aren't my speed." She aimed her mumble at their empty plates and crumpled napkins. "The last time I dated, social networking didn't exist, and my girlfriends argued over whether letting a boy put his hands under their shirts was okay, not whether they should give a guy a blowjob in his car or invite him inside."

Red crept up her cheeks. The mix of boldness and innocence swirling around her drew him like lightning to a mountaintop. She might embarrass easily, but she powered through with courage and sass. Two more points in her favor. His Nora needed a smidge of old-fashioned high school wooing and confidence-building. Inspiration struck.

"Let me take you out Friday night." He squeezed her hand. "No blowjobs, I promise. But I might let you put your hands under my shirt."

A charming giggle erupted from her, and he smiled back. Her laughter had lost the sharp edge. Victory. "I'm gonna hold you to that, Robin."

From her lips, his given name didn't sound so bad.

"My fair maid Eleanora." His chair scraped the floor as he rose. He planted his feet, heels together, and bowed over her hand.

She shivered at the press of his lips. Goose bumps speckled her wrist and disappeared into her sleeve.

He half-closed his eyes in pleasure, the surge of possibility, at her reaction. With a gentle tug, he urged her to stand. He dipped his mouth beside her ear. “At least I know you’re already thinking about holding me.”

Chapter 3

Eleanora's heart thudded with all the weight of a farmwife's coin jar. Scurrying around the bedroom Friday evening, she rushed to get ready for her first real date with Rob.

They'd texted back and forth all week since their Monday coffee. Nothing substantial, a handful of short notes and cute greetings, but she'd assigned him his own chime, and her phone belting out the cheerful tune boosted her mood. She'd forgotten the joys of a man's attention, how his noticing her added a lightness to her days and a hunger to her nights.

David had started his boyfriend tenure thoughtful. But time dragged behind them like an anchor, until even birthdays and Valentine's days passed without comment.

"Rob will be different. He *is* different."

She tugged a pair of comfortable, soon-to-be-for-yardwork-only jean cutoffs over her hips and tucked in her spaghetti-strap cami. Without knowing where he intended to take her tonight, she lacked more to go on than his suggestion for, "Something real relaxed. Outdoors-friendly."

She brushed her hair into a ponytail, topped it with a worn baseball cap, and moisturized her exposed skin with sunscreen lotion. A gauzy, long-sleeve button-down added protection for her arms. Playing rec league softball on the bank's team had taught her fear and respect for the Iowa evening sun.

Jamming her heels into broken-in cross-trainers with help from her fingers, she hopped to the entryway with three minutes to spare. She'd left work at five, and he'd insisted he couldn't pick her up any later than 5:45. The tight schedule didn't leave time for showering or extensive beauty rituals.

Rob's shirt, washed and folded, lay on the hall table beside the door. Her keys rested on top. She pressed her fingers to the fabric. Still soft.

But if she raised the shirt to her nose now, its dryer-fresh scent would disappoint. No hint of him remained.

The rumble of an engine drew her to the door. Rob pulled into the drive smooth and sure, behind the wheel of a pickup truck.

Sharp, blistering heat chewed under her ribs and shredded vital organs. If she'd misunderstood and dressed too casually, he'd label her old and frumpy and never ask her out again. Or he'd think she wasn't trying hard because she didn't want to date him.

Dammit. She'd forgotten anxiety and second-guessing went along with the giddy excitement. Waiting on a man's approval, alluring as the fantasy proved, lacked the same thrill in reality.

He stepped down from the truck, casual and easy, laid-back and lanky, a confident man in a body built for sex appeal.

She swung between the highs and lows like a teenager in the throes of her first crush. Excruciating, exhilarating, and too overwhelming to stand for long. Scooping up his shirt and her keys, she yanked open the door to the hallucination-inducing 90-degree heat of Iowa in July. She almost smacked him in the face with the screen.

He flung his arm up and caught the frame. "Well that's a good sign." He looked her over from head to toe. "And that's another."

"Oh God, I'm so sorry." She squeezed her eyes shut, willing away mortification. "I swear, I've been operating doors all my life. I have a great safety rating."

"Only decapitated two previous suitors, did you?" He tapped his head against the wood below his hand, his flinch exaggerated with raised brows, an open mouth, and a double take. Goofy man.

"Three, but they never made the charges stick." Playing along wrapped her in Rob's teasing humor, welcome insulation from the echoes of her ex-husband's exasperated corrections.

Laughing, he backed up a step. "I'll be on my guard, Miss Dangerous."

She followed, locking the door behind her. "What signs did you mean?"

He held the screen until she slipped by him on the front walk. Breathing deep in passing, she relished his earthy scent. The heat and humidity thickened smells into tastes, swarming her with a rich and decadent masculine darkness. The screen snapped shut, and she jumped.

"First good sign is you rushing out your door to greet me." He laid his hand against her back as he had at the bar a week ago, guiding her forward with light pressure. "Either you're one of those hoarding folks afraid to let people in the house, or you're awful eager to go out with me. I figure I'll hope for the second."

His light confession swatted her fears. The dating vulnerability game worked both directions. Her chasing his approval didn't sting so deep when he admitted to chasing hers in return.

Delivering her to the passenger side, he pulled the door open and offered her a hand despite the easy step-up running board.

She took his hand. Not requiring his help for balancing faltered beside the more compelling desire to touch him. Anywhere would do. She settled in the seat and reached for the belt. "What's the other good sign?"

He zipped the strap forward. Pressing the buckle into her palm, he brushed her skin. His gaze drifted down her legs and back.

She returned the favor, scoping out his uncluttered, well-worn jean shorts and plain orange t-shirt. Probably the same style as the black one whose neat folds she crushed in her lap.

The belt clicked into place.

"You know what relaxed means." He pinched the brim of her cap between thumb and forefinger and gave her a teasing wiggle. "No heels or pearls or froofy nonsense, as my mama would say. And you didn't keep me standing at the door while you ran through your closet a hundred times. I like a woman with courtesy and common sense."

He closed the door and crossed in front of the pickup.

She exhaled a flood of relief. Not frumpy. Suitable.

The driver's seat receded beneath his solid frame. He turned over the engine.

Leaning back, she crossed her ankles as the air conditioning started flowing. "How long a ride are we looking at?"

He paused his hand on the gearshift. "You wrap your mouth around the nicest words sometimes, Eleanora." Flashing a smile, he winked. "You tell me how long you want the ride to last, and I'll do my damnedest to meet your needs."

Groaning, she dropped her face in her hands. God, she'd actually asked that. "Is everything an opening for innuendo to you?"

He coughed.

Now what had—opening. His sense of humor set her cheeks ablaze, but the naughtiness enticed as much as amused. Something to get used to, this easy charm so unlike David's stuffy idea of wit. "Okay, smart guy. How far away is the place we're going?"

"You afraid I have terrible taste in driving music?" Rob threw the truck in reverse and backed down the drive. His free hand rested on the seat back near her shoulder.

"I'm dying of curiosity. You won't tell me a thing about where we're going or what we're doing." Nervous laughter trickled from her throat. If she'd chosen to trust the wrong man, a lengthy and awkward night loomed. "It's my first date in a decade, and I don't want to end up in a ditch somewhere."

"I don't mean to scare you, Eleanora. I wanted to surprise you. Make our date a thrill." He brushed her shoulder, pulled away, and shifted into drive. "If you're truly uncomfortable, say the word, and I'll spill my secrets. But if you can hang in there for twenty minutes, all will be revealed."

Not far. Somewhere in town.

"I'll wait and see," she croaked from a mouth gone dry. "Don't mind my jumpiness." The last time a man had surprised her, his gift had been the sight of his bare ass featuring another woman's legs wrapped around it. Less thrill and more devastation. "I'm being silly."

"It's okay to be nervous. Hell, I am."

"You don't look it." He looked yummy as sin and confident as the devil himself.

"My heart's whomping like a Huey. I'm trying to impress a pretty girl. She's smart and funny, too, and I'd like to give her a kiss before the night's over."

She stared at him, but he kept his eyes on the road. The onslaught of compliments flustered and emboldened at the same time. He wanted to kiss her. A man's mouth hadn't touched hers in two years. Desire swarmed thick as bees in a hive.

"So I'm thinking every second"—he spoke dead ahead, fixed on the windshield, his jaw popping his cheek in profile—"thinking on how I can ease her mind and show her I'm a trustworthy guy, 'cause I think she hasn't seen many of those." He flexed his hand on the steering wheel, long fingers straightening and re-gripping. "When she makes that choice I want her thinking about how good it feels and not worrying she's making a bad decision."

They pulled up to a red light. A breeze set the signal swaying on the line.

"Rob." She darted toward him even as he turned.

Their lips met.

* * * *

She tasted of mint and smelled of spring, of the sweet honeysuckle that curled around his fence posts and shrouded the wood in strong vines and delicate flowers. Her fingers grazed his cheek.

He groaned his approval, her tentative touch alluring and deserving encouragement. His mind raced ahead, plotting the motions to release her seatbelt, slide her across the bench seat to his side and lay her on her back. Five seconds and his mouth could be wetting her breasts through the thin blue shirt clinging to her skin.

Forcing himself to hold back tested his limits harder than securing a system run by lazy password admins. When she sighed against his lips, he almost tossed caution aside.

A car horn blared.

Eleanora jumped back, tearing their mouths apart.

Pissed-off driver. Right. Because he'd sat at a light, behind the wheel, not moving, while his cock did his thinking for him.

She peered at him with blue-gray eyes wide. Her swollen, pursed lips and flushed cheeks invited him to taste her again.

Damned impatient driver behind him laid on the horn, blasting long and shrill. Curses flooding his head, he zipped through the intersection beneath the yellow light.

A block later, Eleanora was still studying him. Or his general direction, anyhow. Her hazy, unfocused gaze hovered around his chin, and her lips curled inward like a woman evening out her lipstick.

Stare like that'd make a man nervous. 'Specially when he'd gotten a helluva goodnight kiss ten minutes into the date. "Well? How'd I do?"

She took a long blink as she inhaled. "Fantastic."

Her low purr shot an ache up his cock. Please God, don't let her sneak a peek at his shorts. He hadn't fought to hide a burgeoning erection so urgently since ninth grade.

He'd swear on a Bible, a calculator, the federal interest rates—whatever she believed most sacred—his attraction leap-frogged beyond sex. But the enticement of their initial rush of hormones held undeniable sway. A powerful longing claimed him each time he laid eyes on her, and the urge strengthened with exponential force at every subsequent meeting.

"Way better than I anticipated," she added, her tone turning thoughtful.

"You've been anticipating?" God knew he had. Every morning and night for the last week. "That's good. 'Course, you expecting I'd be a lousy kisser isn't doing wonders for my ego."

She chuckled, a hearty laugh and not the fake girlish trill of a woman enduring a bad date with grace. "I thought *I'd* be lousy. It's been"—she dropped her head and twisted the frayed edge of her shorts between her fingers—"a long time. Wasn't sure I remembered how."

"You're doing better than fine, make no mistake." He slowed to cross the train tracks. Iron rumble-bumps succumbed to steady handling. No jolting discomfort for his Nora. "But if you want more practice, you know where my mouth is."

Her smile spread slow and easy as she relaxed into the seat.

He eased his left leg against the door panel. He'd need to invest in roomier shorts if she meant to be so damned enticing all the time.

Green rows of knee-high soybeans and higher than head-height corn flashed past the windows. The turn came quick. Easing the pickup off the main road and onto the crushed gravel, he relished the gasp from the passenger seat. "Figure where we're going yet?"

She bobbed with unexpected excitement, ponytail bouncing against the seat back. "How did you know?"

He pulled up to the end of the line. Five cars idled ahead of them. His rush had paid off. They'd get a spot at the back, a private cocoon for sampling each other's charms if she were so inclined. After her cock-swelling kiss, he had to believe she was.

"I don't suppose I did." The gates wouldn't open for another fifteen minutes, but he left the engine running. They'd be in the hazy heat soon enough. "You tell me what you think I know, and I'll try to convincingly pretend I planned it all along."

In truth, his plan hadn't gone further than finding an activity appropriate for the juvenile feeling he thought she'd like to recapture. No place better than the drive-in movies for a night of cuddling and petting high-school style.

Her tiny snort charmed him.

"You're laid-back. You're funny, but you don't boast." She squeezed her hands together in her lap, her thumb rubbing at the empty ring finger. "It's nice."

He reached across the seat back and wound a lock of her hair around his finger. Addictive stuff, a honey-brown rich, thick, and silken. Man wouldn't go wrong waking to the same view.

"I'm glad you like it." He'd cut out of work early to clean the pickup and pretty things up for her. Lowering his voice, he teased. "So, you come here often?"

She frowned, a quirky little sideways blip beneath flat, shuttered eyes. "Not once."

"Then I'm the lucky man who gets to show you something new." One of a hundred delights he'd show her if she gave the go-ahead. Her ex must've been quite a prize. What sort of man couldn't be bothered to escort his girl to the drive-in when the idea had her bunny-bounding in her seat?

"My parents used to take us. I grew up in Ohio. Dayton has this gorgeous old double-screen drive-in." Her voice warmed, wistfulness calling to him. "We went every weekend, all summer, the whole family."

Ahh. He'd lucked into a corner of childhood nostalgia. A time she'd felt safe and loved, before she'd wilted in a years-long drought. Tender nurturing and irrigation would perk her up. The promise of seeing her in full blossom had already perked him up.

"We've only got the one screen, but the corn dogs and the soft pretzels can't be beat." He brushed the tip of her ponytail against her neck, the ticklish caress a placeholder for the kiss he ached to bestow. "And the caramel corn melts on your tongue."

She glanced at her hands with a small smile. Breathing out, she lifted her head and looked him right in the eyes. "Is that how you're gonna taste it? On my tongue?"

Sweet Jesus. When she found her confidence, she sure as hell found it good. A regular firecracker waiting to pop. "I'll taste anything you want, Eleanora. Any way and anytime you want me to."

* * * *

The arousal pooling between her legs challenged her not to squirm beneath his heavy gaze. She pressed her thighs together. Her breath stuttered.

Did he truly mean *that*?

He held her mesmerized as if willing her to believe him.

She wanted to kiss him again. Too soon after she'd been so impulsive at the stoplight. He'd expect more, faster, if she admitted her desire and surrendered. Had fighting off hormones been this difficult as a teenager? Memory made the struggle seem easier then, or maybe Rob accounted for the difference. More arousing than high school boys had been. Straight-up lust after two years without.

"My mouth is dry," she blurted. What the hell? She'd lost control of higher brain function. Speech took a detour through desire and emerged twisted and nonsensical.

He tipped his head. Playing with her hair, he slid his hand behind her neck. He flicked her earlobe back and forth with his thumb. "If you're saying you want a cold drink," he whispered, "I'm gonna feel awful foolish in a second."

She started to shake her head, but he held her firm.

He swooped down and planted his mouth against hers.

Relaxing into his kiss, she opened her mouth for the swipe of his tongue. The man knew his stuff. He quelled her nerves and enhanced her arousal with a single motion.

The seatbelt and his hand held her captive. Undulating his tongue, he created a wave pulling her under. Their lips slid over and around each other time and again, and her every squeak and cry received an affirming bass hum in reply.

Drifting away, he tugged her lower lip with his teeth. "How's your mouth now? Better?"

"Much." She worked to catch her breath. Her sex throbbed in time with her pulse. The combination added a shake to her voice. "Can I get a prescription for your treatment?"

His gaze, darting to her chest and returning to her face, left a torrent of gratifying confidence in its wake.

She dared a return glance, lower. Faded denim outlined his arousal, a vision for her alone. However powerful his influence on her, she affected him with equal strength.

"Repeat as needed," he murmured. "No more than fifty times per day. Addiction probable."

A sliver of doubt pricked her ballooning confidence. "Common side effect of your kisses?" They hadn't progressed to discussing romantic histories. His charm and skills might've caused the same reaction in dozens of women. With his gentlemanly manners, maybe he meant to warn her about getting too attached to avoid a messy breakup later.

Eyes narrowing, he caressed her neck with firm strokes. One finger slipped under the collar of her cover-up. He traced the edge of her spaghetti strap.

Heat swept through her.

"You'd have to ask my exes about that, I guess." He traced her collarbone and squiggled up her neck, lifting her chin. "I won't lie to you, Eleanora. I've had my share of relationships that didn't work out. Sometimes the sex was bad, sometimes good. But the timing and the chemistry and the emotional connection never came together."

He made tearing her gaze from his impossible. Force of will, the deep intensity in his voice, and the gold flecks in his eyes dancing in the evening sunlight kept her spellbound.

"Our lips touch and I'm like a grain silo in August. One spark and the whole place'll go up." He teased her mouth, outlining the shape of her lips. "Maybe the addiction I meant was mine for you."

Metal clanged.

Rob dropped his hand and turned away. "Hold that thought."

She claimed a deep breath, the spell broken by the theater gates opening.

He eased the pickup forward as the line moved.

Seven days wouldn't make any man addicted to her, but his pronouncement seemed in earnest, a meaningful admission. Desirability buoyed her confidence.

He paid cash at the booth and guided the truck up the gentle slope. All the way back. The cars in front of them birthed crowds of teens, a sea of tank tops and bikinis and summer tans. More followed in the cars behind.

Rob took a spot near the far end of the row, leaving a dozen empty spaces between his truck and the high-schoolers. Arriving minivans discharged pint-sized patrons closer to the screen. The unwritten code of the drive-in—families in the front, fooling around in the back. Parents with young children had better sense than to park in the last few rows.

Keys jangled. The engine fell silent. With the air conditioning off, the cab heated to stifling. They faced a wall of windbreak pines. They'd have a great view of the screen from the truck bed, though. Over her shoulder, the hot metal waited. "Our first date and you're getting me in bed already."

"Well, now I'm feeling the pressure to perform." He nudged her, a sly smile spreading across his face.

She laughed—at him, at herself, at the oddity of dating after so many years. "I'm sorry. My head's all over the map today." Rocking up and down like the seesaw kids clambered over in the playground near the concession stand. Emotional and insecure. God, she hated women who acted desperate and clinging, who manipulated men left and right with wild mood swings.

"First dates'll make you crazy." He pulled the keys free. "Trying to be yourself and everything the other person wants when you don't know what they want."

He popped his door open, and she followed suit.

"Just be yourself, Eleanora. That's the woman I want to spend time with. It's a first date. Things're bound to be awkward." He swung out of the pickup. "If I walk away at the end of the night with nothing more than the two kisses I already got, that's two more than I had this morning."

She hovered between relieved and insulted as he strolled past the windshield. He didn't have expectations. Good, because she feared she couldn't meet them if he did. But he didn't have expectations. That wasn't how this worked. Guys pushed and girls caved. Either the script had changed since the last time she'd dated, or Rob didn't follow one.

He reached across her from the open door, and she jumped.

"Seatbelt." His strong, earthy scent wafted by her nose. "Didn't mean to spook you." He freed her with a click. "C'mon. I brought a Frisbee, or they got mini-golf or sand volleyball, or we could eat first if you're hungry."

She hopped out beside him and surveyed the lot. Two hours until sunset, but the spaces filled in a steady stream. In front of the screen, kids kicked soccer balls, played catch, and ran around in games known only to them. Grandparents set up lawn chairs and crowded the horseshoe pit. Shrieks and laughter and car stereos carried over the crunch of gravel under car tires.

"Mini-golf." Slipping her hand into his, she squeezed. Awkward and perfect. He'd gotten her just right. "I have to warn you, that's one sport I play well."

"A challenge." He returned her squeeze, keeping her hand in his as he walked. "Let's see what you've got."

* * * *

He breathed easier once they had golf clubs in hand, no longer worried she wouldn't enjoy herself.

Eleanora took the game seriously, with a scrunched nose and angled brows and pursed lips as she lined up her shots. Good ones, too.

"You sure you don't play pool?" He prided himself on a superb sense of angles and outcomes, but she banked walls and coaxed curves like nobody's business. "You've got the moves."

Ponytail swinging, she shook her head. "Never tried."

She bent over and scooped her golf ball from the hole—another par—and her jean shorts tightened across her backside.

He clenched the putter in tense hands. If scooping her up were an option, he'd have his hands under her ass in a hot second. "So you don't know you aren't a pool savant." He lined up his shot as she stepped aside. "I'll make a ringer out of you yet."

She scored a birdie on the next hole, extending her lead to two strokes. Her cheerful post-putting dance proved too adorable to resist.

Curling his arm around her waist, he tugged her to him as they waited for the players ahead to finish. "What say you to a wager?"

"You're ready to admit I'll beat you?" She tipped her head back and grinned at him. "It's a little unorthodox to bet against yourself, but okay."

"I was thinking more the loser owes the winner a number of kisses equal to the difference in scores." He puckered his lips and pretended to close the gap, bumping his head against her hat brim instead. "But I see you have an advanced tactical defense system in place."

She giggled, soft and musical. "You make me feel like I'm sixteen."

"Is that good?"

"It's—" She turned her head.

He followed her gaze. Players packed the mini-golf course. Families with kids running wild. Teens in groups and pairs, roughhousing and stealing kisses as if the world weren't watching. Squeals and laughter formed a common bond from the first hole to the last.

"It's different. Fun. Carefree." Her chuckle emerged self-conscious and tight. "I'm not sure I know what to do with that."

"Never too old to learn." Hell, she deserved fun and carefree. If she let him, he'd make sure she got them.

"You calling me old, old man?" Her playful shove failed to dislodge him, but he released her anyway. "You try and keep up." She bent and set her ball on the tee.

He gritted his teeth. With the pretty view she offered, keeping up wasn't his problem tonight. Staying down, now, that one gave him fits.

They tied on the next three holes. She overshot the cup on the fourth.

He lined up his shot. "I hope that wasn't a pity miss, Eleanora."

She snorted. "And lose a kiss?"

"Colin, slow down!" An unfamiliar woman's shout called his attention to the crunch and ping of spattering gravel.

A little boy ran full-tilt across the course to a chorus of gripes from annoyed players. A check the other way confirmed his suspicion. Bathroom. The kid would cross their hole in a few seconds. He waited. No sense taking the shot only to have an unpredictable, pint-sized variable knock his careful deliberation astray.

One red tennis shoe smacked into the low, painted concrete sidewall marking the hole. Arms pinwheeling, the boy pitched forward with a cry.

Rob lunged. The putter fell, ignored, as he thrust one arm in front of the boy's chest to arrest his descent and gripped the back of his shirt in his opposite hand. Swinging the kid forward and up, he set him on his feet on the far side of the hole.

The boy sped off without a glance, though the woman shouted a thanks.

He waved at her and squatted to collect his club. "Think it's safe for me to putt now?"

"That was amazing. Your reflexes—you—" Eleanora stared at him with an indecipherable expression. "Wow."

Standing, he shrugged. Instinct and training never disappeared, nor did Mama and Daddy's admonitions to have a care for the hurts of others. A man did all he could to minimize bad outcomes, no matter if they hit him personal or not. Strong communities got built in those bonds. "I've always been good with my hands."

"Always?" Her tone hinted at coy flirtation.

Half a dozen ready answers jumped to mind. He resisted. He wanted more from her than feel-good surface conversations with no substance. The name of her favorite stuffed animal as a kid. Whether she feared thunderstorms or danced in the rain. How she'd smile, glowing and exhausted, with a newborn in her arms.

"Earth to Rob?"

He blinked, shaking the vision from his head. "Yup, always. Fixed the machinery on the farm since I was no bigger than that kid is now. Had to best my big brother at something."

"Tell me about your family?" She slung her putter like a yoke with her wrists over the metal.

"My folks grow wheat out west of Topeka. My brother works with Dad now. I was hell-bent on tech stuff. Joined the Air Force straight outta high school for the education benefits. Two baby sisters. One married quick and moved to the city, and the other did the wandering artist thing for a while. She's settled down some." He took the shot and sank the putt. "How about you?"

"My parents still live in Dayton. Mom teaches elementary school. Dad's an accountant."

They ambled to the next hole, hips near touching, putters dangling and spinning in loose grips.

"I always took after him. Guess that's how I ended up in banking." Shaking her head, she smiled. "No big brothers, but two little sisters, same as you. One's a stay-at-home mom and the other's getting her PhD in some paleontology subfield way beyond my understanding."

"Nobody around here?" He frowned despite the beautiful view as she lined up with a hip waggle. Working with Brian and the rest of the guys, field-tested blood brothers all, he carried his home with him. Hit the highway for the biggies, spending holidays at the farm snug in a sleeping bag while his nephews packed in the bedroom he'd shared for years with his brother.

"No." She took her shot and hit a bumper at a bad angle. "I moved out here because David—my ex—grew up around here. He joined his uncle's law firm with the notion he'd take over when his uncle retired. Not that he mentioned his plan before he proposed."

Her next shot went wide, hitting the wall with enough force to pop the ball out into the gravel.

"We finalized the divorce three months ago, but I've been living out here seven years now." She sighed through her whole body, going to collect her ball with sagging shoulders and trudging feet. "I have a job I love, and a house I hate, and I plod along minute to minute with no idea where my life is going."

Three months. No wonder she still dealt with the emotional fallout. Alone.

"Sorry. I'm a complete downer. I promised myself I wouldn't drag you through my failed marriage."

"You're not dragging me, Eleanora. I asked."

"Still." Scooping up her ball, she shrugged. "Penalty stroke."

He let the conversation lapse as she re-shot the hole with better focus. If talking strained her comfort with him, he'd take the slow road. But eventually, he'd get her to explain why she hated her house and where she wanted her life to be going. Into his arms would be a nice start.

A few teasing observations about the folks around them had her laughing again by the end of the next hole. She regained her concentration enough to win the game by three strokes.

"Hungry?" He checked the angle of the sun as they turned in their clubs. "The line'll be long, but best be in it soon."

"I hear the caramel corn is can't-miss." She spoke in a light, flirty tone, one without enough edge to be coy. Not the sort to lead a man on, his honey girl.

"I know I'm looking forward to my taste." He held her gaze long enough to make his meaning unmistakable.

Her eyes darkened. She didn't shy away but offered him her hand. "Lead the way."

Clasping her fingers, he slowed his pace to make hers more natural. On the concession side of the building, the line wound around metal barriers. A corral of humans shuffled toward dinner, their gazes fixed on the menu board hung near the roofline.

He guided her in front of him. Slender ribs curved beneath the span of his hand. His fingers grazed the edge of her bra through her shirt. Accidental, but arousing all the same.

Her shiver rippled through them both.

He stilled his fingers. Bending his neck, he teased at her ear. "I'd be happy to pick you up if you can't see the menu over the crowd."

She hip-checked him.

He caught himself, rocking on the balls of his feet. Impressive might for such a little thing. Surprising, too.

"I can manage." Her bright smile as she craned her head back told him he hadn't given offense. "But you make too many cracks about my height, and we're going to have words, buster."

"Sore spot?"

"What girl doesn't want to be the tall, willowy image of perfection she sees in every TV show and magazine from the time she's old enough to toddle? Society has one ideal. If you don't meet it, well—" She shrugged and waved a dainty hand. "You'll never measure up to the picture a man has in his head anyway."

He'd dated compliment-fishers, and Eleanora didn't capture their wheedling tone or their narcissistic praise-me prattle. Somewhere along the way, she'd gotten the wrong idea stuck in her head.

"Maybe society does—the ad folks and the entertainers."

She stepped forward as the line moved, and he followed.

"But I tell you what—every man's got his own image of perfection floating in his head, and they ain't all those half-starved waifs with giraffe legs. The lucky ones, they spot her one day."

Turning shadowed eyes on him, she made looking away impossible. He hadn't managed to put her out of his mind since his first glimpse. Her uncertain stare demanded more, culled confessions and requested revelations.

"Not even looking, and suddenly she's all he sees." The lowering sunlight flickered off the awning and streamed toward her face. The dancing highlights added shine to delicate arches, curves where a man might wander lost and find himself again. "Walked right outta his dreams, with a glow like the universe wants to make sure he doesn't miss her."

Christ, he'd said way too much. He should've stopped at the legs. Closed his mouth and let the general statement stand. Foolishness had urged him on.

The barest part appeared in her lips.

Fuck if he didn't burn to hoist her up on the rail, cement his mouth to hers, and slide his hips between her welcoming thighs.

Distraction. Holy lord, any would do.

"So, you see anything you like?" His frantic mouth stumbled into a bad pickup line. "On the menu." Black letters filled the white board up front with safe, non-erect squiggles. "Pizza, nachos, corn dog, milkshake, deep-fried Oreos—whatever you want." He tossed her his most charming smile. "Hell, I'll buy you one of everything if you can't decide."

Laughing, she shook her head. "Save your money, big spender. My clothes are staying on tonight."

The implication stopped him cold. He'd nearly bungled into telling her their connection had been love at first sight for him, and she'd retreated into Dating 101.

She turned and studied the menu board, still giggling.

She hadn't meant anything by her flippancy. Flirty-skittish commentary. He understood the surface games.

But the way sex became the top commodity on the dating market and building a relationship became somehow secondary broiled him despite the shade. Every date he'd been on in the last decade—hell, the last two, since he'd first brandished his driver's license—had come down to the same exchange.

They shuffled along with small steps, inching toward the counter and its fragrant offerings. He stared at the menu without seeing.

In his head, he was seventeen again. Slamming the door of his daddy's truck and scuffing his shoes through the gravel to the house. Out sixty bucks, a huge chunk of his cash, and nothing to show for his effort. No fooling around. Denied a goodnight kiss. And what had he said when Dad asked about his foul mood?

"I took her out fancy. A sit-down dinner. And the movie after." Ornery and blue-balled as a stallion without a herd, he'd kicked the porch post. "She owes me."

"If I were a different sort of man, I'd slap that horseshit right out of your skull, boy." Daddy'd clamped his shoulder, driving his thumb into Rob's collarbone. No wiggle room. "Taking a girl out, paying for the meal and the movie, they don't entitle you to her body. They entitle you to her company and her attention long as she's willing to give 'em. That's all. Boys'll start asking after your little sisters in a year or two. Hormone-drunk hotheads like you, thinking the same things you think, only they'll be thinking those things about your sisters. You want them thinking they're entitled?"

"No, sir." The comparison had chilled him. Boys letting their dicks rule their behavior. Trying to get in his sisters' pants. "I'd pop 'em in the face the second they laid a hand on Jill or Sara." He'd never again considered dating a numbers game.

"You don't like what a gal offers, no law says you have to take her out again." Daddy's short nod and comforting squeeze had signaled approval since Rob had been small enough to ride on his shoulders. "But I tell you what, Robin. A girl whose company you'd keep for nothing but the conversation, the lightness of her laugh, and the scent of her hair—she's the one you marry."

The one standing in front of him now.

He knew the truth, even if a rocky relationship history blinded her understanding. His first flash of anger at being challenged and insulted, as though his whole standard of manhood and masculinity had been questioned and dismissed, had subsided. Training had taught him to lock down the hothead response and think through problems. He unlocked puzzles for a living.

Eleanora didn't strike him as a mercenary woman who considered sex a business dealing. She must've married a lousy example of manhood the first time around to hold such a cynical opinion. The kind of man who maybe still needed someone to smack horseshit out of his head.

"—don't you think?" Ponytail swaying, she glanced over her shoulder. "You've been studying the menu awfully hard."

"I know you don't mean to say I'm trying to buy your body."

Startled confusion faded to a cringe that twisted her face. "I was—"

"Joking, I know." He didn't aim to lecture, but he wouldn't have her thinking of herself as a tradeoff. A burger and fries for a night fondling her tits. A steak with wine for her lips around his dick. Not him, either. "Two things, Eleanora."

He stepped closer as the couple behind them argued over the merits of licorice whips as drinking straws. "One, my mama and daddy raised me to be a gentleman, and nothing'll happen between us faster than the pace you want to go." He whispered to her, urgent and soft, the need to get the words out stringing him tight as a catch wire. "And two, I hope you wouldn't devalue yourself like that. You have a beautiful body—trust me, I've noticed—but you have a lot more going for you than looks. I'm not gonna grab at one thing like a horny kid and ditch the rest on the roadside."

Her face relaxed, but she didn't speak.

He let her be. Silence fell between them. He kept a covert watch on her as the line wound them down one row and halfway up another. Longer she held her peace, the more convincing the shoulder-demon voice suggesting he'd fucked up grew.

She cleared her throat. "David used to buy me extravagant gifts." Her whisper floated so airy amid the din he had to lean in to hear. "Anytime he thought I was being stubborn, he just…"

Tried to substitute money for love. Her implication came through loud and clear.

"After a while, we never talked anymore, not about anything that mattered. If we argued, he'd come home with pricey junk." The muscles in her cheek twitched with the pull of a bitter smile. "I wanted"—the tip of her tongue touched her lips and retreated—"an apology. I'd have taken less. An acknowledgement he'd heard what I said and understood. But he never understood." Blinking fast, she ducked her head. "I wanted a human connection and he brought me things."

He hadn't intended to push something so emotional in such a crowded space. To embarrass her. He swept her close and tucked her head beneath his chin. Strong arms might set straight what loose lips knocked askew.

"I don't mean to paint you with the same brush, Rob." She shrugged and burrowed into him. "I'm sorry."

"You got your head wired on those paths." He ran his hand over her back. Up. Down. Smooth strokes as he willed himself to ignore the tickle of her breath at his throat. "Change is hard. Trust is hard. I can't give you an easy fix for reasonable caution, Eleanora."

He tugged her ponytail. As she tipped her head back, he leaned away. No tear tracks, thank Christ. He hadn't gone that far astray from his plan to give her a fun, relaxing night. But she wore shadows deep as Jilly's after a damnfool hunter had sprayed their Chessie with shot. Jilly's faith had taken longer to recover than the dog's hindquarters.

"All I can do is show up every day and demonstrate the kind of man I am. Make some new pathways here." He tapped Nora's forehead with a gentle finger. "I think those are paths I'd like to explore."

Hope shone in her eyes. Unless he'd glimpsed the imagined reflection of his own.

She lowered her head and snuggled against his chest.

He hugged her to him, despite the heat and the gap ahead of them where the line had moved. "With caramel corn," he whispered.

She giggled, and he inhaled the honeyed sweetness of her hair.

Conversation. Laughter. Scent. She busted the chart for all three. One of these days, his daddy would be welcoming her to the family as a daughter-in-law.

* * * *

A third hand wouldn't have gone amiss for each of them.

Eleanora toted the drink tray and the bags of popcorn, one sweet, one savory. Rob balanced cheeseburgers, fries, and slices of pie—apricot and strawberry-rhubarb, made fresh this morning—with consummate skill. With impressive juggling, he cradled the food in one arm and dropped the truck's tailgate with his opposite hand.

Speed, skill, deft hands. Recalling the light pressure of his hand at her back, the way he'd traced the lower edge of her bra, made her shiver. Rob broadcast a subtle image of the kind of guy who could unhook a girl one-handed. The sexy charmer who'd gone from fumbling to seductive by eighth grade. He hadn't been boasting about being good with his hands.

"Here, lemme get those." He scooped the drink tray and popcorn from her, depositing them on the end of the tailgate beside the rest. Turning back, he extended his arms and paused. Inches from her waist, his fingers twitched.

She made a show of glancing down, daring him to touch her with her stance if not her voice. Her body begged for his solid, capable grip.

"You gonna hip check me again if I help you into bed?"

She jerked her head up. "If you—"

"Shit." He swore with his eyes closed, shaking his head. "The truck bed, I meant."

"Freudian slip?" Not one she minded, if so. Least she wasn't alone in having trouble focusing. She gave him a broad, teasing smile. Whatever the girls at work—or David—thought, she wasn't some stuffy, tight-assed bitch. "Guess I know where your mind's at."

"It's not only on that, Eleanora, I promise you." Honesty and sincerity poured from his eyes, from the sweet curve of his mouth, from the tiny furrow between his brows.

"I know." Clasping his hands, she pressed them to the top of her hips. God, he felt amazing. The sun's heat had nothing on the heat between her legs. "And yeah, you can give me a boost without fear of reprisal."

She leaned into him and accepted temptation's goad. Fingers slipping up his arms, she mapped the easy strength in his forearms. Teased the soft skin in the crook of his elbows. Gripped the roundness of his biceps and shoulders. Imagined how they'd enclose her as he moved above her.

Imaginary Rob smothered her with kisses and thrust. Real Rob stood unmoving. Thirty seconds passed. A full minute.

"I'm ready, Rob," she whispered. Her brain caught up to her mouth half a second too late.

His fingers dug into her sides, and he uttered what might have become a groan if he hadn't snapped off the sound almost before it began. His quick lift settled her on the truck bed.

Her legs dangled. Hot metal stung the bare backs of her knees. Raising her legs, she scooted deeper into the truck and slumped against the side. Breathing room. God knew she needed some. Rob's nearness fed an uncontrollable spring in her. A bubbling well David had never touched, not once in the eight years they'd shared a bed.

Rob hoisted himself in and leaned against the wall opposite her. One leg of his shorts gaped, showing off a solid thigh and a smattering of brown hair trailing into darkness.

Heart rate rising, she wrenched her gaze away and studied the neat precision of his shoelaces. Same size loops, same length ends, nothing long enough to drag in the dirt. As pleasing to the eye as a balanced ledger.

He passed food from hand to hand until her dinner sat between her tennis shoes.

She fished a ketchup-drizzled French fry from a red-checkered paper boat.

Rob bit into his cheeseburger.

They traded darting glances and ate in silence. She struggled to tabulate the feeling on her mental balance sheet. Not the comfortable quiet of longtime friends, but not the strained resentment of the silences between her and David, either. A tense silence. No—an intense silence.

Pregnant with possibility. Six inches separated their bare legs. He owed her three kisses. And when he'd lifted her, she'd thought she'd felt his—

Flushing, she sipped the old-fashioned lemonade she'd opted for instead of pop. If fitting the word in her mouth went beyond her comfort level, she sure as hell wasn't ready for fitting—him.

But he'd said she wasn't a commodity to him. He didn't think of their date as a transaction, a loan of his resources in exchange for some interest from her, a down payment. A deposit, her mind supplied, and she'd never found banking so filthy. God help her keep a straight face at work Monday morning.

His consideration ought to have put her at ease. Instead, she occupied a heretofore-unknown position, having to square his gentlemanly restraint with the lust she simmered in thanks to his presence. Staring at him out of the corner of her eye raised her pulse. She breathed faster. Sipped her drink more often.

Maybe she was the predator, the one cruising for an easy lay. She'd never been the seducer. Hard to judge without trying the role on for size.

Women her age initiated one-night stands after their divorces all the time. The magazine covers in the checkout line said so.

Conscience tugged at her. Using Rob—funny, sexy, thoughtful Rob—as nothing more than an outlet for the sexuality welling up inside her would make her miserable, not satisfied. Scanning the rows ahead of them, she searched for a spark. Dozens of men. Some of them well-groomed, well-muscled, attractive men.

Not a single one primed a reaction in her body the way Rob did.

If thirtysomething divorcees were supposed to be on the prowl for horny boys, her body hadn't gotten the message. Chalk her indifference up to another failure. The rows beyond the teens and college kids held minivans and dusty sedans, a sea of parents and children all the way to the screen.

She belonged down front with them. Mom had been raising three kids by her age—heck, when Mom hit thirty-one, Eleanora had been starting kindergarten. Lil and Vi had been in diapers.

She didn't hate her career. Arranging loans for aging farmers and eager entrepreneurs and young, in love, first-time homeowners made her happy despite the extra time she had to put in to make the numbers work. But every year she fell another tick behind. Felt a little more like the life she longed for had to be happening elsewhere, in a parallel universe where she'd done something right instead of wrong. The disappointment weighed on her, a lethargy beyond her ability to shake.

"Finished?" Rob squeezed her knee under his palm.

"What?" She cringed at the yelp in her voice. "Sorry, I mean—" Her hands sat empty, and so did the paper boat where her fries and cheeseburger had been. "I guess I am, yeah."

"Good." He tilted his head and studied her. Inscrutable, with his gold-brown eyes, his straight lips, and his squared-off jaw.

He examined her the way she pored over ledger sheets, but what she added up to in his head, she couldn't say.

"We've got the best pie in town waiting, and you have to try both." He switched sides, coming to rest alongside her with his legs stretched to the far edge atop the curving wheel well. The pie wedges sat in a paper boat he nestled in one hand. He picked up the lone fork. "Which one do you want to try first?"

She could've protested. Procured her own plastic cutlery and asked him to divide the slices. Demanded he pass over the fork and let her cut her own bites. "You choose."

He raised an eyebrow and glanced from the pie to her. "You sure about that?"

"I expect I am." She hoped, anyway. The usual effects of his proximity already trounced rational thought. A thumping rush danced between her legs. Her nipples stiffened, her bra rough and tight across sensitive flesh.

"Close your eyes, Eleanora."

She exhaled on a shuddering breath. The gruff-but-coaxing demand in his voice twanged a response low in her belly. Might be enough to overcome her nerves. Trusting David would've been impossible. But Rob wasn't David. He'd been nothing but trustworthy so far. With a slight nod, she closed her eyes.

Anticipation sluiced through her, leaving a cold fire burning in its wake. She strained to hear the scrape of the plastic fork on paper.

"Open up." His low command drowned out all other sound.

Had the first bite been apple or peach or coconut crème, she wouldn't have known the difference. Her heart ran the four-minute mile while every cell in her body, down to the ones in her taste buds, danced with excitement the second her mouth closed around the fork. Her shoulders unclenched, and she moaned without thought.

"Seems you're a strawberry-rhubarb woman." Rob's intimate whisper lacked any hint of laughter. "If you like the apricot half as well, I'll count my evening well-spent watching you sample pie."

Her internal squeeze surprised her, an involuntary response to the passionate warmth in his voice. Leaving her eyes closed, she rolled her arm. Not much, but enough to rest the back of her forearm and her knuckles against Rob's thigh. The resurgent thrill zipped through her.

"Have another taste."

She opened her mouth. Sugary-sweet fruit with a buttery crust and juice coated her tongue.

"Best pie you've ever had?"

Best service, for sure. She licked her lips. "I might be biased. Can I expand the sample size before I decide?"

He fed her small bites at a languid pace matching the laziness brought on by the summer sun. She didn't care to open her eyes, and he never asked.

Stretching her fingers, she curled them against worn denim. The thickness had to be a seam. The bottom hem. She traced the ridge with her index finger and grazed warm flesh.

His thigh flexed. "Last bite. Best make it count."

She closed her lips and sucked the fork clean. Sweet, delicious strawberry. She swallowed it down and loosed an appreciative sigh. "Definitely the best I've ever had."

Rob shifted his leg under her. "Can't say as I remember it ever being this good before, either."

"No, mustard!"

Her eyelids flew open.

A girl ran past the truck, spattering gravel. "Did you hear me? I changed my mind. Forget the ketchup."

Eleanora flung herself out of her lewd slouch and into a proper, David-approved, straight-backed dinner posture. Dozens of people might have spied what she and Rob were doing. In public. God. If she ended up in another video online—

"Nobody's paying us any mind." Rob set the empty dish aside and squeezed her hand. "When you close your eyes with me, you can be sure I'm watching for the both of us."

"I'm that obvious, huh?" She reached for calm with deep, even breaths. He was right. No one stared at her or accused her of enjoying herself too much. She comprised the whole class of people having trouble accepting fun and freedom.

"I'm trained to be observant, Eleanora."

Comforting, but his answer skirted around a blanket *no*. She forced a laugh. "You must think I'm paranoid."

His lips tightened as he watched her. He raised his hand from hers, slow and steady. Turning his torso, he brought both hands to her cheeks. No. Not quite. His palms didn't rest on her skin. He hovered, a hand on either side, a hairsbreadth away from touching.

She met his eyes, and her breath caught. Trapped. He cradled her like a firefly within his cupped hands.

"I think you're noticing things that maybe didn't get so much attention from"—he wrinkled his nose—"in the past. And 'cause you're noticing now, you figure everybody else is." Shaking his head in a slow sweep, he traced her jawline and held her transfixed with two fingers beneath her chin. "But all those others are wrapped up in their own noticing. The things you think shine big ol' flashing lights give off faint sparks. No one's looking for 'em but me, Eleanora." He smiled, his teeth white and even and his lips full. "And I'm looking closer than an electron scope at integrated circuits."

She matched his smile, letting his natural comfort lure hers out of hiding. "Pretty close, then?"

"Mighty close." Dropping his hands, he dug into a pocket. "Here." He passed her his car keys, one held between his fingers. "Pop the footlocker while I toss the trash, and we'll make this perch more comfortable for movie-watching." He gathered up everything but the popcorn and strode toward the garbage can at the end of the aisle.

Opening the box revealed two spongy mats folded accordion-style. She snapped them out, egg-carton side up, and created a soft base in the truck bed. A base not unlike a real bed. More rummaging uncovered a sheet and two pillows. She pulled them free and closed the footlocker.

She snuck in a sniff before he turned back toward the truck. Fresh. Sunshine and grass, as if he'd washed the linens yesterday and left them hanging on the line today. Him planning ahead didn't surprise her. He seemed like a thinker.

But not knowing whether he'd prepared for her comfort specifically or had seduction down to a science bothered her. Maybe years spent honing and perfecting his style had taught Rob to pinpoint to the minute when his date would shuck her clothes so long as he had everything lined up. His insistence about not expecting sex might be part of the ploy, a way to put women at ease.

How the hell would she know? She'd been stupid enough to believe David when he lied to her face, and she'd known him for years. She'd known Rob one week. Kneeling on the mat, she locked her gaze on him. He covered ground fast, more from a long stride than seeming rushed. He walked with his shoulders back and his head up. He dodged distracted wanderers with easy steps. His shirt didn't sport a telltale *all men are liars* slogan.

Closing in, he grinned at her with those kind hazel eyes, their golden flecks too far away to discern. He waved at himself. "Do I pass inspection?"

"I—you—" Fumbling with the sheet, she tossed one end toward him. "Help me shake this out."

Catching the cotton in one hand, he tipped his head. "All right, Eleanora."

She turned her back on his frown and hopped out the far side of the truck. "On three."

Too late, she realized she hadn't explained her intent. But they lifted together in a smooth motion, the sheet billowing with a flick of their wrists. Pale blue cotton rose in a second sky, and she gave in to the urge to lift her arms with it.

Ducking her head under, she gazed up at the falling fabric and imagined playing parachute like a first-grader in gym class. A wave rippled across.

Rob's affable smile and the intense heat of his gaze met her startled glance. He'd raised his arms, too, and shook the sheet again. "My brother and me entertained our baby sisters like this when Mama made us bring in the wash. Can't say we got a lot of folding done." He leaned in, pulling the edge of the sheet down behind his shoulders. "Plenty of smiles, though."

She let the cotton sink, stepping back until the sheet settled into the truck bed. More down-home, putting-her-at-ease, gosh-I'm-a-nice-guy Rob. "You always carry fresh sheets in your truck for emergencies?" Shit, she sounded bitchy.

Rob's smile faded.

"I mean, my parents always sat in lawn chairs at the drive-in." She rushed her words out, as if fast-talking would halt the slumping mouth and flattening cheeks reshaping his face. "They'd spread a blanket on the hood of our sedan, and my sisters and I lined up and leaned back on the windshield to watch."

"It's hot out, even with the sun near down." Rob rested his hands on the side of the truck. "I thought you might rather a padded seat than bare metal, and a thin sheet instead of a heavy, scratchy blanket that'll cling to sweaty limbs in the heat. That's all, Eleanora."

He didn't sound angry, but she must've offended him. Hell, she'd offended herself by asking. Time to change the subject.

"So, how 'baby' are your baby sisters? Mine—" She babbled. Prattled. Went into detail overload about her mother having three babies in four years and how close—and sometimes fiercely competitive—she and her sisters had been growing up.

But she didn't budge from her position beside the truck, and he held firm to his opposite her. The bed grew into a gulf between them even as he divulged his own sibling details.

He'd come along thirteen months after his brother and learned quick to keep up. When neighbors meant miles down the road, playmates were blood or nothing. His first sister had arrived three years later, and the second sixteen months behind.

The screen flickered to life with a ten-minute warning. She took a moment to regroup as they both made bathroom trips and Rob picked up a fresh drink to go with their popcorn. Returning first, she clambered into the truck bed without him, settled a pillow against the footlocker, and leaned back. A quick tug arranged the popcorn bags to either side.

She'd never lain in the darkness beside a man who wasn't David. Rob's expectations remained a mystery. Hell, her own expectations had mystified her this whole week. Thinking of him, wearing his shirt while she—

Awkward guilt shrouded her deeper than the darkening sky. David hadn't liked her touching herself unless the act was for him. With him watching. After a while, inspiring the need got less and less important. Arousal grew harder to find.

Could she—was she ready for…

The crunch of the popcorn bag in her hand startled her, and she laughed at herself. Worse than a fraidy-cat jumping at the wind knocking the screen door. That'd be sure to impress him.

Rob hustled back to the truck, keyed the accessories, and slid open the back window as he tuned the radio to pick up the movie soundtrack. With the first green preview screen flashing behind him, he sauntered around to the tailgate. The mix of fading sunlight and movie brightness set him aglow. "Room for one more up there, miss?"

"What if I say no?" Dammit. She hadn't meant to ask, but she craved his answer in every tense muscle, about matters weightier than seating arrangements.

He set down the drink cup and patted the end of the truck. Cartoon racecars zipped across the screen behind him. "Then I'll be cooling my heels here."

Pulling the second pillow beside her, she paused. He sounded sincere, not like a man cracking a joke. "Won't you be lonely?"

"I expect so." He held his head level and his body still, a marble pillar of honesty and integrity. A man who'd never cheat on his taxes. Or on other things.

This man would put her comfort above his. He'd respect her boundaries. Acknowledge her emotions. Listen to her and understand what she said. Maybe even what she meant. So far from David they didn't seem the same species, let alone the same gender.

"I think you should come sit next to me." She toed off her shoes and flexed her feet in her cotton footie socks. The freedom breathed tingling joy in her veins. "Otherwise all the talking will annoy our neighbors."

He boosted himself into the bed and passed her the drink. "You're the kind of gal who talks through a movie, huh?"

"You didn't invite me on a date so we could spend hours staring at a screen in silence, did you?" She sipped cherry lemonade through the straw.

Shaking his head, he rubbed his jaw. "Talk all you like, Eleanora. First show's for the little ones anyway."

She fell silent as the movie started. Her shoulder brushed Rob's. They passed the popcorn and lemonade between them, grazing hands in the heady overlap of accidental and on-purpose. Squinting against the screen's brightness, she made out the silhouettes of the families in front. Memory and imagination sketched them in greater detail than reality could match.

The kids watching with rapt attention and the ones spinning in circles with no care for the screen. The younger ones climbing into mom or dad's lap, ready to nod off before the credits rolled. The mothers with blankets thrown over one shoulder, babies nursing in the privacy beneath.

They could be anyone. Any family. And in the darkness, every one of them could be happy and perfect.

"Do you ever think about parking down front?" Whispering, she waved toward the sea of anonymous families.

He twitched, his shoulder jerking.

Oh God. The drive-in was his go-to date. He had the details down to a science. Of course he didn't park where kids would see. "I don't mean for, you know, doing things." Please let something stop her mouth. Power outage. Lightning crash. Alien invasion. Anything. "Because that's, I mean, obviously not—"

"Not for making out or putting on a show," he broke in. "I understood what you meant, Eleanora."

Did he? She didn't. Heck, she didn't know why she'd asked the question. Half the things she'd said or done with him remained inexplicable. She got near him and unexpected things popped out.

"Much as I like the drive-in, I don't bring dates here. I relax here, and that's not what a lotta women want from a date." His fingers found hers in the narrow gap between their bodies. "Most of the ones I've met want something fancy, an inch pretentious and a yard uncomfortable, everybody jumping through hoops in a three-ring circus."

He cleared his throat and squeezed her hand. "I brought you here because I think we're alike in that respect. Tired of the fake things. Thinking about"—scanning the rows ahead of them, he rolled his shoulders—"something real."

Fear and hope gripped her. The desire to believe. He made picturing a future together so easy.

With a tilt of his head, he leaned on her. The faint pressure sent her pulse soaring.

"And yeah. I think about parking down there." Low and yearning, like the cool caress of a foggy morning, his voice swirled over, around, and through her. "Car seats and sippy cups and skinned knees. Toothy grins and tantrums from tots running wild, and the one on the way resting safe under his mama's heart."

Shuddering, she sucked in a breath and prickled with goose bumps. Too perfect. Rob presented himself as everything David wasn't. She couldn't deserve him.

"I'm hard-wired to be a family man, I guess. Maybe a little more with every year that passes." He glanced away, his swallow audible.

She tightened her fingers on his. Saying these things might make him as nervous and excited as hearing them made her.

"Haven't had much luck finding the right gal who feels the same," he whispered.

I'm that girl.

The words floated in the space above her tongue, but she held her lips closed. She'd known him one week. Offering to be his wife, the mother of his children—that would be insane. But affection and arousal crashed like the sea in her body, swelling toward high tide and pulling her along. "You owe me three kisses, Robin, and I think you're a man of your word." God, such a sultry tone couldn't belong to her. Where had she dredged those low notes from?

His quiet growl suggested a similar origin. "Whatever my lady desires."

He grasped her with one hand, his palm heating her cheek and his fingers splayed down her neck.

She tensed for a rough kiss, awaiting his delving demand.

He nibbled.

She gasped, air puffing out with her surprise.

Despite the firm command in his muscles, his kiss didn't demand anything. Slow, teasing bites and flicks of his tongue coaxed her open as if the idea had belonged to her all along.

Their bodies slipped down, and the line between seducer and seduced blurred. His hand slipped, too, edging beneath her gauzy cover-up. He fingered the thin strap of her camisole beneath.

She twined her fingers in his orange t-shirt to keep him close. She'd used his black shirt, the clean one lying in the cab, as a sleep aid all week. She'd reluctantly washed the loaner Thursday because manners demanded she return it tonight. Six nights she'd lain in bed with his rich, earthy claim surrounding her, and six nights she'd slipped her hand into her underwear and stroked herself to climax with thoughts of him.

All that satisfaction, hell, more than she averaged in a year—no, in six—should've worn her out. Another message her body hadn't gotten.

Days of orgasms hadn't eased her hunger for him. They didn't stop her arousal from surging in his presence.

The need seemed stronger, as if she'd created some expectation in her belly that now was the time for touching before sleep. She'd advanced from one failed attempt a month at the most to nightly success thanks to Rob.

With a final press of his closed lips, he pulled back.

Her lips stayed open. Her lungs demanded air faster than her nose allowed.

"One," he whispered.

He counted his effort as one kiss? Seven, at least. Maybe eight. But damn. One meant she had two more coming, and not a single part of her disagreed with that idea. She nodded. "One."

"Don't wanna squander the two I have left." He tugged the brim of her cap. "Sun's gone. This an indispensible part of your look?"

"High fashion." Her dry tone raised a chuckle from him. "But you can take it off me."

He leaned in close, his mouth next to her ear and his breath warm. "I like those words, Eleanora."

She pressed her thighs together to quell the spasm between her legs. Not helpful in the least. Whatever he stirred in her overpowered her ability to hold back. Not alone, and not with him, either. She'd gone from David's lackluster wife to Rob's wanton slut in a hot second. What the hell was wrong with her?

Her hat, pulled off with careful attention not to disturb her ponytail, landed somewhere behind her. Humidity had given her bulk and curl. He wound her hair around his hand once and fingered the strands.

His growl made her shiver. The slight pull at her scalp as he rubbed his fingers together tightened her nipples and set them to tingling.

She opened her mouth, and he swooped in.

He delivered the harder kiss she'd expected the first time around. His show, start to finish. He overwhelmed her with raw power. Mouth sealed to hers, he swept his tongue inside and stroked.

Their bodies rocked. He guided her backward on his arm. They no longer lay on their sides, facing each other as equals. Now she rested on her back, and his weight pressed into her side with the burning heat of a blast furnace.

She wiggled to settle herself more comfortably.

He groaned into her mouth and clamped his hand down on her far hip.

He was hard.

She didn't have to guess this time, because this touch wasn't fleeting. The immovable stone digging into her, pressing high on her thigh, was his cock.

Ready for the word, but for the man? Uncertainty warred with desire. He wanted her. The thought crashed through her body like lightning. Shock, heat, and fear.

He pulled his mouth away.

She whimpered at the loss. Honest-to-God whimpered. A sound she didn't realize herself capable of making.

"Two." Hand splayed across her stomach, Rob stroked her through her camisole. The edge had risen out of her jean shorts, and her gauzy cover-up had fallen to the side. Night air caressed a thin strip of skin above her shorts, tickling her navel.

Tension made her stretch in an instinctive search for relief. The motion rippled through her, highlighting every point of contact between them. The roughness of his leg against hers. The press of his erection, digging in harder than a metal belt buckle but a hell of a lot more pleasant. The firm planes of his torso, hidden now beneath his shirt, but familiar from the eyeful she'd gotten last week. His left arm, steady and supportive under her neck. He'd let go of her hair. When, she didn't know.

"Ready for that third prize, Eleanora?" He nuzzled her face, pushing and bumping like the cat she'd had as a child.

His playful affection settled her nerves. She was ready for three. She'd make three count. And after he took her home, she'd touch herself like a madwoman to quiet the jangling need driving the thumping rhythm between her legs and dampening her panties.

"I hear the third time's the charm." Excitement deepened her voice, until he grazed the bare strip of belly above her shorts and made her squeak. "Lots of charm."

Rolling his fingers lower, he circled her navel with his thumb. Slow, and gentle, and not stopping. He tapped his fingers.

Jesus. His touch sank through her shorts, through her panties, an inch north of flesh thumping in reply. If he stretched, he'd be touching—he'd be touching the places she'd touched thinking about him.

Her clitoris. Her vulva. Clinical words for pieces of herself she'd never felt so connected to before.

"Mm-hmm. You have lots of charms, Eleanora." His fingers drifted.

Her muscles twitched. Her body broadcast needs she begged herself to permit. Let him come closer. Let him. Please.

* * * *

Cupping the curve of her sex in his palm, Rob pressed the heel of his hand where he hoped the weight'd do the most good. Thick denim played havoc with his accuracy.

Her gasp and the tense bend at her knee as she curled her leg tighter beside his groin seemed promising.

He captured her mouth and speared his tongue through her parted lips.

She raised her head and gave as good as she got. Chasing the pressure or staking her own claim. He'd take either.

He pushed back harder. Heated passion consumed him, adding intensity to the kiss and his clenching hand between her legs. The denim of her shorts had the softness of a hundred washings, but she'd be softer still beneath them.

She rocked her hips into his motion. The thinnest thread of her moan made him yearn to hear her in full-throated cry.

Not here. She'd be mortified. He jabbed himself with a sharp reminder to take things gentle with her. Creativity would be his ally. No reason they couldn't both enjoy this night to the fullest. Working her up and leaving her unsatisfied smacked of the rude, uncaring treatment she seemed to expect.

He drew his hand toward her waistband and released her mouth. Her mewl an unspoken question, he aimed to reassure. He brushed his thumb across the zipper on her shorts and tweaked the button flap.

"I'd sure like to touch you, Eleanora." With his forehead pressed to hers, they shared the same air. He breathed slow and steady. Her quick puffs teased his skin like the kiss of the west wind. "I wanna feel you under my fingers."

"I, I want that too, but…" She closed her eyes.

"But what?" He had an inkling. Nerves. The location. Ties to her ex-husband, unhappy memories. If she needed to wait, they'd wait.

"It's so"—her whisper dripped out in a halting tremor—"slutty."

No. No. No. Nothing shameful in loving. He gentled his voice and his touch, tracing the waistband of her shorts. "Why do you say that?"

"The people." Opening her eyes, she dug her fingers into his chest, curling his t-shirt in her grip. "They could see."

"It's dark back here." He kissed the corner of her mouth. "And I won't let anyone see an inch of you." They'd both keep their clothes on for this. He aimed to show her a good time, not embarrass her. Not make her feel dirty.

"It's only our first date." She objected without conviction, her tone more confused and uncertain than anything else, and she nestled close rather than trying to pull away from his cradling embrace.

"I could say third." By his count, leastwise. He savored the moments they'd spent together. "We talked at the bar. Had coffee Monday." He forced himself to stop caressing the sweet strip of skin between her shirt and her shorts. So damned soft. "By your standard, you must think I'm a slut, taking my shirt off on the first date. Did you lose respect for me right then and there?"

She chortled, and her breath held the sweet scent of caramel. "That's different. You're a guy. You have different rules."

He rolled his head, a rejection and an Eskimo kiss in one. "Rules are for other folks, Eleanora. Folks who can't be honest with themselves and their partners. I promised you I wouldn't be fake with you, and I won't. Which matters more, the number of dates or the quality of the connection?"

"I've never wanted so much as I do with you." Her whisper came as a hot, eager rush. "I feel like, like I don't know what's happening to me. All week, thinking about you, I couldn't stop, every night, and I—" She stuttered and sucked in a breath, her hips thrusting. "And I don't usually and now it's all I think about."

He bit down, holding in a groan. His dream girl, confessing to masturbating to thoughts of him for the whole week. Christ, he'd unload his balls with every possible permutation of her image in his head for days.

"It's the same for me, thinking of you." He nudged his hips forward. The pressure of her thigh against his cock loosed the low groan he'd tried to silence.

She squeaked, the sound half-swallowed as she clamped her lips tight, but she met his push with her own. A woman testing new territory.

"You're waking up, Eleanora." He dotted her face with tiny kisses, the sort he'd wake her with every morning. The blaring nuisance of an early alarm would be a thing of her past. His body woke him at six without fail, and he'd rouse her with kisses and caresses before their workdays began. "Your body knows what it wants. If you trust me with it, I won't lead you astray."

Never. Only into his arms, where she belonged.

A moan floated from down the row. A giggle drifted in from the opposite direction.

"Plenty of people testing their cars' suspension in this lot. Seeing how much motion those shocks will absorb." Squeaking metal and crunching gravel surrounded them, and the movie soundtrack droned through the open back window of the cab above their heads. "Nobody here'll take notice of one more."

He waited for her answer in stillness, with a mumbled chorus of prayers filling his skull and tingling heat everywhere their skin brushed.

The nod came first. "Touch me, Rob." Quiet but sure, she spoke without hesitation. "I want you to wake me up. I spent too many years sleepwalking."

Relief and eagerness washed through him. She hadn't responded like a woman coerced into giving in. She wanted him. She owned her needs.

"You deserve this pleasure, Eleanora." He thumbed open her jean shorts and dragged the zipper down. The bigger the stakes, the steadier his hands. Worked in the military. Worked at a keyboard. Worked wonders on a woman. "And I aim to see you get everything you deserve."

Sliding into the gap in her shorts, he teased two fingers over her panties and traced the full lips hidden beneath. Fuck yes. Arousal left her panties slick and supple. A deft nudge pushed the fabric between her lips.

She shuddered, her knees rising. Her instincts won silent applause in his mind. His woman didn't lack desire.

He rocked his erection against the outside of her thigh as his fingers worked. Ease her mind, prove to her he hadn't shoved her out on a limb alone. His arousal kept pace right alongside hers. "You like that?" Grazing her ear, he pitched his voice low and soothing.

Her sigh promised an affirmative answer. "More."

He slipped his fingers up and under her panties. Working in the dark without a map, and God, he'd love to have eyes on her right now. And tongue. On. In.

Next time.

She huffed out a breath in the same moment her clit jumped under his index finger. Mission objective located. He rubbed a circle around the edge, testing her sensitivity.

His position at her side pinned her right arm below her breasts, but her other hand danced with the sheet spread beneath them. She fluttered her fingers and clenched by turns.

He added pressure and swept across her clit. Her most sensitive skin rocked under his fingertips.

Rolling her cheek against his bicep, she rocketed one arm upward, bent at the elbow, and gripped his forearm beside her head.

Damn, she could squeeze. His cock thumped her thigh, untroubled by the layers of denim between them.

A deep kiss muffled his groan and hers in reply. He dipped his fingers lower, an easy slide, and kept his senses on alert for changes in her.

Her arousal coated his fingers in wet heat. She squirmed, restless and rocking against him, clamping his arm in pulsing waves.

He stroked her entrance but didn't push. Her choice. Had to be.

"Please," she whispered. "Please, something. More."

"Inside?" He circled with a single finger. "Is that the more you want?"

"I, I think so. Please."

Sinking his middle finger into her heat, he pressed his thumb to her clit.

She arched her back, curving her hips up as if trying to fuck herself on his hand.

His breath stuttered. The slide of her thigh rubbed along his length, a tortured delight. He thrust as she came back down, his finger inside her and his cock at her side moving in concert.

"Beautiful." He teased her earlobe with his tongue. "Sweet and wild."

Surrounded by slick, fast-flowing evidence of her enjoyment, he slipped a second finger in alongside the first.

She moaned, foggy and low, and fluttered around him.

Orgasm potential in his palm. Not half bad for a man coming off a lengthy hiatus. He'd scale the peak with her, help her claim the mountaintop, and God willing she'd ask him to guide her again.

Abrupt silence sliced off her moan.

Fuck, had he hurt her? Scared her? Lifting his head, he tried to catch her gaze.

Eyes squeezed shut, she pulled her top lip into her mouth. Wishful thinking, if she expected to barricade her moans behind her grimace.

"Still feeling good?" Nuzzling her cheek, he slowed his pace.

"Someone's going to hear." She lay rigid and unmoving, her hips no longer following his lead. A wisp of church basement scandal clung to her whisper. "I don't—" Bracing her arm against the sidewall, she flexed trembling fingers. "I shouldn't." Her hesitation smacked of more than a recurrence of a matter he'd thought settled.

"I won't let anyone embarrass you." Not even himself, and sure as hell not to give her an orgasm she feared or to force her vulnerabilities to the surface. She'd confessed to masturbating all week but hadn't used the word. She'd gone out tonight trusting him. He'd take her home by the same route. No detours into distrust or confusion. "I'd never want you hurt or ashamed, Eleanora. You say stop and I'll stop."

She breathed. Deep, slow breaths with a five-count between in and out. Her stiffness melted.

Light from the moon and the screen outlined the curves and peaks of her breasts. His arm crossed her hip. His wrist disappeared into the dark vee of her shorts. The view down their bodies made him ache.

Beyond, at the foot of the truck bed, the lane stood empty.

"No one's watching you but me. No one's feeling you but me." He bent his arm and rolled her farther into his embrace. "No one's hearing you with your face against my neck."

"Nobody else." She tucked in and rolled her hips, calling him back into action. "Just us."

Stretching, he grasped her hand and joined them in a clasp atop her breast. "You and me."

She wrapped her other arm up and over his shoulder.

"You're safe here." He kissed and nipped his way along her forearm. "I've got you."

Shivering, she nodded and clung to him with surprising strength. "Don't stop."

He worked her with patient fingers. More patience than his cock showed, grinding against her side.

Mewling sighs answered him. She clawed his back, clutching fistfuls of fabric as if she meant to pull his shirt right off him.

"You like knowing how hard you make me? That's all you, Eleanora."

She rocked in rhythm, her hips undulating in a wave, and Jesus God save him if her body didn't clamp his fingers with a virgin's tightness.

"You consume my thoughts." His thumb working her clit would break the sound barrier if he stepped up the pace any more. "I wake up hard with you on my mind."

She moaned on every exhale, quiet but audible and vibrating where her face pressed to his neck.

"That's it, you can let go." He squeezed her hand, the two together cradling her breast. "It's all right to let go. You're so damned soft and wet and your heat's burning my fingers. Heaven's on fire."

Straining toward him, she lifted her hips and spread her knees wider. Her thigh jammed his cock. He'd be damned if he finished before her despite the solid provocation.

"Bite down." Whatever held her back, he aimed to provide the soothing solution. "You can scream and moan all you want into my neck. No fear, Nora."

Pain blossomed, but pain had never felt so good.

Her muffled cry coincided with a jolt of tension through her body, her heels drumming at the truck bed. She spasmed around his fingers in a wet rush.

Hard as a rock in his shorts, he groaned and joined her in release. Four shots, his cock jerking with the blaze of cleansing fire. Somewhere in the long line of cars, a teenage boy or two had probably filled his shorts with the same sticky warmth and struggled with embarrassment.

Age brought perspective. Feeling like a man wasn't about where he shot his load. His masculine pride belonged to her whimpers and sighs and her body squirming against him. The way she gave him control and trusted him to keep her safe.

Her shaking took a long while to slow. He planted kisses along her hairline and tasted the salt of her sweat. Murmured nonsense syllables and endearments as her legs fell slack. At her nudge, he uncurled his left arm.

She rolled flat and used his bicep for a pillow. Her eyelids fluttered. Shrouded in shadow, the hollow of her neck invited deeper exploration. She sighed through her smile.

"Good feeling?"

"I'm seeing stars." Her hushed voice magnified his satisfaction tenfold. A wisp of awe clung to her. "Even when I close my eyes."

He kissed the tip of her nose. "Same thing I see every time I look at you."

She giggled, and he leaned in for a true kiss, slow and full of gratitude. He rested his fingers over her sex, relaxed and possessive at once. A treasure he wouldn't relinquish.

"If you want, I can—you know." She curled her hand in a loose fist and shook it. "Return the favor."

Startled, he twitched like a rabbit hearing a rustle in the brush. So caught up in her climax, she hadn't recognized his. Pride burned hot. He set his lips against her ear. "No need," he drawled. "I christened my shorts making you feel good."

Dipping her chin, she gazed down their bodies. "I'm sorry. I should've offered sooner. God, I didn't think about you needing—"

"No apologies, Eleanora." He dropped a hint of steel in his voice. No fucking way would she blame herself for what didn't constitute a problem. Not with him. "When we're together, I want you focused on your own pleasure. If you're having a good time, you can be sure I am. Nothing makes a man feel like a man more than his woman in rapture."

"Your woman." Curiosity cast her before a fancy three-sided mirror, a woman trying on new clothes. They made a good fit, him and his honey girl. She'd see the truth. "You called me Nora."

"I did." He called to her so often in his solo sessions the nickname had slipped out.

"I've been stuck with 'Ellie' since forever." She stretched and yawned. "I like 'Nora' better. Especially for"—a tremor ran through her—"special occasions."

"Glad I rate as a special occasion." He nudged her face in a teasing caress.

"You're one of a kind, Rob. That's where you rate." Dead serious, his Nora stared him straight in the eyes. "Nobody else even gets on the chart."

* * * *

Too much. She'd revealed too much. He'd take her honesty for clinginess and cut her loose like in the articles her coworkers read to each other off their phones when foot traffic slowed. Men didn't want to be called a woman's everything. They wanted to be told they had the biggest—

"Good." He quashed most of her fear with a single word, solid and definitive. "You X off every square on that chart, 'cause I wanna reserve 'em all."

Nagging doubt called his bravado pillow talk, but he backed up his words with an unholy amount of cuddling. The rest of the double feature played out on the giant screen without a scene registering. Rob loomed larger. Closer.

His touch sent her into blissful overload. Desire accounted for a tiny fraction of the whole. He stayed.

He curled her in the crook of his arm, their bodies pressed together, and he didn't once complain about a disappointing night. They lay together watching the stars as the credits rolled and the cars down front trundled off to carry their sleepy passengers to bed.

Taking a chance on the way home, she rested her hand on his thigh.

He lowered his from the steering wheel and clasped hers. His light squeeze kept her quaking nerves at bay until they stood at her front door.

She ought to thank him for the night out. For the…surprise.

The orgasm.

And the still respecting her after.

Except she stood dumbstruck as a high-schooler ending her first date.

"I'd like to take you out again, Eleanora."

A second date. A fourth, if she started counting by his method.

"Next Friday, if you're free."

Silly man, changing the laws of math to make things add up the way he wanted. Rules were immutable. Weren't they?

"I'll clear my calendar." Four words. A victory. Her coworkers would pounce on her the second she bowed out of a girls night two weeks in a row. "Umm." Plague her with teasing innuendo. "Well."

Rob stood waiting. She'd hit the moment. The script dangled between them. Her line. *Would you like to come in?*

But to let Rob inside the house where memories of David uncoiled, to promise him something she couldn't wholeheartedly deliver tonight—the words echoed in her head and lodged in her throat. She tried twice to fit the key in the lock. Finally the pairing clicked, and she pushed the door open a finger width.

"I'd also like to kiss you again." Rob laid his hand on her cheek. "Before I leave."

He didn't expect her to offer. Thank God. She sagged into her comfort zone, breathing easier, her muscles pliant, her mind quiet. "Please."

Time stopped as he leaned in. Unhurried, he kissed her without pushing. His slow, rolling lips relayed her special status, her importance to him.

She replayed the moment again and again when he'd gone. Almost nothing he'd done tonight matched the man behavior Sharilyn described when she recounted her dates in graphic detail. But Rob transformed her every time she glanced at him. Thought of him.

"Rob."

Yup. Even saying his name alone in her bed wrapped her in her own femininity. Checks and balances. Rob's brand of manliness called to the woman inside her, all of the joys and hopes and desires churning so deep she no longer listened to them. But Rob did.

Her phone chimed from the nightstand.

Sleep tight, Nora. Pleasant dreams.

No question they would be.

You too, Rob.

Chapter 4

Rob sent her texts all week long, tantalizing tips for their date.

Think casual. Indoors.

Wear socks.

And something you wouldn't mind getting a little grease on.

When he picked her up at seven on Friday, she danced out the door in shorts and a scoop-neck tee she hoped clung to all the right places.

"Evening, Eleanora." He tugged her belt loop with a crooked finger. "Once again, you've shown brilliant instincts. Got your socks on?"

She swayed closer, letting him reel her in. Her heartbeat had spiked since his truck pulled into the drive. Near enough to inhale his earthy musk, she zipped along like a bill counter spitting out bundles. "Over my feet, inside my tennies, like usual." Laying her hand on his chest, she soaked up the strong and steady thumping under her palm. "This an elaborate setup for a joke about knocking my socks off?"

"And how might I do that?" His whispered question roared in her ear.

She shivered with goose bumps despite the lingering heat of the day. "You could kiss me hello." She'd fantasized about his mouth every night when her phone chimed with his goodnight texts.

"Could I?" He settled his hand on her hip, each finger a searing reminder of his proximity. The pinkish perfection of his lips sported a cocky rise.

She wouldn't mind seeing other things rising. Her face warmed. "Uh-huh."

He leaned in.

She tilted her head. Her eyelids grew heavy.

"Good to know."

Their lips brushed. A week's worth of pent-up passion tightened her nipples and tugged her sex. Initiating a deeper kiss, she tasted him with greater confidence than she'd owned last week.

He cradled her head, pulling her to him when the force of his kiss would have pushed her away.

She retreated for balance and he followed. Lips fastened together, they slow-danced another step and a third. The door handle dug into her back.

The bell rang, high and low.

Her jump broke the kiss. "Jesus." The offending doorbell button lacked the decency to apologize. Noisy nuisance. "Sorry about that."

Chuckling, he eased his fingers from her hair and swept loosened strands from her cheeks. "Can't say I've ever rung a woman's bell with one kiss before."

She fought down embarrassment and reached for a newer, not so timid feeling. The hot churning urged her to forget about the date, open the door, and invite him in. "You sure? If any mouth could manage, I'd bet on yours."

His gaze flicked to the door beside her. Air hissed through his teeth.

"C'mon." He grabbed her hand. "Into the pickup with you before my mouth lands me in trouble." He had the dark-eyed, tense-mouthed look of a man who very much wanted to find trouble.

Maybe she'd invite him in for trouble later.

She squirmed with a little *no* and a lot *yes, please*. Standing on her front walk contemplating—

with a guy she'd known all of two weeks—

and what if he asked why she didn't use the master bedroom—

and she didn't have condoms handy, for God's sake—

and *shut up and get moving.*

"Yup. Pickup. Time to go. Just what I was thinking." She danced two quick steps from her door. "You coming?"

Open mouth, insert foot. She'd come in his truck. Lying in the bed beneath the stars with Rob's solid frame beside her and over her and in her. He had beautiful fingers. Delicate instruments.

"Right there with you, Eleanora."

She shook off the memory and let him guide her by the elbow to the passenger seat.

The side mirror revealed his hand skimming the heated metal of the bed wall as he rounded the truck. Pausing at the far corner, he tipped his head back, closed his eyes, and took a deep breath.

She held hers in tandem, breathing out when he did. What in the hell was this man doing to her?

He slid into the driver's seat and cranked the engine. The vents blasted lukewarm air. Cooler than outside, anyhow. He backed them into the street. "Figured out where we're going this time?"

"Absolutely." She had, but straight answers subtracted from the fun, and she needed a lighthearted night. A subject far, far away from sex to give her panties time to dry out wouldn't hurt, either. "You've Crisco'd a floor and we're gonna go sock-sliding."

He shot her a glance. "That's a thing?"

"It is if you're seven, the kitchen floor is linoleum, and your parents are gone for the night."

"You were a wild child, Eleanora." He *tsked* with a decent imitation of sincerity. "Who was minding you?"

"Teenage neighbor." She and her sisters had tortured their sitters, battering them with incessant questions and making mayhem after the inevitable command to shoo. "She spent most of the night in the traditional way, tying up the phone and kissing her boyfriend. My sisters and I stood by the couch making *ewww* noises until she chased us out. We found something better to do in the kitchen."

"Was your mama mad as a hornet at the mess?"

"More when she saw my fat lip." She'd sported a pouty smile for days despite efforts to manage the swelling. "I slipped too close to the counter."

"Ouch. You seem to have healed up nice, though. Soft and plenty kissable."

Her laughter spilled out. She couldn't pick a topic that didn't lead back to romance to save her life. Not with Rob, at least. Riding in the car with David had been like traveling in a funeral train toward the end. "All praise belongs to a towel full of ice."

"Ah. Yeah, that one's saved me a time or two."

She teased the story out of him as he drove, learning the myriad reasons behind the inadvisability of hanging a swinging rope from the barn rafters to play Tarzan—starting with trusting your brother's skills.

"Boy Scout, my butt. He didn't deserve his knot-tying merit badge, I tell you what."

* * * *

The parking lot stood near filled as he swung the pickup along the rows and into a space. He helped her down from the seat, an excuse to tuck her hand in his own.

"Well?" A flashy sign illuminated the plain, squat building. Smokers clustered to the side of the bar entrance. Children skipped through doors ahead of their parents at the other end. "This about what you expected?"

She nodded, her ponytail bobbing.

He hadn't seen her hair down. Pulled back when they met, and in some fancy twist that suited her work clothes at coffee, and now twice in a ponytail on their dates. He itched to spread her honey-brown locks in a loose, flowing halo around her face. "Ever been?"

"Once or twice." She wrinkled her nose. "David didn't like bowling. Too lowbrow for him. He wanted to teach me golf. Real golf, not mini."

He glued his tongue to the roof of his mouth. No sense badmouthing her ex-husband, even if the man's behavior screeched certifiable ass. She'd loved the idiot somewhere along the way. Probably.

"No, that's not exactly true." Head tilted as if remembering weighed her down, she struggled upright and squared her shoulders. "He bought me clubs and lessons for my birthday one year, after I made the mistake of saying we weren't spending enough time together anymore."

"Why didn't he teach you himself if the gift was about togetherness?" He would've stilled his mouth, but the words fell out soon as the curiosity cleared the first synapse.

"He said we'd play once I got good enough to keep up." Pursing her lips, she emitted a disdainful chirp. "I never did use those lessons. He never bought me a birthday gift after that year, either. Said he didn't like me being so picky."

Oh hell no. The temptation to pop the bastard roared loud as an F-16 in his chest.

"I know it's not my business, but you ever notice when you talk about your marriage, it's all about what your ex liked?" He rubbed his thumb across the peaks and valleys of her knuckles. The softness of her skin made a soothing contrast to the rigid frame beneath. "What about what you like?"

He braced for an explosive reply. Nosing around old relationships wasn't always the wisest strategy. No, scratch that—prying never was. Women got right prickly about guarding their past. He'd dated one or two in his time who'd returned to a former flame after a few jealousy-making dates. But Nora had a unique way about her, a special something unlike the rest.

Her laugh cascaded like a hiccup, a series of stutters before her happiness flowed free and easy. "God, I needed to hear that. We tried the whole marriage counseling thing, but I never believed the counselor when she said the same damned thing." She tossed her head with the furious discomfort of a new-bridled horse. "Never could answer the question, either. I put my life on hold to be what David wanted me to be. Having my career became the only thing I refused to concede. The longer I stayed, the more our mismatched visions chafed. When I started pulling away, he"—her volume dwindled to a thin whisper—"replaced me."

He knew the sound of her shame, knew the taste, knew the blinding drunk anger and the long hours at work to forget. A decade past now, but betrayal scarred. "He cheated on you."

Shrugging, she pulled away. Her hand slipped free.

"I've been there." Sharing might help his honey girl open up. Fuck all if he'd let her believe herself unattractive or unwanted or cover herself in shame for her ex's wrongheaded jackassery. "She left her email open, almost daring me to find out."

A grimace twisted Nora's face, but she clung to stubborn silence.

He tried again, beefing up his tone with deeper authority. "It's not your fault he cheated."

She shook off his declaration before he'd finished. "I'm not legally allowed to say those words."

Falling silent, he slapped a neutral expression over the confusion and surprise tumbling beneath the surface. His gaze stayed trained on her unchanging face.

A car belting country-pop passed on its way down the aisle. Children's laughter sounded near the front doors.

She closed her eyes and held her breath. Thirty ticks passed before she bled her air out in a trickle. "My ex is an attorney." Jaw and shoulders tight, she met his gaze. "We divorced over irreconcilable differences. I can't discuss the terms."

Nondisclosure clause.

The words flashed a *game over* screen in his head. He signed the annoyances on a regular basis, secrecy being an unavoidable consequence of his work. Handling encrypted data necessitated careful protections.

But here? No.

His gut told him her fuckwit of an ex-husband had bedded down with another woman. Which meant he'd used his legal knowhow or his connections to ram an unfavorable agreement down her throat. The guy had cheated on her and made telling anyone impossible for her.

He nodded, stuffing his anger down deep. No wonder she doubted her desirability and struggled with sexual shame. Trying to move beyond a betrayal she couldn't talk about gave her no respite. The sharp edges gnawed at her self-worth and confidence.

"Oh, sure, I sign a lotta NDAs for work." He kept his voice light. Making this harder on her wouldn't help. Better to let her know he didn't hold her reticence against her. "Nature of cyber security, you know."

Of course, the agreements he signed compartmentalized information. They didn't brutalize him emotionally.

"Ready to try bowling?" He held out his hand.

With a growing smile, she accepted his invitation.

He curled his fingers around hers as she asked playful questions about the secrets he kept. They approached the front door slinging a well-established call and response pattern.

"And is your chair comfy?"

"I'm sorry, miss, but that's classified." He used the forbidding tone he'd used to keep the slick sleeves in line once he'd gotten kicked up to staff sarge. The voice had shut the noobs up something fierce.

Nora giggled and played finger-footsie. Her relaxed body language gratified him more than the snap-tos and order-followers ever had.

"What kind of candy dish do you keep by your keyboard?"

"I'm sorry, miss, but that's classified." Releasing her hand, he opened the glass door and sent a blast of cold air over them both.

She shivered in retreat, plastering herself against him even as she stepped in front to enter.

He fought the urge to wrap his free arm around her.

"Co"—he coughed, courtesy of her interrupting shudder snugging her ass against his hardening dick—"Cold?"

Christ, if she didn't step forward soon, he'd have a visible problem of the sort unwelcome in a family-friendly establishment.

"Half of me is." Her voice matched the cozy warmth of her rounded glutes. "Feels good on both sides."

He bit down on a groan, and she stepped away. He'd planned to have a cold beer or two tonight. Right now, a cold shower would do.

* * * *

Lighter than air. She led the way to the rental counter with Rob's hand resting on her back, and her feet bounced in her shoes as if she danced on a cloud.

His penis had flexed.

Unmistakable, when the sudden temperature shift had startled her. She'd bumped into him, and he'd responded to her with desire. Emboldened by his interest, she'd spoken her mind. He'd nudged her backside with his—his cock.

She itched to yank his shorts down and shout her discovery to the beige panels of the drop ceiling. Her touch had gotten a man hard. He wanted to sleep with her.

Face heating, she glanced at the fugly patterned carpet. One date with him—more accurately, a single date in which she'd let him slip his fingers inside her and pleasure her better than David ever had—and she'd turned into a slut.

She craved sex with discomforting persistence, thinking of Rob as she sat at work and went over repayment schedules with new loan signers. She crawled into bed at night imagining his bulk beside her and wondering how he'd feel in her hands.

The loss of control shook her between terrifying thrill and welcome relief. The cat jumping out of a dark basement in a horror film when the audience expects the knife-wielding maniac.

Rob's steady confidence and gentle handling raised her eagerness for the moments when he took charge as he had last week in his truck bed. He hadn't treated her like used goods afterward, and he'd asked her out again without making her wait and wonder.

His behavior didn't match the men Chelsea and the girls complained about, not the ingrates who ducked out in the middle of the night and never texted and not the moochers who emptied the refrigerator and downloaded porn on the girls' computers as though they owned the place.

"Two pairs of shoes and two games apiece to start, please." Rob rubbed her back in the space between her bra strap and the waistband of her denim shorts. "We're joining the pair on lane sixteen."

"We are?" Trotted out like an ornament. Smile and look pretty. Laugh, but not her unladylike horse laugh. Be witty, but don't outshine the clients David meant to woo. They'd never become members of the elite upper class if she kept dragging him down. Rob hadn't said anything about a double date. Nothing about the couple she'd be meeting tonight.

"Mrs. Kulp?" The man behind the counter smiled wide beneath a trimmed, graying mustache. "Almost didn't recognize you without your fancy lady suits. This feller your husband?" He extended his hand toward Rob. "Jake Bruner. Your wife's got a fine head for numbers."

Shaking his head, Rob grasped the offered hand. "Rob Vanderhoff. Eleanora has a sharp mind, right enough."

"Vanderhoff?" The older man's gaze swung her way.

"I, uh, Mr. Bruner, I didn't realize you'd be running the show tonight. I thought you wanted to spread the responsibility around. And it's—" Digging deep, she drew forth a smile in return, a falsity tugging on her cheeks. "It's Miss Howard now." She flashed her bare left hand. "Things have changed since the last time you dropped by the bank in person."

"That they have." He patted the counter, and his wedding band clinked on the orange laminate. "Well." Squinting at Rob, he pursed his lips. "Smart woman's too much for some to handle, I suppose."

She scrambled for something, anything, to escape a conversation guaranteed to drag her through awkward territory. "You know, if you want to refinance, we could talk about extending the loan to add your indoor skatepark proposal." Discussing work put her on firmer footing.

Rob rolled his thumb in relaxing circles on her back.

"Is your grandson still practicing at the outdoor park in Ames?"

"He's playing pin monkey tonight, Mrs.—Miss Howard." Jake waved toward the lanes. "But now you mention it…"

The proprietor rambled on about the family and the business between checking their shoe sizes and requesting their own shoes in trade for fresh-sprayed loaners.

She lifted one foot and jammed her fingers behind her heel.

Rob touched her wrist. "Let me." He sank to the floor beside her in a wide-set crouch and untied her tennies.

She tried to hold up her end of the conversation.

He stroked the back of her leg along her sock line.

Sucking in a breath, she leaned on her elbows.

Rob slipped her shoes free. His brief massage eased the tension from wearing heels at work all day. The firm press of his thumb in her arches made her toes curl and her thighs clench.

Laying her cross-trainers on the counter, he gazed at her with darkness swallowing the brown and gold of his eyes. His mouth never moved, but she'd swear he promised to run his hands from the soles of her feet to the hair on her head. Every inch. Strong fingers. Steady hands. Stroking her flesh as he had last Friday—

Bowling shoes clattered on the counter. "These oughta do ya."

Rob pulled his stare from her and slid bills across the counter for the rental. No discussion about who would pay. He seemed to accept the responsibility as given, but he didn't flaunt or complain. He took care of things in his quiet, direct way.

David would've thrown the money out with a sneer or a joke, the way he'd tossed the house in her lap to buy her silence. Discussing his affair would lose her the house and cost her a penalty payment besides, neither of which fit in her budget.

•

But Rob had backed off. He'd let her statement stand, redirected the conversation, and made her feel comfortable. He took her feelings into account instead of badgering her. David used to interrogate her. Practicing contract law, he didn't have much call for courtroom skills, though he'd sure enjoyed testing them on her at home.

Rob scooped up both pairs of shoes in one hand and returned the other to her back.

"C'mon, we'll get you something nice and light to start with." He guided her away.

She waved her belated thanks to the owner.

"Take things slow and ease into the heavier game."

Mouth drying, she nodded. If he meant bowling, her body had missed the message. Her mind taunted her with the knowledge of his weight against her. What games did he want to try?

He could ease into her. A growing certainty promised she'd like that.

* * * *

He found her a ten-pounder fit for her slender feminine fingers, and she insisted on carrying the ball to the lane herself. Fair enough. She cradled the weight under her breasts like a gal who didn't care about smudging her shirt with grease, a woman who wouldn't balk when life got messy.

They stepped down to the pit for lane sixteen. Lucas sat slumped in the scorekeeper's seat, flipping the bird, while Brian danced on the lane, shaking his ass. The digital scoreboard dangling from the ceiling flashed a pixilated image of a turkey doing the same. The place needed new graphics something fierce.

"Damn, man, put that away." Wasn't a time or place Brian couldn't find troublesome ways to amuse himself. Least civilian life hadn't fattened him up, or he'd truly pass for Thanksgiving dinner. Shit. He ought to cover Nora's eyes before she decided blonds in plaid board shorts flipped her switches. "Nobody needs to see your tail feathers."

Lucas swiveled in the seat. "Finally, somebody else he can beat on. You know how many times I hadda watch his stupid dance?"

"Sherwood, you made it." Brian pushed off and slid toward them. "And you brought someone way prettier than this fella." He jerked his thumb at Lucas. "He doesn't appreciate the allure of the turkey dance."

Eleanora craned her head beside him, her brows furrowing. Introductions, right. With the bodily fluids flying around, she'd missed out on the full meet-and-greet at the bar.

"Eleanora, meet Brian and Lucas." He waved toward each in turn with a shoe-laden hand. "I promise, they're nice guys when they aren't hanging out on bar floors." Better company than the girls she'd been spending her time with, he hoped. Relaxed, not making her prove something.

"Oh! It's nice to meet you." Shoving her ball into the crook of her arm, she extended her other hand to Brian. "Sorry, I just, you look like brothers. I didn't realize you were a couple."

Brian busted out laughing. "Please." He wiped lane grease across his shirt and shook her hand. "Like I'd let this twerp near my junk."

"Ugh." Lucas kicked the back of Brian's knee. Sibling love tap. The kid would have to try harder to knock Bri off balance. "As if I'd wanna be near your scrawny old junk. I'm thrilled you moved your ass out before we had to share a bathroom."

"When I moved out, Mom was still wiping your stanky ass." Brian shoved Lucas in the shoulder and, when the twerp tried to retaliate, wrapped him in a headlock. "Lucas is my baby brother, Eleanora. Emphasis on the baby."

Cringing, Nora shot a squinch-eyed prayer glance at the ceiling. She gained a toothy grin on the way down, her head shaking while Lucas drummed his brother's elbow to no effect.

Good. The need to put her at ease, let her enjoy herself, hit him fucking sledgehammer hard. Brian and Lucas wouldn't poke at her for one conversational fumble. These clowns would keep the dating pressure off.

"Rob said we were joining the pair on lane sixteen, so I thought he meant a double date." Her gaze held shrewd speculation, and her pursed lips invited a kiss. Full, pink lips.

"Yeah, a date with Heckle and Jeckle." He dropped the shoes by her feet and grabbed the ball from her arms. Safer than picturing where he wanted her mouth. "They get too rowdy for you, you let me know, Eleanora. I'll boot 'em off the lane."

"Oooo, Sherwood's got it bad." Brian let Lucas break free. "He's gonna toss us aside for a lady."

Lucas snorted. "Would you blame him?"

"You knuckleheads ready to start a new game or what?" He loaded up the carousel with his ball and Nora's, basic black and neon orange. Alongside the alien green waiting and the ball return spitting out another in black, the place looked decked out for Halloween. "I've got me a ringer here, and she's gonna put you both to shame."

"Big words, airman. Let's see what you and the lady can do."

Tying her rental shoes, his girl ignored the teasing. Her smile as she ducked her head seemed genuine enough.

Lucas's fingers flew over the keyboard, and new player names jumped to the display. Ringer. Airman. Buttface. God.

Rob slung himself into the seat beside Nora. Pressing his hip to hers, he bent down and slapped the bowling shoes on. Smooth, creamy skin ran from her ankles to the edge of her shorts. A road his tongue ached to travel, her honeysuckle scent goading him on. He'd been so damned mesmerized at the counter, resisting the urge only because he'd given his fingers permission to massage her calves.

"Okay, Ringer, you're up first." Brian delivered an expectant drumroll. "Show us what you've got."

Her breasts dropped into his eyeline as she leaned forward. Jesus. Shirt-covered, but still. Round, firm, and the perfect packet size for his capacity. Christ himself hadn't been so tempted.

"You know I'm not a ringer," she whispered. "I don't know the first thing about bowling. What do I do? Tell me what to do, Rob."

Blood surging to his dick, he clamped down on a thrust. Way too early in the night for those thoughts. "I'm sorry, miss, but that's—"

"Classified." She giggled.

He stood and pulled her to her feet. "Let's get you situated first. Stance, steps, and release." Release. An uncomfortably accurate word choice. "That's all there is to it."

He lined her up a smidge off-center as he explained the guide arrows and the benefits of spin. Good excuse to touch her. Nudging her elbows and knees into alignment, he tucked her body into a compact pose ready to launch from a short runway. "Mind the fault line. It'll buzz if you go over, so you wanna measure your paces first."

She gave the sequence a try without the ball, four steps, hips swaying and arm swinging. Twice more. "How'm I doing, coach?"

"Beautiful. Let's add the ball this time and see how she goes." Grabbing the orange ball, he ignored the snicker behind him. He waited for her to get into position and handed over the ball. "That's it. You want to cup the ball firm but gentle, too. Don't push. Let the weight roll off your fingertips."

"Yeah, cup his balls gently," Brian teased. "Fingertip precision. Rob needs delicate handling."

A snapping shutdown leapt to his tongue.

Blushing, Eleanora glanced over her shoulder. "You seem to know a lot about how to handle Rob, Brian." A flash of boldness lived in her eyes and her smile. "But I don't hear anyone in here offering to cup yours."

Brian groaned, and a chair creaked. "You wound me, Maid Marian."

Eleanora's smile gained an extra mile. The night seemed headed in the right direction. Squeezing her in his arms, he kissed her cheek.

Lucas chortled. "Rob's girlfriend scored off you, bro. You better up your game."

"Find me an unattached girl in here as pretty as Rob's, and I'll throw out my best pitch."

* * * *

She picked up steam by the end of the eighth frame. Might've gotten the hang of bowling sooner if she didn't spend ninety percent of her time checking out Rob.

He strode up with confidence and cradled the ball in large, long-fingered hands. Captivating, the way his fingers disappeared and the heel of his hand bumped the surface. Stimulating. Every night, thanks to him. Like he'd turned her on and her fumbling kept missing the shutoff valve.

A bottle of beer dripping with condensation thrust under her nose.

"Here." Lucas dropped onto the curving bench beside her. "I, uh, kinda owe you one. For—you know."

An apology round for the fiasco at the bar. Sweet kid, when he didn't stink of vomit. Maybe Rob had put him up to apologizing, but his open baby face and hunched shoulders blasted embarrassed sincerity.

"I think you owe her more than one." Brian swiped the second bottle from his brother. "Nice to see you make the return trip without spilling your stomach."

"Shut up, bro, can't you see I'm having a serious thing here?" Lucas flamed pink as she imagined she did a dozen times a day. More since she'd met Rob.

"Look, Eleanora"—Lucas cleared his throat—"you're like, real nice, and not super-old, and I'm sorry about ruining your night. So thanks for not bailing on Rob and for, you know, not being a bitch about the whole vomit thing."

She hadn't missed much by skipping the dating scene until she'd hit her thirties. Stumbling incoherence passed for manners at twenty-one. Wait 'til a guy hit maturity, and the excitement and uncertainty grew more attractive.

Standing at the ball return, palming the ball rocking into his hand, Rob winked at her.

Exponentially more attractive. Two weeks old, and their fledgling relationship seemed certain to sprout wings.

"The night turned out the best I've ever had at that meat market." She twirled the bottle in her hand. He'd brought her out for a night with his friends like she belonged in the gang. "So don't apologize." Not hiding her like a shameful secret, not hustling her in and out of his bed, but introducing her like someone who'd be sticking around. Not the impression she'd gotten from anyone else in the bar week after week. "But for God's sake, don't do it again."

"Don't worry, E. Next time I spew, I'm aiming at my big brother. Unlike you, he deserves it."

"Maybe you oughta help him out." Small clusters of bowlers crowded the pits from here to lane forty, and every hand without a ball held a beer. The families had packed up for the night long ago. "Some of these hot thirtysomethings must be single. Target one of them, and let Brian rescue her from your inexcusable youth."

"Yeah, it's old fogeys night here." Lucas ran a hand down the back of his hair. "Uhh, no offense. Just, you know, all the cool kids are at the drive-in getting fucked on Friday nights. Too many lights here."

"Jesus, Lucas." Brian smacked his brother on the forehead. "Try not to swallow your feet while they're crammed in your mouth."

"What? 'Cause I said 'fuck'? E's chill, she's not like the rest of these mom-types."

What the hell. She'd bitten her tongue so often around David. With Rob, she wanted to loosen up. "Rob and I went to the drive-in last weekend." She swigged her beer, calm as could be. "He knows how to show a girl a good time."

Bluster, mostly, and a spell of blushing, but the guys cracked up with catcalls and hoots. Fun, though not as gratifying as the heavy stare Rob had going. Heat and pressure pinned her back in her seat. Promised her a stupendous night, better than the last.

Every drop of approval and desire in his eyes egged her on to new boldness. A woman she'd never been, but one she yearned to be.

Rob sauntered off the lane toward them. The display above his head announced his spare. Up next, Brian bounced to his feet.

"You dog." Brian punched Rob's shoulder in passing. "You didn't tell us about the good bits."

"Sure I did." He settled next to her and draped his arm around her shoulder. "I said I went out with the woman from the bar. Everything about that was good."

* * * *

Nora fit right in. Eased up, enjoyed herself, teased Lucas like a kid brother by the end of the night. Not the sort of date he'd have picked for a short-term gal, but Nora he meant to keep.

She didn't act too good for bowling with the guys or demand attention and compliments all the time. Fact, she seemed happier not being the center of attention. Cuddled into his side, letting the conversation flow around her, she tossed out quips to wind Bri up and inspired Lucas to new heights of goofy kid antics.

She understood how family worked. Doing the chicken dance out on the lane with Lucas when Brian choked on the turkey.

He'd half-calculated the gas left in his truck and the five-hour drive to his folks' place before reality asserted itself. Taking Nora to meet the family when he'd known her all of two weeks would spook the shit out of her. But damn if he didn't want to. Give Mama a call and tell her she'd be setting an extra place at Christmas this year.

They closed down the place, herded outside with the rest of the stragglers a tick past midnight. Time to take his girl home and put her to bed. His cock jumped at the suggestion, an eager volunteer making a desperate bid to wave around in his shorts.

He walked her to her door, same as after their movie date. Kissed her goodnight and kept some distance. The trembling, tongue-tied woman he'd bid goodnight last week met his eyes with bold determination tonight.

"Do you want to come in for a drink?" Nora blinked like she didn't believe she'd gotten the words out, but she'd done it.

"I'd be right happy to." No pressure. Down boy. He'd show her a good time without putting his dick in her. Maybe get the drink he'd been hungering for all week. Only if she wanted, too.

"Good. Okay. Good." She bobbed her head as she unlocked the door. More nervous by asking than she'd let on.

God send a lightning bolt to strike him down if he fucked up the best gift he'd ever gotten by rushing her. If she woke up ashamed of herself the next morning, he might as well castrate himself for all the good his cock was doing him.

* * * *

She led him by the hand, her fingers too tense to let go. She flipped the light on with her free hand. Nerves firing, heart racing, panic blocking her breath.

The door thudded shut behind her.

Too late to turn back. The first time she'd invited a man in for fooling around. Sex, maybe. No, that'd be trashy. More slutty than asking him for—for what, she didn't even know. He might.

Spinning around, she swallowed past the terror in her throat. "You know I didn't invite you in for a drink, right?"

"That's a shame." Warm and seductive, he wrapped her in his voice. He teased her with his chest, the barest brush against hers. Entwined their fingers and stroked her palm.

"It is?" Desire blazed a path from their points of contact. Her breasts ached with tugging insistence.

"Mm-hmm." He nudged her back to the wall.

Good. She needed the help standing. Especially when he leaned his weight into her and the thick heat against her lower belly registered.

"I'm awfully thirsty for you, Nora." He kissed her.

She welcomed his invasion with her whole body, swaying her hips for the thrill of his erection rubbing her belly. Arousal erupted as if he'd pressed passion into her with his tongue and his cock. A communicable disease, a fever heating her skin with blistering speed.

He crushed her lips and stabbed his tongue between them. More than a kiss now. A devouring. He meant to gobble her up.

She meant to let him. Exhilarating and terrifying in a single breath. Scrabbling for the edge of his shirt, she found the hem and shoved her fingers underneath. Her quaking body demanded she yank the shirt off him. She'd take everything off him and take him and finally be free of this pent-up passion—

He clamped her wrists and pushed her arms against the wall. His kisses slowed until he caressed her mouth with the dreamy, languid warmth of a summer evening. The pull and retreat of a porch swing.

Cotton whispered along her skin. He slipped her shirt from her shorts, his hands slow and sure as he stroked her stomach.

The tumult drumming between her legs eased.

He kissed her cheeks.

Her lips parted for air for the first time in what seemed hours.

"Forgot myself for a minute." Shuffling his feet, he drew his hips back. "You make gorgeous music, honey girl, and you've got dangerous, dangerous fingers."

Cotton dragged higher. Cool air touched her ribs in territory left behind.

"What say you keep them to yourself a little longer?"

Her shirt inched over her breasts, up to her underarms. He rolled his thumbs across the top of her shoulders.

"To myself?" Maybe her fumbling fell short of his expectations. His touch enthralled her. She'd give him the same incredible experience, if she could.

"Uh-huh." He lifted her arms with the steady press of his palms, taking her shirt with them. "Give me a chance to touch you without going crazy."

"I make you crazy?" She poured her panic into the hope he meant the good kind of crazy.

As her shirt swept over her face, he groaned. He flattened his hand against the wall above her head, pinning the fabric and her arms in tandem. He'd need help to undress her now.

She wriggled.

"Wait." His rasp might've been command or plea. Pressing their cheeks together, he nuzzled her ear. "You drive me insane. I'm eighteen again around you, hard at the drop of a hat and aching to pop. So please, Nora, let me keep those oh-so-eager fingers of yours far from my shorts awhile longer."

Heart hammering, she whispered agreement. Her inexperienced attempts couldn't possibly arouse him as much as his confident caresses did her.

Bunching her shirt in his fingers, he drew her arms together over her head. He flexed his forearm with tantalizing strength. "That's right, tip back and show me your beautiful neck." He scraped his teeth down the side of her throat and chased them with his tongue.

The dual sensations reawakened the throbbing deep in her belly. A riot starting. Sneaking out for the night to meet up with a boy, a trespass she'd never tried, though her sister'd gotten away with plenty, and oh God, the appeal. Threats of groundings and phone bans wouldn't have kept her out of Rob's arms, either.

Delivering sweet and sucking kisses, he traveled toward her breasts in an unhurried descent. He traced the upper edge of her bra with his heated tongue. The teasing dance set her squirming, bumping between the wall at her back and the man at her breast.

He cupped her breast in his free hand and peeled part of her bra away.

She raised a silent plea not to disappoint him now.

* * * *

Her flesh overflowed the top of her bra, nipple straining in the open air. Soft, supple skin under his fingers. Gorgeous blushing tips.

"There's the tight bud I want to taste." He filled his mouth with her breast and lapped across her nipple. His cock banged at his zipper harder than a hacker at a firewall. Access denied, impatient bastard. Less than ten minutes of kissing her and he'd been ready to break his promise to himself. To pop his fly, shove down her shorts, and take her against the wall five feet from her front door.

She squirmed. God how she wriggled and arched closer. Her ass thumped the wall.

He'd have a hand inside her panties caressing her backside in a hot second if he had an extra. One fondling the breast not in his mouth. One clenching her shirt so hard his knuckles ached, but fuck if he'd let go.

Her breathy alto moans cascading with every nip and suck dragged him near enough to coming. Freeing her sweet little fingers would invite more trouble for him.

The volcanic surge in her, the way she'd swarmed him with grasping hands and searching fingers, had set him straight. He'd been out of control, and he'd made her out of control. They couldn't do uncontrolled. Not yet.

She hadn't been with a guy since her husband. If she wasn't a hundred percent sure, he'd be Mr. Rebound instead of Mr. Forever. No fucking way would he settle for being a fling, not with Nora.

"You comfortable here, Eleanora?" He groped for an excuse to navigate deeper into her house. The front hall didn't lend itself to sustained action, and her beautiful breasts deserved extensive attention. The more he sucked and teased, the more she sagged against the wall.

"My legs are pins and needles." Laughing, she shivered from toes to fingertips. "The good kind."

"You got my nerves firing too." With her body vibrating against him, sweet Christ. He ached to sink deep and feel her vibrations from the inside. "Not sure how long I can stand."

"Arch behind you." She flapped a hand, her arms trapped in her shirt. "Living room."

Making out in the front parlor, furtive as a pair of horny teens. Good for now. Room enough to lay her down and feast. Nourishment. He still had that thirst to quench. Forcing his hand to unclench, he freed her arms and let the shirt fall.

She wiggled her fingers in front of his face. Her sassy stare lent her a cute-as-hell glow. "Not so scared anymore?"

"Terrified." He swooped in for a kiss while he got his hands positioned. Distraction. Misdirection. God, she deserved so much magic. He lifted.

Squealing, she flung her arms around his neck and clamped her legs around his waist.

He ground against the heat between her thighs and groaned. Should've accounted for the temptation of everything lined up and ready to go. Pre-flight checks complete. "Hold on tight, honey girl."

She clung to him. Her breath warmed his neck.

He stepped back. "We're taking a short trip."

She nuzzled closer, kissing her way up his jaw as he navigated the hall. "I like where you've taken me so far."

Her arms tensed across his shoulders, and her breath came hot in his ear. Plotting something, his shy scamp. She closed her mouth around his earlobe and tugged. Scraped her teeth on his skin. Copying his moves on her. Christ she learned fast.

He took a shaky breath and squeezed, his spread fingers brushing the denim covering her ass cheeks. "I got ideas for plenty more places I'd like to take you." Two loveseats and no couch. Springy carpet would have to do if he meant to lay her out. "Right now it's somewhere with a more relaxed dress code. That all right with you, Nora?"

She dragged her teeth across his neck, nipping as she went. "Someplace dangerous?"

"Mmm, your mouth is as dangerous as your fingers." Her kind of dangerous pasted his boxers to his cock with pre-come. "Gotta know where you are at all times."

He set her down but kept her close. Ran his hands up the backs of her thighs and cradled her ass. "So I guess it better be a place where you keep telling me what you like. With words if you got breath for 'em, or those sweet little moans when you don't."

"I don't, I mean, I'm not—it's kind of quiet." Arms twined around his neck, she fiddled with the wisps of hair at his nape. "With me."

Sure didn't seem she'd expected to stay quiet at the drive-in. Nervous about being overheard. Biting deep into his neck and shoulder. Five'd give ya ten if she thought herself quiet, the blame sat square at her ex's feet. Lazy, selfish ass hadn't exerted himself enough to pull a moan out of her.

"Nothing wrong with either way." Hooking his thumbs into her shorts, he grazed the skin above the edge of her panties. "You do what feels right."

Someday she might nod without the doubting eyes. So long as he kept providing reasons to believe. For now, he'd take the fingers curving inside his collar and the hesitant caresses.

"This dangerous place we're going—" Her gaze dropped to his chest. "Is your dress code as relaxed as mine? You're my shirtless gentleman, Rob. Fair's fair."

Excitement hummed in his blood and set up camp in his cock. Every new boldness brought her closer to him, flashing through the cracks of the insecure, jilted wife. He'd never give her cause to worry about him straying.

"Mine's as easygoing as you say it is." Beneath his hands, her back radiated soft warmth, a spur to touch every inch. "You want someone who'll stand buck naked in a rainstorm with an apple in his teeth, I'm your man."

"Too bad it's not raining." Giggling, she slipped busy, teasing hands down his chest and raised his shirt.

Not quite the powerful six-pack he'd owned a decade ago, but he kept himself muscled and trim. His bare chest had seemed to please her at the bar. Hadn't turned her off, leastwise.

She dropped his shirt by the nearer loveseat.

Reaching the clasp of her bra, he rocked the tight band against her back. "Dress code."

"Off." Tone distracted, she rubbed circles on his pecs. Fine place to focus if she liked. "Shouldn't ever be allowed anywhere anyway."

"You won't hear me arguing, honey girl." He slipped the hooks and pulled her bra down her arms. Christ, she redefined beauty. The bra fell from his fingers. He sank to his knees and cupped her breasts.

"Look at you. Curves flowing right into my palms, deep pink tips and these hard little nips like candy on my tongue." He stole a kiss from each, leaving her wet and shining in the light spilling from the hall. "Begging for appreciation. Ripe. Delicious."

He sucked each breast in turn.

She writhed toward him, slow at first but gaining passion.

Confidence, he hoped. Angels knew she made him feel like a god. His cock leapt into overdrive on a zipper-busting mission.

Skimming her waistband, he fingered the buttonhole of her jean shorts. A tiny tug, and the metal slipped through. Palm flat, he brushed lower, into the soft curls he'd played with last week. "Dress code." The zipper ticked down. "Gotta confiscate these."

She folded into him, knees buckling.

He lowered her to the floor with steady hands and stripped her shorts. Left the panties, their light lavender a match for the bra on the floor somewhere already. Except for the darker patch in the center.

"Gorgeous." From her wet pussy to the womanly slopes of her belly and breasts to the pale perfection of her neck and the nervous anticipation in her eyes. All but that last one, and he aimed to bring her hidden bold streak into the bedroom every night of their lives. "You know what I am, Nora?"

She shook her head.

He itched to free her hair from its ponytail. Straddling her on his hands and knees, he leaned in and coaxed the hair tie loose. "I'm a man who sees everything I want in the world staring right back at me."

Her sigh shuddered through her body. "The places you take me," she whispered. "I don't think I've ever been here."

"Is here good, honey girl?" He kissed her cheeks and sat back on his heels. Spreading his knees wide helped some. Sliding his fingers through the sides of her silky panties compounded the problem. Especially when she raised her hips.

"It's wonderful." She pierced him with her blue-gray eyes, a thin ring around the blackness swallowing their centers. "I wanna stay awhile."

"Long as you like." He breathed out slow and dragged her panties down in a controlled slide. Caressed her smooth legs on his way back up.

Her plump lips clung together, a deeper pink than colored her breasts, waiting beneath golden-brown curls crying out for him to part them.

"Long as you like, Nora. No need to rush."

He stretched out over her, face to face, propped on his forearms, and angled for a kiss. But his mouth watered for the honey flowing between her legs and filling the room with sweet, heavy musk.

* * * *

Naked. She'd let him strip her naked and gotten him half-naked, too. Any minute now a prankster would jump from behind the curtains to point and laugh.

She didn't date. She didn't invite men into her home. Men didn't kiss and caress her like they'd been starving without her.

But the floor-length drapes hung silent and still while Rob made her squirm. Weight and heat. Firm hands and wet kisses. So incredibly better than she'd imagined night after night in her bed alone.

He worked down her body in sinuous motion and sucked at her breasts. Left them darker and more pointed than they'd ever been, swollen and beating in rhythm with the pulse between her legs.

He kept going. Lower. Kissed her inner thighs.

"Oh! You don't have to." Panic seized tighter than passion in her gut. "I mean, it doesn't work. On me, I mean." Her heart begged him not to be dead set on doing that. "I don't"—she wouldn't be able to convincingly fake proper enjoyment—"you know." Not once. "It's never worked on me."

Hand splayed across her belly, he hovered above her sex. "How many guys have tried?"

"One." Her ex-husband, begrudgingly, with a chorus of annoyed sighs as an accompaniment. "There's—" The words lodged in her throat. Not enough experience or too much—somewhere between existed a magical fantasy world where women lived free of shame. "There was only ever the one."

Rob rolled his thumb downward, sliding over her clit.

Her hips bucked. God. Two years since any fingers but her own had touched her, and now his tempted her for the second time in eight days.

"Maybe he was doing it wrong. Let me try." Lowering his head, he placed a light kiss on her sex. "If you don't like it, we'll do something else."

Maybe David had been wrong. Not maybe she was faulty. Not *if you didn't take so damned long to heat up, I wouldn't have to look elsewhere.* Not the shame of her husband rolling over and getting himself off while she curled up in a ball, dry and sore from trying to satisfy him before she admitted defeat. Or the cringing pain of letting him use her body as an apology for her failure and the time he'd wasted on her.

Rob dabbed an arc of gentle kisses low on her belly, above the pale brown tangle of her pubic hair.

She hadn't considered grooming before her date. She hadn't thought he'd want to put his face there. Should she have shaved? Waxed? Should've asked the girls at the office what men wanted, that's what she should've done.

He captured her gaze in a contest of wills and desire. Sincerity welled deep in his quiet voice and kind eyes. "It's fine to say no if I'm making you uncomfortable, Nora." Here lay a man with abiding patience. Growing up on a farm might've taught him to appreciate slow nurturing the way she'd learned to value compounded interest. Steady growth. These things took time.

"But maybe you're the right kind of uncomfortable." He circled her clit. "You're beautiful as sin, honey girl, pink and flowing."

The hint of pressure, the broad tip of his thumb, rocked her hips.

His nostrils flared. "Your scent's driving me crazy. My cock's gonna bust through my shorts and the floor beneath." He rolled side to side, and beyond his sleek back tilted the firm roundness of his denim-encased ass. His groan pushed warm air across her stomach and shivers through her body.

Nothing would happen that she didn't want. He'd promised.

"Try," she whispered. Part of her—lots of parts of her—wanted this. Enough to outweigh her cowering fear that he'd give up and label her a lousy lay too. "I want you to try."

His nod pressed his nose and chin into her skin. "Nice and open for me, Nora." He laid his hands against her bare inner thighs and pushed with gentle, unrelenting force. "Let me see your beautiful lips for a proper kiss."

Tense anticipation gripped her. Rob spoke to her in ways no one had before. He told her things her body cried to hear.

Warm and wet, his mouth closed over intimate, tender flesh. The drag of his tongue lifted a moan from her throat and gave it voice.

Images snapped in the hazy flashes between her fluttering eyelids.

Her back curling, pushing her hips toward his face.

His hand running along the inside of her thigh, his palm heated and his fingers spanning the top of her leg.

His tongue extended, the point sliding between her parted lips and emerging glistening.

Over and over again.

Pressure built between her legs. Tension ruled her frame. She rolled her neck and bent her knees. Her calves pressed tight to her thighs, Rob's arms and shoulders wedged and holding her wide.

She curled tighter, her body drawn to a central point. The point of Rob's tongue, sliding and circling. He prodded and dipped inside her. Oh God, it was too much, too much, she couldn't—

Pleasure raced in unending waves. Her shoulders and hips thumped the carpet. She dug into the plush pile, desperate for a solid and familiar base in a frenzied world of intensity and sensation.

Framed to perfection beyond the shudders rolling down her breasts and belly, Rob rested between her thighs in mid-lick. Closing his eyes, he curled his tongue and pulled it back into his mouth. His moan amplified her trembling whimper.

The frenzy retreating from her body stole the fear away and left behind calmer heat. Her wrung-out satisfaction surpassed the aftermath of the massage and a sauna visit they'd done for her sister's bachelorette party. Trust Rob to discover an incredible way to top the chart.

"Delicious." He stroked her with light-fingered sweeps. "Feeling all right?"

"Never better." Her whisper might have held a touch of awe, but embarrassment didn't swamp her. "You're amazing."

Shaking his head, he crawled up her torso. "You, not me. You taste sweeter than the first rush of water to a man who spent the day running drills or tossing hay bales."

He settled his weight on her, welcome as the thickest down comforter in mid-December. Cozy and snug. A place she longed to stay for hours. Or forever.

She traced the rounded ends of his shoulders. Strong and firm, curving over her, he provided shelter and warmth. He created a clandestine bower, an oasis in her living room.

He stretched, extending his neck over her face and laying a kiss on her forehead.

She inhaled his earthy musk. No stubble greeted the brush of her nose.

"You shaved before our date." The intimacy of their position hushed her words.

"Mm-hmm." Ducking his head, he trailed kisses down her hairline and across her cheekbone to the corner of her mouth. "Be silly to mar your sweet skin with beard burn." He rolled his cheek against hers. "Not on your beautiful face and not on your gorgeous, clenching thighs."

Speaking the words brought about the action. She squeezed his hips between her legs, and the urge seized her to touch him, to undress him as he'd undressed her and lay her hands and maybe her mouth on his bare flesh. His jeans had stayed on last time. Well. He'd come in them last time, too.

"You didn't, um, jump the gun?" She snapped her mouth closed with a click. Smooth. Smooth as the backside of a porcupine.

* * * *

Silence reigned for half a second.

His laughter erupted in a snort past her ear. Christ. His girl's euphemisms had their own gentle charm. Pulling himself together, he planted a kiss on her cheek and lifted his head.

Uncertainty swam in her eyes, thin silvery-blue rims around fuck-drunk pupils.

"Nope." He ground his cock against the wet crest of her pussy through his jeans. "Still loaded and ready."

Fuck if she didn't mewl like a kitten.

He groaned. He wouldn't pressure her to seal the deal tonight no matter how much his cock ached to be inside her. She needed slow, and he'd damned well give it to her.

"Could I—would you mind if—" Her featherlight fingers on his biceps teased like the lick of flames.

Given the chance, he'd immolate himself in her heat with a joyful heart.

"Can I touch you?" She rocked her hips. No mistaking her meaning, but she shied from her own request sure as she leaned into him. Her gaze rose and dropped. Her body tensed to flinch. "I mean, without your jeans between us?"

He raced to define the variables in the calculus of Nora Howard. What he'd learned of her shouted emotional abuse, not physical. Skittishness borne of curt rejection or whatever bullshit her ex-husband had fed her when he'd been getting his on the side. "I'd sure like it if you did, Eleanora." He softened his voice to match hers, steady as he cradled her head and slipped his other arm under her back. "You've got me dreaming of you."

His swift roll left him sucking in his breath at the delicate weight of her nude body draped over him.

"I dream about your slim fingers." His grip kept her breasts flattened to his chest. "Your sweet mouth."

Her bare legs straddled his hips, a tantalizing pressure centered on his cock.

"The beautiful blush between your legs."

She jerked upright, her eyes wide and dark.

His hold slipped to her hips.

"You do?" Her tongue peeked between her lips and retreated. She fingered his belt buckle, her grip firmer than her voice suggested.

"I surely do." He tensed his thighs to redirect the energy begging him to thrust into her hand. "If you'd rather touch me with your breasts or your stomach or your feet, even, you say the word. Your choice."

"My feet?" Her giggles gave way to speculation. "People do that?"

"They do."

The heel of her hand came to rest on his arousal. She seemed unaware of the contact, relaxed and giggling once more. "Feet."

He gave a slow nod to hold her attention. "You do what feels best to you, and I promise I'll tell you whether I'm liking it." He flexed his cock.

She sucked in a breath, her breasts lifting, their sweet tips tight and tempting.

"I'm not a hard man to read."

A delicate flush spread across her cheeks. "You seem like a hard man to me, Robin."

He would've guffawed with delight at her bitty boldness if she hadn't chosen the same moment to squeeze his shaft. Fuck, her touch sent him soaring. Denim and cotton aside, her hand was the first besides his own on his cock in months.

"C'mere, Nora." Voice hoarse, he swept his hands up her back and tugged. "I wanna kiss you so bad I can't see straight."

* * * *

She gave him the kiss he wanted. Then she took the kiss she wanted, pushing her tongue into his mouth and reveling in his guttural moan.

As she pulled away, he chased her, raising his head from the floor. A firm grip on his shoulders set him straight. She broke free.

"My turn to play." A whole new ballgame. "You gotta let a girl lead sometimes, right?"

David never had, but then David'd never left her limp and shaking with his face buried between her legs. Maybe his other criticisms had been as off-target as his mouth.

"I one-hundred-percent-for-sure do." Rob brushed her back and shoulders on his way to her face. Cupping her cheeks, he held her mesmerized. "I'm your prisoner, Nora." He wiggled, thick and hard behind the teasing scratch of denim. He let his hands fall. "Conquer me."

She ground her weight against him. Against his cock. The outline kept drawing her back to his jean shorts and the need to ditch them. Courage would carry her through. Courage and Rob's faith in her. And maybe a teensy bit of curiosity and passion. A smidge.

Gripping his waistband, she pushed the metal rivet through the buttonhole. "What if I wanna set you free instead?"

"Free me, and I promise I'll stay right here." His zipper ticked open a few teeth on its own. Pushing into the gap came cotton shorts molded around the obvious ridge of his cock. "No place I'd rather be just now."

She inched free her promised prize. The zipper's ticking descent echoed in her spine with jangling anticipation. She'd won a carnival game. Only Rob wouldn't be the substandard stitched-in-a-developing-nation junk she'd claimed her first time around.

Her grand prize revealed itself under tight-stretched navy cotton.

"Must hurt to be all tied up." The zipper hit the end of the line. "No room to breathe."

He rocked his hips and thrust upward. Muscles rippled in his abdomen. His shorts rubbed her thighs and lips. The band at the top of his underwear rolled and flipped, exposing his cock. Smooth and round, his head peeked out the top.

God, for as hard as he was, skin so smooth had to be soft. The urge to find out goaded her. She stroked the tip.

He sucked in air through his teeth. "Sweet Christ, honey girl. I'd say I was breathing just fine, but you make me catch my breath."

Warmth grew and filled her chest. Soft skin twitched beneath her. "You made me lose mine." The temptation rose to return the favor. She curled her fingers around his shorts and boxer-briefs together and lowered them while he shimmied free. Abandoned them at his knees. Too busy. His cock stood waiting.

The second cock to be bare in her presence. The illicit thrill beaded in her blood, a twin to the dot of fluid at the end of his erection. Thicker, taller, with a wider flare and the slightest upward curve at the tip. "You're so beautiful."

"First time I've been called that." His smile promised he'd taken no offense, held no stinging words to deliver.

"You should hear praise all the time." She cupped him lengthwise. Even with her fingers extended, he overflowed at top and bottom.

"So should you." He squeezed her knees in his palms. "Beautiful inside and out, Nora, and don't you believe anyone tells you different."

Tough trick to master. The minute she started anything, he'd recognize her lousy man-handling skills. How her grip and pacing never turned out good enough.

Rob moaned.

She froze. She'd only pressed the heel of her hand up his shaft from the base to the tip a few times. Maybe he'd show her how he wanted it done.

"Mmm, don't stop on my account." He flexed his cock. "The pressure feels fantastic."

Her hand jerked, a rough squeeze as surprise bounced through her. He liked what she'd done. And he didn't mind saying so. She tried again, a slow slide, his heat burning her palm. He thrummed with life in her hand.

"Yeah, just like that," he whispered. "Makes me wanna be bigger for you. Harder for you."

He wanted to be more?

"You pulling and pressing at me." He shuffled beneath her, arching into her touch. The gold flecks in his eyes shone. "So damned hot."

Careful not to catch his hair, she lifted his cock away from his stomach. The bead had grown into a dime-sized pool left behind. She squeezed, and new pre-come leaked out. Dripped. Dangled in a shimmering line from his cockhead to the lowest curve of his abs.

"See how eager I am for your sexy fingers?" He rubbed the heels of his hands up her bare legs, knees to thighs, same as she'd done on his cock. "Feels good, doesn't it? I'm flowing fast as a high schooler on prom night, and I've got an unbelievably gorgeous naked woman straddling me and playing like I'm her favorite toy."

Carnival prize.

"Carnival prize?"

Shit. Thoughts escaping without permission. "Nothing, I mean—" She stroked him. Rhythmic, soothing action. Hypnotic, the way his cock swayed. "I feel like I won the grand prize. Winner's choice, the biggest prize at the whole fair."

He rocked his hips, thrusting his cock higher and faster, popping the head in and out of her hand. "Hell, might come from hearing you talk, if you keep saying such sweet things."

"I have that kind of power?" She slid easier, slicked with pre-come.

"So much, honey girl." He groaned.

Must've been caused by her rubbing. Best be sure. She passed her palm over the top of his cock again.

He barked out a laugh. "Was gonna say you didn't know how much, but maybe you do. You're so fucking good at this, Nora."

Nothing but honesty in his face, a pleasure-strained smile and his eyes focused on hers. David's dirty talk had catalogued where she'd gone wrong. He'd made touching him a chore. Rob made foreplay a delight, an exciting exploration and surprise to see how she affected him, how each act she chose made him move or moan.

No fear, Nora. Not of her desires and not of his criticism. She closed her mouth around his cock.

"Fuck, oh honey, Jesus." His garbled praise flowed in a stream feeding a river of confidence rushing through her.

She let him thrust through her hand and sucked when his cockhead popped beyond the edge of her fingers. Testing her tongue on him, she rolled around the ridge.

Groaning and shudders greeted her.

"Nora, fuck, I'm—" He tugged her hair, his hand fisted tight by her ear.

Same as David. In a second, he'd force her deeper, 'til her breath ran out and she gagged on him.

"Lift your head, honey girl. Christ, so fucking good. Let go beautiful, I'm gonna come."

His first splash of salt touched her tongue before he covered her hand and redirected his cock. They stroked together, fingers interlaced and slipping, as he coated his stomach.

She savored the tang in the back of her mouth. Nothing bitter about Rob. Hot and salty and with more evidence of her prowess spilling across his skin.

Peeling her hand from his cock, he levered himself up and slapped a hard kiss in her palm. "My bold, beautiful Nora. You amaze me."

"You amazed me first." She crawled alongside him, lying down and stretching her legs.

He kissed her with a sweet thoroughness.

She nestled her head on his shoulder and breathed in his earthy musk. Maybe he'd stay the night.

On the floor?

She'd have to let him into her bed. An invisible line she hadn't crossed. Only one man had shared her bed, and he'd trashed their trust, and she'd burned the damned mattress to ashes.

A nap. A living room floor nap. Why not?

* * * *

Heaven. He lay in heaven with a naked angel curled at his side, her curvy hip under his hand and her slender fingers grazing his chest. Sleepy contentment stole over him, a thief cutting short his time with Nora. Hell, he didn't know how she'd feel about him staying the night. He hadn't asked, and she didn't seem inclined to move just now.

He wanted to stay. Carry her to bed, wrap his arms around her, and sleep. Wake her in the middle of the night and make love to her the way she deserved, sweet and slow. If her ex's demands formed the be-all and end-all of her sexual experience, he'd show her different.

Except she hadn't asked, and a gentleman didn't invite himself into a woman's bed. Even a woman sliding her hand across his chest in a super-slow-mo game of air hockey. She skirted the patches of come cooling on his stomach. Itchy when it dried.

Have to let her go to get up, though. Not yet. He squeezed her tighter and dropped a kiss on her honey-brown hair.

"Rob?"

"Hmm?"

She stopped her skittering back-and-forth and flattened her hand over his chest, dead center. "You didn't make me swallow."

Caught him flatfooted with that one, she did. He fumbled for a response. "I wanted to see your face." Truth, but not the whole of it. He'd been guessing. Trying to lay down new pathways in her head for shared pleasure. "This fun's about both of us. You're the woman I'm sharing myself with."

"Sharing." Quiet, as if she'd sampled the word.

If her ex was as big an ass as he figured him for, he'd have demanded blowjobs, and the asshole probably got off on making her swallow or take a facial. Either way, his own stomach had seemed the safest bet. "Gorgeous as the top of your head is, I prefer your smile."

She resettled her shoulders. "You're full of—"

Lord, don't let her think him some smooth-talking bullshitter.

"—compliments."

Miles better than plenty of words she could've picked.

"I'm not used to—" She rubbed her face in his side and inhaled. "I mean, I don't know what to make of you, Robin Vanderhoff."

Him. A man who wouldn't breathe a hint of the mental calculus behind the split-second instinct to pull her off his cock. Hardest move he'd ever made. "A'course, I made a mess of myself." He patted his chest above the splash zone. "Typical guy."

She snorted, a laughing burst of air warming his ribs. "You're anything but typical."

"Oh-ho, I'm special, am I?" He tickled the swell of her hip.

Squirming closer, she launched her hand south so fast he almost tossed up a reflexive forearm block. She cupped his balls and tugged. Light enough to love it, hard enough to feel it. She'd have him redefining threat if she kept on. "You know what they say, Rob."

Christ, he didn't know a thing when her hand formed a strong cradle for his balls. Even left his name in doubt. He grunted in question.

"Go big or go home."

He rolled her over and pushed into tight, wet heat in a single motion.

No.

But the urge ripped through him so hard his dick tried in vain to stand up for her. Too soon, but hope sprung eternal. "I hope you aren't saying you wanna send me home just yet."

She shook her head, her hair flowing across his arm. "I'm saying I know you can go big." She squeezed, and he mock growled for her giggle in return. "And maybe I want you to stay. For awhile. If you want."

Her short-term request looked a damned sight better than not at all.

"I got nothing but you on my mind. My whole calendar's full up with Nora Howard." He nudged her with a teasing elbow. "You point me toward your bathroom, and I'll make myself presentable again. Less sticky, at least."

She rolled out of his embrace, her cuddly warmth abandoning him, and pushed herself to her feet. Naked, standing beside him like a goddess, and him a sacrifice for her pleasure. Give it time. An hour, and he'd worship her in new ways.

"Out to the hall, first door on the left." Her grin and cascading hair softened her face into relaxed lines. "Come find me in the kitchen when you're done. All that exercise must've made you thirsty. I'll get you that drink I offered."

He dragged his shorts to his hips and left them hanging open as he stood. Leaning in, he kissed her with unhurried appreciation. "I'd rather have another shot of the first drink you gave me." See if he could get those clenching muscles rippling around his tongue more than once. He nipped her ear. "If that's on the table."

Her breath rushed past his neck. "On the table?"

Not what he'd meant, but her adorable, arousing, hope-to-God insatiable curiosity had him building a mental picture file. A towel or two for his knees might come in handy, as much time as he intended to spend on them. "Anywhere you want. We're playing by your rules."

She pushed his chest. "Go clean up and meet me in the kitchen in five, then. I want to see these table skills of yours."

"We'll make a pool player out of you yet." He kissed her forehead and sneaked one more breath of her honeyed scent. "I'll show you how I run the table."

She swayed as she walked away, the sultry swing women seemed to naturally possess. One of God's bountiful gifts to the men who loved them. He'd happily keep eyes on her lift-and-wiggle all day long. Smooth and plump. His dick twitched closer to that encore.

He hustled down the hall. Four doors. Two left, one right, one at the far end. Brief glances, not a full recon, and he slipped into the bathroom. Piss first, cleanup second. Dried come wouldn't be making a break for it down his abdomen.

Door on the right had been a bedroom. A lived-in one with rumpled sheets and a dresser with women's things and a set of dress clothes tossed at the end of the bed, probably what she'd worn to work today.

He flushed and dropped the seat back in place for her. The little niceties of married life. Washed up at her sink with its vanilla-scented pump soap and cream-colored hand towels.

Second left, a spare room matching the empty spaces at his place. Did she long to fill hers with children, too? Soon?

He worked a solid job with negotiable hours. Saved money in the bank. He made a fine candidate for fatherhood. Plenty of folk he'd grown up with hadn't been so ready and boasted two or three rugrats by now.

Yet here he stood, a childless bachelor wiping semen off his stomach at thirty-six. He hitched up his shorts and zipped. Her doing the undressing made for half the fun. Well, not half. But a nice chunk.

Flipping the light off, he stepped into the hall. The closed door nagged his instincts. Had to be the master suite. Nothing else the room could be with this layout, a basic three-bedroom rancher. But she didn't sleep inside.

A shrine to her bastard ex? Or hiding that the fucker still lived here, if their finances pinched so hard. Divorced couples splitting expenses wasn't unheard of. No other car in the drive, but her ex might've gone out if they had some date-night arrangement.

His thoughts conspired with his feet. Both times he'd picked her up, she'd met him at the front door. Hadn't given him a glimpse inside the house. Trained instinct, some of his need, sure, the inability to leave a closed door shut, to see the danger, eliminate the threat, and secure the system. A quick peek wouldn't hurt. The knob turned under his hand.

"Rob, wait—"

The door swung open.

"—please don't."

An empty room lay before him. Barren, with an undisturbed layer of dust on the floor. No worse than the empty rooms in his place.

"I'm sorry, honey girl." He dropped the knob and turned. "I wasn't meaning to intrude." Only assuage his own petty fears and jealousies.

She stood naked at the end of the hall, tight lines etched around her eyes and a small gap frozen between her lips.

"My mama told me time and again curiosity would land me in hot water." Nothing he said registered in her spooked face. Two sweeping steps brought him within reaching distance. "Hey, I'm sorry. I didn't mean to upset you." He wrapped his arms around her tense frame. "You've got every right to be angry at me for snooping."

No response. Her thoughts stayed bottled up behind her blue-gray stare, opaque and unreadable.

"My house is fulla empty rooms, too. You wanna come snoop in every corner, that's fair. Nora?"

Shuddering, she pushed his chest. Hard and meaning it. Twice and a third time.

He let go.

"I was gonna ask if you wanted ice in your drink." Her wobbly tone sank in thick undercurrents, her words mired together and struggling to reach him. "And which side of the bed you like."

Oh, fuck. No way in hell would she ask him now. Not after those unreadable eyes filled with darkness so heavy she bent her neck under the load.

"Be angry with me, honey girl." The plea straining his voice ran unchecked, gone beyond his ability to rein in, and why the fuck not. She ought to know how much she meant to him. "Let me have it, both barrels, 'cause I swear to you I will respect your privacy—"

Shaking her head, over and over, she backed away.

God in heaven, let her slap him across the face and get the anger out rather than simmer in regret.

"I'm sorry, Robin, but I need you to go." She wrapped her arms around herself. Hiding her body from him. Clutching her hip and her shoulder with a white-knuckled grip. "Please."

No. Dammit. He'd opened one goddamned door to an empty, meaningless room. A mistake, but not the end of the world. "Nora, please, we can get dressed and talk about—"

"Please don't fight with me. Please." Her voice cracked and fell to a broken whisper.

His outstretched hand only pushed her further away.

"I can't do this." She hunched like her stomach pained her, the arms she'd crisscrossed insufficient bandages for what ailed her. She hovered on collapse and him the cause. "Not right now."

"Okay. All right." He raised empty hands beside his face. No threat, not to her. "Promise me you'll talk to me the first minute you're ready. The very first. I don't care what time of day or night or what you think you'll be pulling me away from. I told you my calendar's full up with Nora Howard and I meant it. Every minute I have is yours, even the ones when you don't want me here."

Two of those minutes, longest of his life, passed before she nodded.

"I promise," she rasped.

Leaving her went against every protective instinct in his gut. He walked past the living room, his black shirt an inky blot on the pale carpet. He'd marred perfection and couldn't name the crime. Managed the fooling around beautifully and somehow launched a bunker buster at the emotional side.

With a wordless apology, he left the shirt where it lay and tugged the front door closed after himself.

"Still your shirtless gentleman, Nora." He cranked the truck's engine. The radio spitting classic rock didn't give a damn for his confession, and his phone stayed stubbornly silent. "Whatever this is, we'll fix it together."

* * * *

Her date ended with a gentle thud and the snap of the screen. Outside, Rob's truck engine turned over with a low rumble. Faded. Left her alone with the monsters pouring out of the open master bedroom.

Scrubbing the place clean months ago hadn't erased the memories. Rob's house might have empty rooms, but hers seethed with ghosts. Hatred for that fucking room tangled her in knots and left phantom pains two years couldn't banish.

Stale, dusty air flowed into the hall, tendrils grabbing and dragging her forward. The doorframe towered over her.

She lined her toes up at the edge. One more step, and she'd be inside the room she hadn't opened in almost a year. Even the emptiness mocked her.

In her shock, she'd stumbled against the door. The solid *thunk*—that and her gasp—had alerted David. No apology. No leap to distance himself. He banged away with his bare ass hanging out and his hateful smirk. "You should stay, Els. Join us. Maybe you'd learn something."

The words rang in her head every time the damned door opened.

Feminine laughter trilled beneath him.

Shaking away the memory, she dropped to the floor and jammed her back against the doorframe. Hard and unyielding. Goddammit.

"Why did you open the door, Rob?" Hugging her knees to her chest, she forced herself to look. "Why did I?"

The question she'd tortured herself with for two years. If she hadn't come home early. If she hadn't heard the noise from the bedroom. If she'd never walked down this hall and pushed open this door and discovered the depth of David's dishonesty.

She would've slept in the same bed with David that night. Let him use her body how he liked in the hope of holding on to a marriage not worth saving. Accepted his belittling and strove to be a better wife. Counted the hours until her workday started, until she escaped to the one place in her life that valued her.

Two, now.

Rob valued her.

He'd fucked up, but he respected her as more than a doll to manipulate.

She traced a line in the dust. Added another. R.

An imperfect man. Was that what stung the most? That Rob was human and not some all-knowing god come to fix her mess?

She'd half checked out the second the door unlatched, David's voice flooding her head. Shame and despair. Closing the door wouldn't shove the nightmare back in. Pieces of herself she despised. Things she didn't want Rob to see.

Circle in the dust. O.

Having a relationship with Rob required letting go of David.

Living in this house made a genuine break impossible. If she sold the house at a loss, she'd have to move back to Ohio and live with her parents. Ready for Rob, and ten hours away from him.

Perfection didn't exist, but Rob came incredibly close. God, he must think her crazy. Flipping out on him and getting all emotional about a damned door.

But he hadn't said so. He hadn't berated her or made demands. He hadn't shoved excuses at her or blamed her for his screw-up.

A bubbly, bouncy B joined the other letters in the dust.

Those moves belonged to David. Rob had a whole different set. If he messed up, he owned his mistake. Apologized. Offered to talk through the trouble. Things she'd begged David to do, things he hadn't done despite a marriage counselor steering them, and they'd been Rob's go-to response.

Straight lines. One long, two short crossing top and bottom. I.

When she'd ordered Rob out, he hadn't lost his cool or fought with her about her decision. He'd respected her without understanding all the door represented. Without any explanation, and he clearly appreciated going after answers.

He'd urged her to talk to him when she was ready.

Straight line. Diagonal. Straight. N.

She dragged herself to her feet. Leaving the damned door open behind her, she trotted down the hall and turned the corner into the living room. Her shorts lay bunched on the carpet.

So did Rob's shirt.

Kneeling beside the clothes, she fingered the hem. Black, like the shirt he'd worn the night they'd met. The one she'd worn home that night. Maybe the same one.

Face buried in fabric, she inhaled a hint of beer and bowling alley grease, but mostly Rob. Deep, earthy, aroused Rob. The cotton slipped over her head with ease.

She fished her phone from the pocket of her shorts.

* * * *

Buzzing. Text message. Time to stop staring at the ceiling and calling it sleep.

Rob launched himself at the phone, tangling his legs in the sheets and cursing the delay. Family tragedy or Nora. Only reasons for his phone to go off at two forty-seven in the morning.

I'm sorry about tonight.

Tonight. Christ, don't let her be regretting the sex. She might follow up with an "I don't think we should see each other anymore." His stomach flew straight into turbulence.

He started typing. A new message blinked in.

Not the first part. Just the throwing you out part.

Thank God. He started over.

I'm sorry, too, Nora.

He waited. Two minutes. Three. The phone's clock oh-so-helpfully kept track for him. Cyclone winds churned in his gut.

Nora's ringtone sounded.

He stabbed the screen. Accept, goddammit. Accept already.

"Rob? I'm so sorry I woke you. I thought you'd see my messages when you got up in the morning." She rushed her words faster than he could break in.

"Wasn't sleeping." As if he could've, with her panicked response and his theories about why spiraling darker with every passing minute. "Been lying here wishing I had you next to me, feeling sorry I opened the wrong door."

Nothing but breathing from her end of the phone. Gulping breaths with a hitch in them.

"I didn't mean to hurt you, Nora, but I did, and I'm so damned sorry." He ached to rewind the night, to lie with her in his arms in the afterglow. Drop off to sleep flopped on her living room floor and stay 'til morning.

She gave a watery laugh. "Stupid to say I wasn't hurt, I guess. You'd know I was full of shit."

"You strike me as an honest woman." Nice and gentle. He'd coax the answers out of her. Brute force attack lacked the finesse this cracking job demanded.

"I spent too many years not saying things I should've said." More shaky breaths followed her words.

He needed to see her face and touch her skin. This conversation didn't belong on a string of cell towers between two lonely lovers.

She cleared her throat. "But the hurt, it wasn't about you, Rob. It's that door. I can't open it without seeing them in my bed."

Them. Jesus wept.

That's why she'd looked so damned spooked. Her sonuvabitch ex needed a lesson in the worst way, and she still lived in the house where he'd been sticking his cock in another woman. No wonder she didn't sleep in the master bedroom. "Let me take you to breakfast."

"What? When?"

"Now." He kicked the sheets down and swung his legs over the side of the bed.

"It's not even three in the morning."

"So it's morning." He played up his teasing tone, trying to reach the woman who sounded startled but not upset by his suggestion. *C'mon, Nora, go with me here.* He refused to crash and burn over things they should've said. "I'm thinking a 24-hour place that makes mean pancakes."

"I know the place. You really want to eat now?" She broadcast more hope than skepticism in her rising lilt.

He latched on to the kernel of her faith with his whole heart. "Food or not, I want to meet you on neutral ground so we can talk face to face and not fight ghosts 'round every corner."

He'd let irrational fear consume him, standing outside the bedroom she'd shared with the jackass, and he'd overstepped. Imagined for a minute she clung to some shred of love for the guy, that she'd go back to him. The wrong damned minute.

"No ghosts." Her voice faded into a quiet musing as if she'd drifted from the phone. "I'd like that."

He snagged a pair of jeans and a fresh shirt. She must've seen the one he'd left behind by now. Hopefully taken it as the peace offering and comfort he'd intended. "I can pick you up in fifteen."

"I'll meet you there." Separate cars, and she didn't say whether efficiency or distrust had decided for her. "See you soon."

She disconnected.

Good thing, since he'd been within spitting distance of closing the call with an "I love you."

Even if she meant to say things that'd make sitting in a car together after awkward. Boldness might be driving her. Eagerness. Or not wanting him at the house again tonight. A hundred reasons, and only one Nora to tell him which rang true.

"Drive safe, honey girl." He slipped his phone in his pocket, scrubbed his face in the bathroom, and grabbed his keys on the way out the door.

* * * *

Five to three in the morning, and aside from the occasional tractor-trailer speeding through the darkness or drunkard navigating his way home from the bars, the roads stood free and clear. Cool enough outside to drop the windows and let the summer breeze buffet her face.

Maybe the air would freshen her skin. Barefaced honesty. No falsity, no gloss, nothing but unvarnished Nora. She'd show Rob the truth of what he'd be signing up for. The crazy, flawed, casual woman.

She parked her cramped workhorse beside Rob's sturdy beast. The restaurant's cheery lights revealed the man himself seated in a window booth and staring in her direction. She hustled to the door and swept past the hostess station.

Standing next to the table in faded jeans and a baseball shirt with moss-green sleeves, Rob stopped her heart. His slow smile bolstered her confidence. His extended arm welcomed her home. She walked into his embrace without pausing.

"Thank you," he whispered.

Mmph. Warm, solid male. One who offered words and comfort instead of draining their savings with shit she didn't want or need. "For what?"

"For calling. For not giving up or running away." He kissed her forehead and rubbed easy circles on her back. "For wearing my shirt."

"Mine now." She pressed her cheek into his neck. Still smooth-shaven. Still all earthy-smelling. "Somebody left it on my floor."

Finders keepers.

He wrapped her in his arms and lifted. *Eek.* No floor. Her feet dangled.

Holding her tight, he bowed his head to her shoulder. "Maybe somebody didn't want you thinking he's the kinda guy to take his fun and run."

His low, gruff rumble startled her. Tight with emotion, like he'd choked off a deeper fear. Women who'd accused him of being a player before. Desperation for her not to believe the worst of him and disappear.

"I know you're not that guy, Rob." She squeezed. Blind luck his friend's brother had stumbled into her chair and brought him to her side two weeks ago. Hard work and honesty from them both would keep him there. "I see you aren't."

With a gusting exhale, he set her on her feet. "Better let you go before I forget how."

He guided her into the booth and took the seat across from her. Respecting her perceived need for space or getting distance of his own.

"I don't think I'd mind if you forgot how to let go." Forever. The promise David had broken. Different man. Different woman, too.

"Christ, Nora, I—you—sometimes the things you say toss my heart in my throat." He grasped her hands across the table. "I lose my footing. Think about throwing caution to the wind."

Caution. Like he thought he had to tiptoe around her. As if she were weak. Damaged. “Would a reckless step or two be so bad?”

“When I open the wrong door?” Tension raised thick lines down the back of his hands. He rocked forward and back. “Yeah, I’d say that’s bad.”

She flexed, and he released her. She reclaimed him, wrapping her hands on the outside. Being the comforter instead of the comforted sent a surge of determination down her backside. “You think it’s bad because it hurt me.”

“Aren’t you two just the cutest couple.” Their waitress sauntered over with more energy than three in the morning called for. “What can I getcha, dears?”

They settled on juice and pancakes without as much as a glance at the menus.

The woman laughed. “You lovebirds need me, you give a yell.”

Love. She’d believed she’d had the romantic ideal with David. Tried so hard to make the marriage work, but every year the feeling slipped further away. Best and brightest at the beginning, when everything had blazed like a bonfire, new and exciting.

Rob leaned in, his face serious above the paper placemat urging them to open their complimentary crayon box and solve the maze to escape the Flapjack Forest. “I trampled your trust, Nora. You invited me into your house, and I carried fear and jealousy in like a Trojan horse.” Clenching fists tightened beneath her hold. “I’m competing with a man who’s gone, and I let my weakness hurt you.”

Where to begin? She’d done her good man wrong. His sweet mix of respectful and protective made her feel safe with him. His coaxing, lustful edge curled her toes and dampened her panties.

“You’re not, you know. If you’re in a competition, it’s against someone who doesn’t exist.” An imaginary David, one who’d disappeared years ago, if he’d ever been real. “You’ve already won that contest, Rob.”

He fixed his gaze on her, earnest hazel depths in an unlined face. Listening. Giving her his full attention. Better than passion flaring between them. A slow, steady burn fueled by something deeper. More meaningful.

“But I’m not—I won’t be an object men fight over.” No better than being a doll controlled by one. She needed to be a different woman, not the same one. Not the silent one. “I want to be me. Really me, for the first time in my whole grown-up existence.”

Following old patterns wouldn't lead her to her goal. Avoiding meant running away, like Rob said. Time she tried a new strategy. Opening up instead of shutting down. Maybe then, she'd find the give-and-take her parents shared. The kind that led to smiling faces around the dinner table and decades of happy anniversaries.

"I want that for you too, Nora. The you I've seen is an amazing woman." Rolling his shoulders, Rob fell silent as the waitress set their drinks in front of them and departed. "One I don't want to make mistakes with."

"Not a mistake." Nuh-uh. A step in the right direction. "You opening that door let out the ghosts I kept shoving down inside myself. Bad memories."

"I'm sorry." The pinching around his eyes and the tightness in his lips pained her as much as him. "You trusted me, and I let you down. But I swear to you, it wasn't intentional."

A hundred miles from the point she wanted to make. Interlacing their fingers, she knocked their hands against the faux-wood-grain Formica. "I know, Rob. You've respected all of my boundaries without me telling you a word. I just didn't expect the bedroom to be the one you'd—" Not cross. That smacked of intent. "Stumble into. It's not like I hung a sign on the door."

"You aren't angry?" Rubbing his thumbs against hers, he flexed his forearms.

The beauty distracted her, his toned muscles as solid and real as they'd been on her and under her mere hours ago.

"I never was. Not exactly. Stunned and frozen. Seeing the door open blindsided me." Her chest tightened, and she breathed through the residual ache. "But I think it's good. Maybe I needed the shock, because I'm not moving past what happened by shutting the door. After you left, I—well, okay, I stared and cried at first—but I confronted some things I think I needed to."

"You don't have to do that alone."

God save her from the caress of his voice, deep enough to drown in. "I did, though. I had to straighten things in my head first." A relationship built on a man saving her would never deliver the equality she wanted. The strong woman they both deserved. "You respecting my distance, that's what made me call tonight instead of waiting or backing off. I trust you."

Their pancakes arrived. She held her tongue, Rob thanked the waitress, and privacy returned to their squeaky vinyl booth.

"And 'cause you're trustworthy—" She gathered her courage, set to elevate Rob to a level beyond even sleepover secrets and thirty years of sisterhood. Neither of hers knew why she'd divorced David. "That thing I can't talk about. Opening the bedroom door was how I found out. I came home to David fucking his paralegal in our bed."

The first time she'd said the words to anyone outside the marriage counselor's office. Lightness made her giddy. Fluffier than the stack of pancakes on her plate.

* * * *

He throttled the immediate urge to smack a shit-eating grin off the man's face. Find out where he worked, walk right in and bust his nose and a few of his teeth. Or crack his accounts, play awhile, and send the feds after his ass for laundering dirty money or defrauding the government on his taxes.

"Betrayal must've hurt something fierce." He'd been the cheated-on partner. Felt the stabbing pain. Not so vivid as her exposure, but a shadow of her agony. "What'd you do?"

"I froze, first, and then I ran." She busied her hands shaking out her napkin and lining up her silverware. "He said—" She inhaled with a hiss, like he'd probed a wound and found the shrapnel stuck inside. "Said I might learn something if I joined them. And I bolted."

"He's a damned fool."

She snorted. "What, for thinking I'd smile and hop in bed with his mistress because he told me to? I did a lot of things he demanded in bed. Badly, from what he said."

"No. For telling you he had anything to teach you." He'd have to watch himself with her. Make sure he didn't repeat the jackhole's belittling behavior if she'd take any suggestion as a demand. Let her explore at her own pace like she had in choosing to blow him hours ago. Christ, the phantom flick of her tongue held the power to rouse him now. "Your skills aren't lacking, honey girl. They sure as hell aren't bad."

She waved off his words. "You don't have to stroke my ego, Rob. I know I'm not the kind of woman men lust for."

"Bullshit." Bluntness might succeed where delicate handling failed. He leaned half across the table, the sweetness of maple syrup flooding his nose, and lowered his voice. "You wail and moan like a saxophone symphony. You taste of honey and caramel on my tongue. You strangle my cock with those slim fingers, and the sweet suction between your lips makes me wanna crawl inside you and never come out. I'm hard as hell in the middle of the damn pancake house thinking about proving to you how sexy you are in bed and out."

Such stillness. A prey animal, albeit one with a fork clenched in a death grip. He might've gone too far.

She shivered through her whole body. Rippled like an orgasm crashing over her.

His cock begged to crack that code and study her from the inside.

"Rob…" She wrapped her mouth around his name in a low moan.

"You're so beautiful, Nora. I can't explain how much." He'd never wished so hard to have a head for words instead of math and mechanics. "You add up in all the right places."

Her smile grew from a tiny lift at the corners to a full-on, white-teeth-gleaming grin. "You're the biggest asset on my balance sheet, Rob." She giggled. "I like the way our numbers look."

"Me too." Hell, he had a pair of numbers on the brain himself. And they'd look pretty damned sweet in her bed, or his, or anywhere else she wanted to try them out. Their languages meshed fine without fancy words. "I promise you I'm a solid investment."

Laughter turned her cheeks red and left her gasping for breath. "So I hear." She sucked in a deep breath and let it out slow. "I'm not gonna run the numbers at the table, though. Might shock our waitress."

Mmm. Boldness enough to keep him on his toes for the rest of his life. Way too many disappointments between sixteen and thirty-six, short-term pleasures and women who'd told him his career choices lacked ambition or he wanted a family too soon or he had too many old-fashioned notions. Like monogamy.

"I can wait." He picked up his cutlery. "'Sides, the pancakes'll get cold. A man's gotta have an appetite for something other than sex sometimes no matter how much he's dancing in his pants."

She cut her pancakes without taking a bite. All of 'em, lines and crosswise, like a mom making a plate for a kid too young to handle the knife. An older sibling thing. Or a babysitter thing.

He'd done the same for his baby sisters at pancake breakfasts while Dad talked weather and yield and Mama shared recipes. The little habits of a lifetime lighting up pattern recognition in his brain. The output statements saying *she's the one* and listing their similarities as proof.

"You won't try to convince me your sexual needs take precedence over everything else?" She swirled pancake bites in a syrup lake. "Whine about being neglected if I don't strip off my clothes the second I walk in the door after work?" Her fork paused its backstroke. "I mean, hypothetically. If you were living with someone. I have a house."

A three-bedroom rancher full of memories with a jackass who'd treated her like shit. Supposed a ring on her finger made her his property. Missed the mark.

"Nora, if I whined about being neglected, I expect you'd set me straight right quick. The way I figure, a relationship's an invitation, not an expectation." Marriage yoked a couple in harness. Made them pull together in life. Not one holding the whip and the other carrying all the weight. "The answer doesn't always have to be yes, and the asking doesn't always have to come from the same side of the equation."

"Rob?"

"Hmm?"

"How come you aren't married with kids by now?"

Kill shot. The bullet fragmented in his chest and ricocheted like nobody's business. Took out his heart and lungs.

"Not that you have to be—it's just you're so perfect." She laughed, shaking her head and setting her hair to swaying. "Not perfect-perfect, I mean, everybody's got flaws, but you—I'm surprised nobody's taken you off the market yet."

Hell. She'd opened up about her ex-husband. He wouldn't repay her with evasion or silence. "I always wanted too much too soon." The house. The picket fence. The kids and the dog in the yard. "Wasted my early twenties bedding women who chased men in uniform. The minute talk turned serious, they scooted out the door."

Smile slipping south at the corners, she slid closer to the table. Elbows near on, skirting the line Mama'd *tsk* for and Daddy'd laugh and call a compliment to the cook.

He'd had fun, sure. Buzzed enough to be charming, not so drunk to make his dick fall down. Getting by on almost enough alcohol to make him not care when the pretty face he'd taken to bed one week walked out with another guy the next.

Nora laid her fork down gentle as a mother with a sleeping babe.

"Or ones who didn't understand why I didn't want a promotion, wasn't interested in the higher pay for more admin work and less hands-on puzzle-solving." Those had been tougher. Weeks of relationship-building and forging deeper connections only to find out she had ambitions he didn't share. "And now, well, I'm thirty-six and I've never been married. Not even engaged."

She studied him with narrowed eyes, their blue lost in the steel-gray intensity.

Full disclosure. Terrifying, because he'd offer Nora a ring on the spot if she'd take one, and telling a woman he fell short for other women smacked of stupidity.

A rustle under the table brought nudging weight to bear on his shin. One slim leg cross-braced his.

"On paper, I'm a reject. If nobody wanted to take a chance on me yet, something must be wrong with me, right? So I end up dating women who move on after a few months." Confusing, unstable girlfriends who treated a misstep like a landmine. Hurled hateful words at him and rejected his apologies as insincere or not understanding the real issue when they wouldn't tell him the problem. "I don't know what they're looking for, but I know I'm not it."

"Then those women are damned fools." She tossed his own words back at him. "And I'm lucky they are."

The tightness in his chest eased. "I'm lucky you think so."

Her smile settled them in a comfortable rhythm. Eating their pancakes, swapping questions, exchanging past disappointments and future hopes. Laying out a plan for a life together, phrased behind subtlety and hedging.

They'd emptied their plates long before sunrise hit, near on six in the morning and the real breakfast crowd trickling in. He ought to let her get home and sleep after keeping her awake all night. Could use a nap himself. Be a little much suggesting they take one together, though, even if he managed to keep his hands off her.

Nora swiveled in her seat, scanning the crowd. Probably equally aware the disappearing darkness signaled the time for sharing secrets had passed. "What're you doing with the rest of your day now I've stolen your whole night?"

"Can't steal what I'd give you freely." Pride and contentment rolled along under his skin. They'd threaded the needle, found the flight path to carry them home safe. Her trust and faith in him walloped him fierce and heavy, a true aphrodisiac.

"No big plans today anyhow. Softball with the guys." And their spouses. Kids. "Lots of standing around, drinking beer, bragging about that time the bat cracked and the crowd roared." Picnicking. Kisses for luck. "More the merrier, if you wanna come along."

"Sounds fun." She fingered the edge of her napkin. "If I wouldn't be intruding on your guy time."

"Not one bit." Whole company was like family. Sooner he introduced her around, the better, assuming she felt the same. "A'course, you show up at softball, the boys are gonna know you're my girl." He traced the tendons on the back of her hand. "Are you my girl, Nora?"

She laid her other hand over his and squeezed. "Maybe you're *my* guy."

Damn straight he was. "I am. All of me. From my imperfect, too-curious head to the crooked little toe I busted dropping a wheelbarrow when I was eight."

"Might be too late for a kiss to make that boo-boo better." Her teasing smile sure as hell warmed him like a healing kiss. "Are you asking me to go steady, Rob?"

"Don't have my class ring to give you, but we have been to the drive-in. And you're already wearing my shirt." He'd have his mama send up his varsity jacket if she wanted the old thing, fancy-swagger leather sleeves and all.

"The shirt's better. Softer. And it smells like you." She shrugged, and his shirt collar bunched in ripples around her pale throat. "A ring's not a great measure of a promise anyway."

Would be if he gave it. He lifted her left hand and kissed her ring finger. No games between them. She'd almost caused a heart attack saying she didn't want him to let her go. Popped a marriage proposal into his head and nearly out his damned mouth.

"So you'll keep the shirt. And come to softball."

"I will."

Good. He reached for the check.

"Wait, let me get that. I'm the one who got you out of bed at half past two."

"And I suggested breakfast."

"Please, Rob. Let me buy."

"I'd rather you didn't." He tapped the plastic tray. Old-fashioned, maybe, and her needing independence. Like separate cars. Compromise. Mama and Daddy had taught him that, too, by example, and he didn't need a better model for the kind of marriage he wanted. "But if you need to, if it feels like I'm trying to buy your time otherwise, I'll let you pick up the tab."

"You're not buying me, I know." Chewing her lip, she shook her head. "This is about me, not you. For today—just this time—I need breakfast to be my treat." She smiled at him, and her eyes danced. "I've never bought a meal for a man before. Don't you wanna be my first, Rob?"

Sweet Christ. He scraped together a nod. Tough with all his blood sitting in his cock.

She dropped enough cash on the table to cover the bill and the tip. Twenty-five percent on the dot. She must've done the math in her head and compensated for the hours they'd kept the waitress from serving new arrivals. His generous accountant.

A few concentrated breaths evened out his blood flow. He stood as she did.

"Can I take you out fancy next week, then?" The art of negotiation.

She gestured at herself. "More fancy than this?"

Mmm. Permission to look, more than a stolen glance. His shirt draped across her breasts and swayed around her hips. The slim-fitting cotton below outlined her thighs and calves. The girl-form of sweatpants, less casual workout and more thin barrier to skin he aimed to touch again soon.

He curled her hand in his and weaved around the tables. "Real fancy. The kind of fancy where I wrestle with a monkey suit and watch YouTube videos on how to knot a necktie." He held the door open. "Ladies first."

She laid a hand on his chest and stood on her toes. "Don't make your tie so complicated I can't get it off you later."

His bold Nora, back to torment him in the best way.

"If it comes to that, I'll hand you the scissors," he whispered. "Or you can leave the tie on and lead me around like a dog on a leash."

Her eyes sparked lightning in a summer storm. "Maybe I will."

He kissed her, right there in the diner entrance. Too tempting not to.

She leaned into him, her weight a delicious pressure holding him against the door. Maybe she'd like to ride him, her beautiful breasts bouncing and swaying and his cock sliding in and out as she soaked him with her pleasure.

Their lips parted. Her hair framed her face in a honey-brown wave.

He resisted the urge to hoist her up and carry her out to his truck.

She tugged him outside by the hand.

The cooler air cleared his head. Heat and humidity wouldn't hit 'til noonish.

He kissed her again at her car, parked right alongside his like they should be in a driveway or a garage every night. They said their goodbyes, and he closed the door behind her. Locking himself out.

But he'd be picking her up this afternoon for softball. And next Friday for dinner. They'd see what happened then.

Chapter 5

Sex on the brain.

Nora floated between her bedroom and the bathroom on a cloud of nerves. The door at the end of the hall stood open, a personal challenge. Sunlight on the hardwood turned Rob's name warm and gleaming amid a dusty sea. Hall-crossings sent hope and panic soaring.

He'd be here soon for their fancy date night. After their relaxing, low-key outings, tonight should be a breeze. They'd done getting-to-know-you talk. She wouldn't be going in blind or fearing a dating disaster.

Except the sex question loomed. Silly to pretend otherwise. She'd gone out and bought a new bra and panty set, for chrissake. New dress, too. Everything fresh, clean, and new for Rob. Even her.

She stared down the open door. The wedge heels on her sandals echoed. Long, confident strides, same as she'd done every night this week. A careful step across Rob's name.

Throttling back her distaste for the room and its former occupant, she made a slow turn in the barren space. "I am not a failure." Not as a woman, a wife, or a sex partner. David's laughter rippled in the silence of memory. "You don't get to decide who I am."

The girls at work damn well didn't get to decide, either. Once they'd shaken her down for the real reason she hadn't joined them on the last two Friday nights, they'd teased without mercy.

Oooooh, third date.

Ellie, you're so old-fashioned.

That's like the sex date for old people, right?

"I decide."

Even if the girls were right, and she was old at thirty-one. She hadn't looked forward to a man's touch in years. Not until Rob swept in with his sexy smile and his firm abs. His thoughtfulness. His gentle coaxing and his steady, demanding faith in her.

She twirled. Swaying silk tickled her ankles. No laughter. Only blessed silence and the expectation of Rob's appreciation. He'd clasp her waist and slide free the decorative tie before she guided him to the zipper at the neck.

Mmm. Cloudbank of nerves throwing lightning.

The doorbell sang its two-toned greeting.

Panic jangled at her side, an unwanted companion down the hall to the front door. Could she invite him in for the sex first and enjoy dinner after without the question hanging over her head?

No, he'd probably made a reservation. Besides, if she chickened out during the sex, she wouldn't get the dinner afterward. She'd be giving up laughter, conversation, and Rob's sexy smile and gold-flecked eyes.

Third date.

She pulled open the door.

Sweet honeysuckle wafted through the screen. He'd brought a beautiful bouquet of orange, yellow, and white blossoms. "They're gorgeous."

"You're gorgeous." He swung the screen aside and held the petals under her nose. "The flowers wish they were so beautiful." He kissed her cheek as she inhaled. "Probably fretting about whether I got the dirt off their stems."

Wildflowers he'd picked himself, from his own yard, maybe. She accepted the bouquet with a shaky hand. Far better than store-bought roses, the insincere apologies David had always brought her. Inhaling again, she met the intense eyes watching her over sweet honeysuckle, butterfly milkweed, and lemony evening primrose.

"They must not know about your weakness for dirt." When she'd admitted to playing softball in high school, Rob had tossed her a spare mitt and they'd added her name to the informal roster. He pulled her into his life so easily. "You told me last week I looked beautiful with half the infield ground into my clothes and hair."

Grinning, he tugged one of the curls spilling from the top of her head. She'd worn the rollers overnight—a dead giveaway of her date plans at work—and swept the curls into a loose bun for tonight.

Rob's agreement rumbled in his chest. "I like the way you dive for home when the pressure's on."

Home plate. Home run. The reason she'd bought sexy panties. Fun with no room for David's snide remarks in her head. "I should put these in water before we go. I'll only be a minute." Three steps, and she turned back. "You can come in. There's not—I mean, nothing's off-limits. If you want to come in."

She scurried into the kitchen without waiting for his answer, but the screen door snapped shut a second later, and his shoes tapped on the hall floor. No vase handy. She half-filled a tall glass and set the bouquet in the center of the table. Rob brought life and color into her house.

And now he stood in the hall to the bedrooms. Gazing at the floor.

Oh Christ.

She paced up behind him, echoing sandals and all.

"I like the redecorating." Arm outstretched and angled down, he framed an L with his hand as if measuring her progress. "Bold steps on such dainty toes."

Her feet had left dusty outlines from her nightly ritual. The first part. The second, after she'd told memory-David off and slipped down the hall to her bedroom, involved less writing Rob's name in the dust and more calling it to her ceiling. No need to tell him.

"Lots of redecorating." Mostly inside her head. "I'm ready for something new."

Something like Rob in his charcoal-gray suit and powder-blue shirt with the gold-flecked tie that matched his eyes.

"I'm glad, Nora." He captured her hand. "C'mon. Let me take you to dinner before your new no-limits policy gets too tempting."

Be a shame to cut that tie off with scissors. But she'd see him without it tonight. Whether the night ended with sex or more casual fooling around, she wouldn't deny the heat curling around her spine.

"Dinner first." She let him lead her out the door, grabbing her clutch along the way. "We can talk policy while we stuff our faces."

Rob coughed.

She cringed. Lord, let the sun melt her right into the front walk.

No. New policy. Own it.

She dug a teasing elbow into his side. "Could get pretty hot."

"I'm thinking it's awfully hot now." He jiggled the knot in his tie. "Feels like I'm burning up."

"We should make our next date at the pool." She waited for him to open the passenger door. Stepping on the running board, she ducked inside. "Be a great way to cool off." And spend hours staring at the sleek physique hiding under his dressy duds.

"Shucks, Nora, I'll throw a liner in the truck bed and fill 'er up from the garden hose. Your own private pool." He closed her door, rounded the truck, and swung in beside her. "I dunno how that dress'll fare in the water, though."

Silk? Not well.

He slipped the truck into reverse, his hand landing beside her shoulder as he turned to check the back.

She cleared her throat, drawing his attention. "Poor Robin." She dared a pat above his knee.

He tightened under her touch.

Lowering her chin, she glanced at her dress and back up at him, trying for a flirtatious smile. "You've never been skinny dipping?"

He raised a skeptical eyebrow. "You have?"

Pulling her hand back, she shook her head. Too many things she'd never done. "But I'd try with you. A girl's gotta have a bucket list."

* * * *

Sweet Christ. Boldness roamed her eyes and her teasing words and her too-brief caresses. Lust would snap his dick off in his boxer-briefs if she kept on.

Lust and something more tender, the hope flaring in his chest from his name spelled out in thin letters on a dusty floor. Her sweet smile of acceptance at the flowers he'd plucked from his yard with his own hands.

"What else you got on that list, honey girl?" He glued his hands to the wheel. The flowing dress she wore tempted him more than water in the desert.

The dress matched her eyes. The deep blue with embroidered silvering-gray spirals resembled Air Force colors. Ones he'd dressed himself in. She capped hers with tumbling curls flashing hints of honey gold in brown depths. If he took his hands from the wheel, he'd unpin those curls and drag her onto his lap.

"I dunno yet." Her quiet wonder floated high as the stars in the seductive, infinite expanse of possibility. "Nobody's ever asked me."

A million questions crowded his mind. He'd ask them all, every single one, over a lifetime. "Wild adventures? Trekking to the south pole?" He'd gotten the travel bug out of his system in the service. "Skydiving? Swimming with sharks?" Adrenaline, too.

Her laughter sparkled. "Probably not those. I'm a homebody. Simple is exciting and fancy enough for me."

He might've miscalculated tonight. The restaurant he'd pointed the truck toward was fancy, a rarity without driving her all the way to Des Moines. He'd discarded Plan A soon as he'd found himself surfing hotel room reservations. Too much pressure for his skittish girl. Last thing he wanted was her saying yes because she felt she had to. Like he expected sex in exchange for dinner.

"Hope you're not offended I wanted to take you on a fancy date." His Nora got touchy about being bought, but she deserved to shine like a gem. Tough to find new ways to show a woman what she meant to him. A man's wallet carried the cultural currency for that.

He took advantage of the red light to indulge in shameless appreciation of her fancy state. Probably give himself joint trouble from clutching the wheel so hard.

She shook her head. "Not offended."

"But you're not impressed, either."

"You've impressed me a hundred times over, and not one way had to do with the size of your wallet." She gripped his knee.

God himself wouldn't put the judgment on him for pouncing if she slipped her hand higher. Her bare neck needed adornment. Dozens of bruising kisses.

She curved her lush lips in a sweetheart smile. "Light's green."

Shit, so it was.

"Sorry about that." He hit the pedal. "Seems a mighty fine distraction in a pretty blue dress took the seat next to me."

"Good reason for a fancy date." She drew circles on his knee, her left hand paler below the line on her wrist where his spare mitt had covered her skin Saturday. The sun had warmed the rest of her peachy arm to a pale gold. More reasons to kiss her. Trace every tan line with his tongue.

She sighed. "You look delicious in a suit."

The urge to make a meal of her in that dress sent him scrambling for a safer topic. Too bad good manners wouldn't let him take her to bed and then dinner. His folks had taught him better. He had more class and self-control than a sex-crazed teen, didn't he?

Barely.

He pulled into the parking lot. Stout's Steakhouse, the only top-notch dining experience in town, with prices to match. Linen napkins. Elegant service and all that, with trendy craft-beer panache. He cut the engine.

"Mmm." Her low moan plunged into his shorts and made his dick jump. "Their dry-aged rib eye with roasted red potatoes is fantastic."

Aw hell. Sure she'd eaten here before. Her ex was a lawyer wining and dining the too-good-for-you crowd. The place might be full up on bad memories of playing the dutiful wife and schmoozing with clients.

He laid his hand over hers and squeezed. "If you wanna go somewhere else, I'll take you anywhere you want, Nora."

"Nope." Dangling curls bounced around her face as she shook her head. "New policy. Part of the bucket list, I guess."

"Yeah?" Whatever she named, she'd have. He'd keep her list safe in his head, bytes and packets tucked away for later retrieval. Make every last item come true. "What's that?"

"Remind myself the past is done and be thankful for the happiness I have now." Her gaze darted between his eyes and his lips, her eyelids fluttering with every shift.

Her sweet scent luring him closer, he brushed her lips in a kiss. "This makes you happy?"

"You do." She kissed him back, her tongue tentative and searching. "*Us* makes me happy."

"Me too," he mumbled into her mouth. Habit-forming addiction, her kisses.

He dragged himself free and escorted her inside. She outshone the rest of the diners by miles, a gleaming beacon of beauty. More than one head turned. He kept a hand on her back as their waiter pulled out her chair.

"Pack of wolves in here." He ducked his head and nuzzled her ear. "Have to be sure none of them tries to carry off my Nora."

Her laugh floated atop more than a touch of disbelief. "So long as you want to whisk me away, that's all I need."

"We haven't gotten in our seats yet, and I'm already thinking about how much I'd like to take you home." Dangerous words, but he refused to hold back. If his boldness encouraged hers, so much the better for them both.

A true burst of laughter escaped her, a little loud, a lot charming. Redness colored her cheeks as she sat and gave the waiter her drink order, a raspberry wheat shandy.

Soon as the waiter departed, she leaned across the table. "I had the same thought, you know. When you rang the bell."

His dress pants hadn't been so tight when he'd put them on. "A gentleman is always ready to follow his lady's lead."

"What if—" She tilted her head, speculation tinting her eyes. "What if she doesn't know where she's going?" Her knuckles tightened around the leather-bound single-sheet menu. "What if she's never been there before? Or, or thought she'd been, but they turned out to be completely different destinations?"

Places and things she'd thought she had. Good sex? A loving relationship? A solid marriage? Best to start simple. But if she was thinking on marriage with him, he'd set the date whenever she said the word.

He engulfed her hand in his sturdy grasp. Tiny. Impossible to believe she'd whipped a grounder from shortstop to first base with no more than a hop and a scoop last week.

"Then they find their way someplace new together." He nudged her menu. "You've been here before—tell me what I want for dinner."

She wiggled taller, an S-curve in brilliant blue, even as she ducked her chin and half-hid a slow-growing smile. "You want me to order for both of us?"

"Why not?" Compromise. Sure, handing over the decisions smacked of backward duty-shirking when his responsibilities included seeing her needs got met, but her bright eyes confirmed the rightness of his offer. He'd let her pay for breakfast Saturday. Swallowing manly pride and trusting her to order instead of bulldozing over her preferences with his own wouldn't hurt him none. "I don't need a hatful of outdated rules, Nora. I need you."

Her fingers trembled. "I like that," she whispered.

Getting down to business, she quizzed him as she narrowed the choices.

Their waiter didn't bat an eye when Rob directed him to take his marching orders from Nora. Three hours they sat, tasting from each other's plates and trading little touches. Oddly comfortable for a fancy date. For once, he hadn't spent half the night searching for an excuse to drop pretenses and cut dinner short.

They ordered a shared dessert, some flourless chocolate torte with an orange sauce. Two bites in, he declared the concoction too rich for himself and started feeding her the rest. Not quite a lie—the dense cake was super-rich—but mainly a ploy to bring the fork to her lips and feast on the pleasure in her face.

She closed her eyes with a graceful sweep of her eyelashes above her cheekbones. Her pink tongue curled around the fork tines. Her cheeks hollowed as she tugged the bite into her mouth, and her tongue cleaned her lips when she'd finished savoring the taste.

God help him, he'd put that look on her face a time or two later tonight minus the cake.

He raised the fork again. "Can I tempt the lady with another?"

"You—" Her gaze drifted, and her smile faded.

Coming on ten o'clock, the restaurant was busy still. A server stood beside an empty table, seating a party of four.

A man with a big-titted blonde in a red dress on his arm shot Nora a contemptuous stare. He made a remark to his dinner companions and headed over. The fancy fella carried himself with the big-swagger importance of a miniature poodle in a pack of full-size mutts. Strutting chin out and arms swinging, he filled the aisle and forced passing waiters to reroute without glancing or slowing.

Rob laid the fork down. He and the glaring ass would be of a size if things came to a standoff, but a quiet exit might suit his woman better. "Nora? You want—"

She shook her head. Her nostrils flared wide like a horse scenting danger.

"Eleanora." The man poured a five-gallon bucket's worth of disapproval in those four syllables. "I thought we talked about this."

After hearing her given name from Pointylips McBlowhard for the last ten years, no wonder Nora would rather a nickname. She spread her hand flat on the table and swallowed. "Did we?"

The intruder leaned in, his shadow falling across Nora's arm as if he owned the rights to her personal space. To her. "If you enjoy playing the whore at some dive bar, I won't stop you, but for God's sake, keep your shenanigans out of my circles."

Rob pushed back his chair. Nora's ex couldn't go eight seconds without bullying someone to make himself bigger. Almost be worth the trouble to smack the shit out of his slick smile.

* * * *

Oh God. David's name-calling wouldn't sit well with her shirtless gentleman. She sprang to her feet as he stood. "Rob."

"Seems introductions are in order." Rob played calm, smiling at her, his voice smooth, though she'd guess he longed to deck David right about now. His loose posture gave no clues, but her gentleman, well—he championed real civility and good manners, not the fake show her ex put on. "You know this rude yapper, Nora?"

"Such temerity from a jumped-up beer-swiller." David delivered disdain in his angled brows like he'd been born to it. Small-town kid playing big-city lawyer with fancy words and clipped syllables. "You screw married women in bar bathrooms and I'm the ill-mannered one?"

His reputation around town mattered a hell of a lot to David, but the sharp edge in his voice cut deeper. She'd tortured herself for months imagining him with his mistress. Maybe he'd spent a night chewing over unwanted thoughts of her and Rob. Fuel for his offended martyr act. As if she'd been holding out on him.

Rob raised his chin. "I don't, actually, though I wouldn't be surprised if you did."

The gel slicking David's hair gleamed like grimy coffee grounds clinging to a filter under the restaurant's muted lighting. "Is that the plan, Els?"

Using the damned golf nickname he knew she hated. Envy, plain as day. Thinking she'd done sexual favors for Rob she'd never done for him.

David's sneer cut hard, ugly lines in his cheeks. "You brought your bar boy here to service him in the men's room?"

It was the ladies' room. Try to keep up. The retort zipping through her skull nearly tumbled out.

Rob shifted closer, shielding her with his shoulder. "'Bout the only thing from you that'd surprise me is common decency." He nodded toward the other table. "Your date's waiting. You sure you wanna do this now? Here? In your circles?"

Bearing a robotic smile, Jennifer the paralegal sashayed over. Now she carried out the wife duties, put on display entertaining David's business clients and their spouses.

"Is he threatening me, Eleanora?" The three diamond studs on David's tie clip flashed. Still the same piece she'd bought under his supervision to celebrate him passing the bar exam on the second try. His sidestep ate up the space between them. "Because that sounded like intent to commit slander, if not bodily harm."

Rob pivoted and raised his hand. A strong hand, a gentle hand, made for cradling her curves and clutching bountiful bouquets of wildflowers. "Take a step back, Davey."

David's huffing laugh came through clenched teeth she'd footed the bill for. Sparkling white, all surface perfection. "If you're going to pick up pets in such low-class places, put them on a leash. I won't have my wife parading—"

"We're not married anymore." She launched forward, shoulder to shoulder with Rob. "We're over."

David opened his mouth. "We—"

"No. You threw away our marriage, and the only reason you want to get in a pissing contest over me now is because you think Rob has me. Too bad for you." No being afraid of a goddamned door or the man she'd pictured behind it every day for the last two years. "If I crawled under this table and gave him a blowjob better than anything I ever gave you, it still wouldn't be any of your damned business, you pretentious, arrogant ass."

He'd never taken her for a romantic meal focused solely on her. Never fed her from his fork. Rob's open, honest beauty made him a man worth keeping.

"Is that how he's teaching you to talk?" Frame rigid, David eyed the long tablecloth as if she might duck beneath the concealing linen. His arm twitched, primed to drag her away for a private scolding. Denied the chance, he fixed his smirk on Rob, his just-us-boys amusement the same as every time he'd landed a party joke at her expense. "Her mouth is nothing to brag about. She doesn't know how to use it, and she refuses to learn."

Rob twisted toward her, kissed her hair and nudged her ear with his nose. "Your ex always that stupid, or am I just that lucky?"

Warm and soft, his words cloaked her like a blanket draped over her shoulders on a chilly night. She muffled her laugh in his arm. "Maybe you inspire me to new heights." High enough to let her ignore the sideways stares and increasing whispers at the nearby tables.

"I'm warning you, Eleanora." David snagged his paralegal's wrist as she cozied up to his side. "I want you to stop this behavior—"

"Guess you should've negotiated that in the settlement." God, not caring elevated their conversation to the best she'd had with him since he'd been a pre-law student flinging charm and compliments. For once, his wasn't the only voice participating.

"How are you enjoying my house, Els?" Shark grin widening, David threatened to tear her into the manageable, bite-size pieces he'd manipulated for so long. He'd sharpened his teeth on her ever-more-tattered self. "Sometimes I feel like I never left."

"Lavish but empty, like its former owner." Holding her tongue hadn't gained her a damned thing in the last ten years. And honesty grew addictive. "I overpaid for what I got."

Jennifer sneered. "I always found your furnishings a little cheap."

"How would you know?" The nerve. Had she gotten the silver service appraised between rounds of David's monotonous drilling and constant corrections? "The ceiling's not decorated."

Rob snorted.

"Maybe the ceiling's the only thing you ever see." Jennifer ran her finger down David's lapel. "I give my man more than that. I bet that's why—"

"You check the sheets every night to see how many women he's sharing your bed with?" Rob's words dropped into sudden silence.

"You told him? I will own you for that." David glanced at the nearest tables without turning. Air hissed through his teeth and cheek-stretching smile. Always the showman. For a man who loved being the center of attention, he hated being a spectacle.

"I told him the truth. You wanted to force me to live a lie." Hiding everything about David and his trophy. Letting their dirty secret stain her, too. "I would've thought you'd have had your fill after fucking her in our bed for months behind my back. But good for you. Unless you've found a replacement and haven't told her yet. That's your style."

A cheat stayed a cheat. He'd use his paralegal the way he'd used her, taking until she had nothing left to give. A sliver of pity slipped under her skin for the woman who'd taken him off her hands. "I hope you're billing him for the extracurriculars."

Jennifer shot her a look beneath lowered, thin-plucked brows. "You've got more moxie than I thought you did."

More than she'd thought she had, too. No. She'd had courage once. Before she'd let David smother her under the weight of his bullying disapproval. No woman deserved that slow death. "You could do better than him."

The envious gaze scouring Rob from buzz cut to shoe leather projected the other woman's assessment. *You already have*, her look said.

"Better?" David led with his chin, his grand, sweeping headshake an elaborate performance with a toothy veneer. Blasphemy to suggest the world didn't start and stop spinning on his say-so. No one bested David—not law clerks correcting his exaggerations at parties or waiters who served him meat a hair too pink and not her, never her, because the world would wink out of existence first. "You've slandered me in public, Els. You do realize what you're going to lose?"

The right to stand in this fancy-schmancy restaurant much longer, for one, given the wait staffer hustling into the back and probably fetching the manager. Might as well finish strong before they tossed her on her ass.

"You can have the damned house, David. And the penalty payment." She'd find the money somewhere. Sell the car. Garnish her paycheck. Borrow from her folks. "I know what I'm gaining—my self-respect."

He'd made her complicit in his affair. She'd handed him the power to manipulate her, signing his divorce agreement with its penalty clauses and demands for silence.

"My integrity's worth a lot more to me than upholding your bullshit reputation." Scraping off the snake oil clinging to her from his frauds left her cleaner. Lighter. She'd rent a motel room by the week before she let him control her again. "You're a liar and a cheat, and you can't buy my silence anymore."

"You goddamned bitch." An ugly scarlet flush painted his face. He clashed horribly with his wine-dark shirt. The lights added a spotty sheen—sweat.

She'd made him sweat.

"You say one word, and I'll make sure every person in this town knows you're a lying bitch."

She waited for the apologetic urge to swamp her. The cowering agreement as a powerful monster sapped her strength. Not this time. She deserved so much better than an emotionally stunted man with the temperament of a cranky child.

"You'll lose the house." He yanked his shirt cuffs. "Your job." He'd done his best with her, he'd tell the concern vultures, but she just hadn't been good wife material. "You won't find another, not here."

Opportunistic wealth-chaser. She'd thought him ambitious in school. A hard worker. But the work had never mattered to him. Ostentatious appearances and monetary rewards would do fine.

"You'll lose, too." She'd see his persecution ended in mutually assured destruction, if their fight came to that. "The difference is I won't care."

David reached for her.

Rob growled. "You want to walk away."

"You think this bar-hopper is better than me, Els?" David's bite slipped off her tougher skin. His gummy grasping projected as much menace as an infant coating a teething ring in drool. "The minute you take your clothes off, he'll picture someone with bigger assets and better technique. When you fail to satisfy, he'll find another."

Pathetic. Rob witnessing the depression and failure of her marriage didn't shame her. He'd seen her weakness at the house when she'd thrown him out, and he'd listened to the truth. Now he'd see her strong. Confident. Ready to commit to a relationship with him, not holding pieces of herself back.

"No, Rob is a gentleman. Him, I can trust. You…" So many things to say. Not one mattered. David didn't matter. "I'd trust a copperhead not to bite me before I'd trust a word out of your mouth again."

The suit-and-tie employee entering the dining room wore the officious look of a man about to tell them to take the mess outside.

Rob had paid the check while she'd been luxuriating in chocolate dessert heaven. If she'd eaten faster, she'd have avoided David's petty baiting altogether. But then she'd have missed this freedom. "Rob, I'm ready to go when you are." Not an escape but a promise. "We have better places to be."

* * * *

She danced in the parking lot. God love her, under a full moon and twinkling stars and fancy lamppost streetlights, his Nora twirled with abandon. Beautiful. Giddy and laughing.

He popped the locks on the truck without tearing his gaze from her. Independent and free like a wild mare, and her smile. Christ, her smile. So wide her cheeks had to be aching. Stuffing him with the urge to kiss her, to press her against the truck and devour her.

Her dress fluttered as she changed directions and dashed into his arms. Sweeping a woman off her feet had never seemed so natural. Her soft contours settled in all the right places as he raised her up and tipped his head back. "Feeling good, honey girl?"

"Light as a cloud." She looked it, too, a gorgeous blue sky denying the night its darkness. "Like everything was in shadows." She scrunched up her nose. "Heavy. Oppressive." Lowering her forehead to his, she sighed. "And now the shadow's gone, and I feel your warmth like the sun heating my skin and making my heart race, but more than that."

"Love," he whispered, and almost dropped her. Sonuvabitch, he'd thrown everything on the table now.

She squeezed him tight, curling her arms around his shoulders and pressing her breasts flat to his chest. "Love."

Their lips touched. Impossible to say who'd moved first. Did it matter? If they moved as one for the rest of their lives, he'd be damned happy.

She made his dress pants tighter by the second, and no way she didn't feel him, not with her body flush against him and her feet dangling.

"Those better places you wanna be," he murmured between kisses. "Where to, Nora?"

The night gleamed with possibility. She'd gone toe to toe with the pathetic jackhole haunting her and laid him out by TKO. Satisfying as punching the shit out of that sack himself would've been, watching Nora hold her own and come out on top, confident and determined, took the prize. A victory on points and one on power both went in the win column.

"Take me home." She pulled back and gazed at him with wide, dark eyes, the blue-gray rings around her pupils rolling in like a summer storm. Her shining lips begged for more kisses to muss their deep gloss. "Your home."

His legs moved, carrying her around the truck to the passenger door before his brain relayed the signal. Nora. In his house. Under his protection.

"Anything you want."

He peeled one hand from the slope of her hip and clutched her tighter with the other. Hell if he'd put her down just to open a damned door. Driving, though, that'd be harder. Not as hard as him, banging at his zipped fly.

"Anytime you want."

Cool night air slipped between them as he lifted her to the seat and she swung her legs inside. He stole another kiss and ached to touch soft skin instead of flowing silk when he pulled the seatbelt across her stomach.

"Any*where* you want."

"I want our first time to be in your bed," she whispered, urgent and fierce. She clutched his jacket, her fingers curling around the lapel, and tugged him in close. "I want to make love with you until the sun comes up."

First time together. The chance to bury himself inside her heat and show her how right lovemaking could be, what she'd been missing all those years. To be the best lover she'd ever had. To be the only one she'd want from now to the grave. "Same thing I want, honey girl."

He forced himself to close the door on her smile and hustle around the truck instead of dropping to his knees and spreading hers. Drink up the sweet scent and taste of her while she squirmed in his bench seat and her moans and squeals drowned out the hum of highway traffic behind them. Her damned ex'd be on the phone in two shakes getting the cops out here to cite him for public lewdness. Seen enough through the restaurant windows, likely.

Starting the car, he shook off growling pride. Nora wasn't some trophy, some frat-boy mascot he'd swiped for a prank. Claiming her didn't mean putting her beauty on display for her ex-husband and rubbing his nose in it. That fucker got within ten paces of rubbing anything on Nora from now on and he'd be regretting his stupidity.

He drove past the strip of big-box stores with their eye-piercing lights and sanitized, one-size-fits-all design. No challenge to 'em. No love in 'em. Not like his old farmhouse, the one waiting for Nora to help him make a home. Starting tonight.

Office supply store to the left. He'd stowed his gear and put fresh sheets on the bed before picking her up. High hopes. Drugstore to the right. Preparation never hurt a soul.

Nora swiveled toward the window, her curls bouncing. Swinging back, she blurted, "You have condoms, right?"

Same wavelength, same eagerness, a touch more panic on her part. Christ, he loved she'd had the courage and the sense to ask. "If I didn't, we'd be in the drugstore parking lot right now, that's for damned sure."

Giggles greeted his vow. "I don't think that lot's as secluded as the drive-in."

Groaning, he let memory flood in. The boldness she'd wielded only in flashes then ruled her now. No holding back. She'd won the battle. Hadn't needed him, but wanted him. So strong on her own, and she'd entrusted herself to him.

Traffic thinned out to nothing, his headlights the lone illumination on the asphalt. Passed his near neighbors' place, the spotter hitting the gravel where their teen had best be getting his clunker back before midnight. Kid wouldn't be bringing his girl home. Sixteen or thirty-six, didn't make a spit of difference: dropping the girl off made for a long, lonely drive after.

But tonight he had Nora beside him as he pulled onto the crushed stone drive a half-mile farther on. Had her unashamed curiosity, the way she leaned forward with her hand on the dash and gazed out the windshield.

The tilt of her head exposed the graceful curve of her neck, skin crying for his hard kisses. Would she be pissed if he marked her so often she needed sleeveless turtlenecks for the rest of the summer?

He cut the rumbling engine, and the rolling beat from the radio died alongside the wide front porch. The clicks of seatbelts unfastening snapped like a double-barreled shotgun.

He opened his door. The chorus of crickets chirping from the fields proved he wasn't the only male engaged in mating rituals tonight. Giving in to impulse, he brushed his knuckles down her bare arm and savored her shiver. "Wait here."

Long strides brought him 'round to her door.

She reached for him soon as he'd pushed the metal aside. Twined her arms around his neck and slipped into his cradling hands without a prompt. Her dress scurried up her legs when she squeezed his hips between her thighs. Christ, yes, she held on with a tight grip promising to destroy him.

He shoved the door closed and carried her up the porch steps double-time. Pressing her to the butter-yellow siding, he snagged the screen door and jammed his foot in to hold the gap.

She rocked her hips, panties sliding at his waist.

Jesus. Not tonight, but some night soon, they'd finish quick and clothed on the porch, his pants open and her panties pushed aside. His wild, hungry Nora.

"Almost there." He turned the knob and gave the solid red oak a push. "Last door."

"Good." She teased her fingers inside his collar. "I don't want any doors holding us back."

"Me neither, Nora." Stepping over the sill with her in his arms cemented his cock and swelled his heart. "No obstacles in our path."

Not doors, not fears, and not fabric.

Fusing their lips, she tugged at his tongue and dug her fingers into his shoulders. Her desire battered him with urgency, made his blind shuffling toward the stairs too slow and his bedroom too far.

He backed her to the wall at the foot of the stairs and released his grip.

She clutched at him as she started sliding. "Wha—"

"A brief stop, honey girl, I promise. Can't wait." He rubbed her bare thighs, her skin warm and soft under his hands with her dress bunched between their bodies. "Let go for a minute."

With him holding her dress at her waist, she snaked her feet to the floor.

He dropped to his knees the second she'd steadied herself. "Wanted to do this earlier, but I didn't figure you'd appreciate it much with an audience." He hitched his fingers under the sides of her panties. Paler blue than her dress. Lacey patterns over sleek silk. "And some things a man's gotta keep for himself."

He peeled the covering away, down her legs, and inhaled pure, honeyed desire.

"The way you taste, how you squirm and call out with my tongue inside you?" Spreading her lips with his thumbs revealed blushing flesh wet and waiting. His new home. "That ain't something I'm willing to share with anyone."

He swept her curls aside and dropped a tender kiss on her clit. Her whimper stiffened his cock, jerked him as if strings tied them together.

"Just like that," he whispered. "Make music for me, Nora."

* * * *

He devoured her the way she'd inhaled dessert, with deep appreciation and a greedy mouth. Felt but not seen. He blocked her view, his head almost still, his hair bristle-brush short and his knuckles clenched around the folds of her dress. But hidden below, his tongue worked wonders.

Thoughts flitted faster than a filmstrip flapping around and around. Never a movie day like this one. Interactive. Stroking and driving. Curling her toes in shoes too tight for the motion. Lifting her heels.

Pressure behind her knee, and she slammed her hands against the wall to keep her balance.

Rob draped her leg over his shoulder. Her dress tumbled down, a blue waterfall rolling across the solid man beneath.

He squeezed her thighs.

She sucked in a surprised breath.

The tugging rhythm between her legs stopped.

"All right, honey girl?" Her dress rippled, and Rob's short hair tickled her belly. "Something I do you don't like, you go on and tell me."

"Mmmph." She rolled her neck. Nope. All good. Adding up to a sizeable balance. Ready for a payout.

"Nora?" Lumpy movement under her dress.

"No, don't stop." She dropped her hands, scrambling for the back of his head. "Don't—dangit, sorry, I forgot you can't see me shaking my head any more than I can see what you're doing that feels so good." The silk shrouding his neck and shoulders slipped through her grasp. "Please keep going."

The breath from his laughter woke shivers in her blood.

"So good, huh?" He nestled closer, his cheek smooth and soft against her inner thigh. "Must be because I'm eating such a delicious meal. Gonna need seconds later."

"You can—" Oh God, whatever he'd done, let him do it again. "You can have all the servings you want, Rob."

Breakfast, lunch, and dinner. Midnight snack. Afternoon munchies. Mealtimes she'd invent the second her brain started working.

Tension stole up her spine, shoved her shoulders hard to the wall, and tipped her head back. Need choked her, tight and burning, with a welcome invasion, Rob's tongue thick and thrusting while he rubbed her clit with heavy fingers.

So wrong to believe her body incapable of finding pleasure this way. Wasted years. She clung to the edge with a desperate grip. Too quick for this to be over, not ready, not—

Agonizing bliss seared her, a rush of heat and tremors swallowing her whole.

Long, slow strokes along her thigh shook her loose. Her arms hung slack at her sides, her fingers tingling.

Rob held her dress bunched at her belly in one firm, splayed hand as he rubbed her in slow circles.

"You're so beautiful, Nora." His hushed tones belonged in a church pew. Maybe he basked in the same awe kneeling here, at the foot of his staircase. A cocky smile crawled across his face. "And you wail like a five-alarm fire."

"I do not." She wasn't a screamer. She'd never moaned and screamed in the bedroom. "Nobody does. They make that up for porn. Like women who wax everything."

"Nuh-uh." The kiss he planted made her squirm. "Nope." Another kiss, this one on her thigh. "Honest-to-God truth in your case." He squinted up at her. "So, you're a big porn-watcher, are you?"

"No." David trying to push the videos on her as educational hadn't made them appealing. "Girls talk." Chelsea and the girls at work did sometimes, anyway. "Men like that, don't they?"

"What, girls talking or watching porn?"

"No, waxing." She'd meant to ask last week. Now he'd buried his face between her legs twice, and he hadn't said a word about her grooming habits. "Would you want me to?"

He slid his cheek along her thigh. "You feel plenty smooth to me."

"Not all over." A twinge of inadequacy fluttered in her belly.

He raised an eyebrow. "You asking what I like, Nora?"

"I guess so." Guess? What was that bullshit?

Rob waited on his knees in front of her. The man who loved her confidence and her honesty.

"I mean, yes. I'm asking. I want to know what you like and don't like." Not limited to that, either. "And I want to learn what turns me on. I want you to help me figure it out."

"Tall order." He gazed at her with eyes deep and true, their every flicker an invitation and a promise. "I tell you what, though. I'm damned good at following orders and not half-bad at taking command."

Dipping his shoulder, he lowered her leg to the floor. "I like a woman comfortable with how she looks, however she chooses to display herself. There ain't a thing wrong with the way you look tonight."

He shrugged off his jacket and stood. "But you wanna shave sometime, you let me know, 'cause I'll grab a front-row seat for your show." Leaning in, he nuzzled her ear. "Maybe ask for a little audience participation."

"You'd like that?" The boring repetition of beauty routines gained new allure. "Really?"

"Absolutely." He dotted her neck with tiny kisses. "You making a decision because doing something makes you feel sexy or bold or daring? Guaranteed I'll be harder than a titanium strut."

She pressed her hand to the front of his pants, and his moan flooded her with heat. Boldness-response guarantee confirmed.

"The lady requested a bed, remember?" He tugged her hand away. "You touch me now, and I won't make it that far."

She stepped out of her shoes. Her legs wobbled as she followed him up the stairs. "For the first time."

The blank walls begged for photos. Every family saved the wall along the stairs for year after year of portraits. Weddings and anniversaries. Birthdays, school pictures, and sports teams. Smiling faces.

"Then all the other rooms." Maybe she'd finally met the man who'd make those memories with her. "I get a tour of the house, don't I?"

Groaning, he squeezed her hand with desperate strength. "In the morning, Nora." Turning at the top of the stairs, he paused and glanced down. "Way I'm feeling tonight, we'll christen every room in the place by this time tomorrow."

And every day for the rest of their lives, if her luck held. "Best get started, then."

Flipping on the light, he led her into his bedroom. Cleaner than hers. She teased him out of his tie and sent the smooth silk sailing to the floor. "You could do with a little mess, Rob."

"Trying to impress a special gal." He peeled off her dress and tossed it aside. Unhooked her bra and cupped her breasts with warm, firm pressure. "She's always impressing me."

Sincerity poured from his eyes. His intensity flattened her, sucked the air from her lungs while his belief supported her.

She slipped the leather tongue of his belt free and rubbed the button beneath. Smooth face. Raised threads. The slightest push enough to guide the disc through the buttonhole.

Rob built her up without tearing her down. His steady strength made her strong, too. With the last tick of the zipper, his pants dropped to the floor, leaving tented boxers attempting to contain his arousal.

She dipped inside. His cock bounced against the cotton. Much as she enjoyed watching him dance, the view would be better without the shorts. Gone in one fell swoop.

He squeezed his balls, and pre-come beaded at the tip of his cock.

"I gotta apologize." His tone teased. "I didn't shave for tonight. It's like a cover crop down here."

Giggling, she shoved his chest. He stood firm.

"But I trust you, Nora." He curved his hands around hers. "You wanna wield the razor on me sometime, I'm all yours."

Trust. God, she needed that. To trust and be trusted. The currents of honesty and respect, invisible until a twister tore through and shredded them. Swallowing hard, she shook her head and gently scratched his chest. "Another time."

She wiggled a hand free. Down his oh-so-firm abdominals. She grasped skin softer than men had a right to have and stroked.

He whistled air through clenched teeth.

Her confidence surged, a dizzying swirl of power and pleasure. "I've got more important places for this to be right now."

"Thinking of a few myself." He backed her to the bed, stepping out of his shoes and over his clothes.

Letting go, she tumbled onto her back and bounced on the mattress. Her feet dangled. She spread her arms wide. "I hope your thoughts all start this way."

"They surely do." He bent and opened the nightstand's top drawer. "With one addition." He tugged, growled, and tugged harder.

A strip of condoms unfurled with a snap. Long line. Two, four, six—

"Only one missing is the one in my pants pocket, honey girl." He tore free the top square and let the rest fall.

"You bought a new box for me?" A curious sort of pride filled her.

He winked. "A man can dream."

So could a woman. Too many nights imagining these moments a hundred ways. Now she'd gorge herself on every variation. "With that much inspiration, guess we will be trying every room this weekend."

He rolled the latex down his cock. A transparent shield between them. "You're on."

Gripping the back of her knees, he pushed her farther across the quilt. She kicked her feet up and tickled his ribs with her toes. "I feel like a wheelbarrow."

"Squirmiest wheelbarrow I've ever handled." He crawled over her, walking his hands up the bed along her thighs, her hips, her chest. "Prettiest, too."

The mattress dipped with his weight, rocking her side to side.

"Sweetest." He pressed in close, his heat warming her as he steadied himself on his forearms.

Every nerve ending in her body clamored for his touch.

"Softest." He sank down with the welcome scratch of chest hair against her straining nipples. His hard heat pressed to her clit and belly. He kissed her forehead. "Most loved."

"Most loved." Too long since her body had melted for those words and the truth behind them. Joy leaked out in a surprising rush, and she choked on her gratitude. "Thank you, Robin."

"Hey, shhh, easy," he crooned. He kissed the corners of her eyes. "I love you, Nora."

He dragged the tip of his nose down her cheek. "Love you."

Kissed her mouth in a nibbling line. "You're gonna get tired of hearing me say so."

Nipped at her jawline and teased her throat with his teeth. "But I'm gonna keep on."

Rocking his hips, he teased his cock forward and back. "All the time, because I love you."

He stroked her side and slipped his hand between their bodies. "People everywhere'll be asking you, 'Eleanora, who's that handsome stud following you around and shouting how much he loves you?'"

"Oh God." She hadn't told her hips to thrust like that. Instinctive reaction to his fingers on her clit. Must be. Her brain contributed a whole lot of nothing to this discussion. Girly bits operated alone. Clit, lips, pussy, and heart. All of them talking to him.

"Nope. Just your Robin." He rolled, taking her with him. Now she straddled him, her legs hugging his hips and her hair falling in curls around their faces, shutting out all but their intimate nest for two. He cradled her in his broad hands. "Your choice, honey girl."

No, not her choice alone.

She pushed herself up and snagged his hand. Guiding him, she wrapped both of their hands around the base of his cock. Raised her hips. Nudged him between her lips, seeking the perfect alignment.

"Our choice." She sank.

He groaned and blinked, his mouth wide and his gold-flecked eyes dancing. His cock lodged deep. Sturdy. Strong. Rob. He flexed his hips.

She shuddered. "I love you."

* * * *

Home. Tight and trembling above and around him, soaking his balls and his thighs. Been a while for her. Him too, but his dry spell just made him quicker off the draw. He'd wanted her good and relaxed, orgasmic and laughing, so he wouldn't hurt her.

"Love you right back." With a fierceness and a certainty he'd never found before.

After a deep breath, she caught her lower lip between her teeth. Moans poured forth anyway. She'd deny them later. Thought herself quiet as a church mouse, his unrestrained screamer. His Nora.

Eyelids drifting, lip slipping as her mouth opened and her curls swung free, she ground her hips and clamped down on his cock. On purpose or couldn't help herself, either way, goddamned hot.

He surged beneath her. Near lifted her off the bed.

Rocking forward, she slapped her hands down on his pecs. Fuck, the sting upped the urge to grab her waist and drive himself into her until neither of them had thought enough to take a breath.

No need. She found the rhythm herself, bouncing on his cock with sudden speed.

Unhh, Christ, he oughta look anywhere but where he disappeared inside her. Too close to unloading every time she pulled him deep.

The flare of her hips and the ripple in her stomach proved no safer. Nor the hypnotic jouncing of her breasts or her fingers kneading his chest or the brilliant smile on her face.

Jesus, turn her on and let her loose, and her instincts and eagerness promised him heaven. Land of milk and honey. Moans, laughter, and mind-blowing pleasure.

"Love the way you ride, too." He inched toward her center. He'd give her a hand, push her over the edge before she took him. "Not gonna last long like this." He thrust up as she slammed down. Fuck, her fingers'd leave divots in his chest in another minute. "You feel how hard I get for you?"

She gasped and groaned. Her clit jumped under his fingertips.

"That's all you, Nora, taking me inside your slick, sweet pussy."

She spasmed. Victory for them both. Her feet beat an incoherent rhythm on the mattress beside his knees as she milked him.

Pinning her thighs beneath his palms, he emptied with a shout.

Lungs heaving, she sagged.

He wrapped her tight and pulled her to his chest. Her breath gusted past his ear as he kissed her cheek.

"Mmm, take a breather." Soft, warm skin with a hint of salt under his lips. "You more than earned one." Her heartbeat raced below her jaw. "My turn to do all the work next time, hey?"

She shivered and wormed her arms around his back. "Promises, promises."

The smile in her voice didn't dispel the flicker of a question. Bunching her straying curls in his hand, he turned her head and kissed her with firm, crushing lips. "I keep my promises."

Supple arms and legs crushed him in return. "I believe you do, Shirtless Gentleman." She nuzzled him like a kitten, bumping his nose and cheeks.

"I wouldn't be here if I didn't." Lifting her head, she giggled. "Definitely wouldn't be naked. In your bed. Holding you inside me."

She tightened already-tight muscles. Deliberate this time, for certain.

He exaggerated his groan. "It'll be a sweet death when your appetite kills me."

"Am I too much for you?" His woman teased him with a bold tone and a smile verging on smug.

She'd shed so much shyness since their night at the drive-in. The night his fingers had ventured where his cock rested now.

"Just right." And how. He'd have to pull out soon, before he lost the firmness gluing the condom tight to his cock. All well and good to imagine Nora with his ring on her finger and his child in her belly, but spooking her with a pregnancy scare their first night sure as hell wasn't the way to go about getting there. "You are right on the button for me, Eleanora Howard."

Her satisfied hum rumbled against his neck. They lay together in growing quiet. Not the awkward, empty silence of a bad first date but the filling silence of comfort, of summer evenings on the porch swing.

The smooth expanse of her back flowed under his hand. Stopping himself from petting and stroking her would take more effort than he cared to muster. 'Til he softened, leastwise.

He rolled her with a growl, pulled his hips back, and made a quick grab for his cock. Missed her tight heat soon as he'd left her. With the latex pinched between his fingers at the base, he twisted to sit up. He tied off the condom and pitched it in the trash. Now he had a sticky dick and a girl waiting. Boxers. Perfect cleanup. He bent over and snagged them.

A slow wolf whistle sounded behind him, followed by a giggle.

He wiped off his cock, dropped the undershorts, and shook his ass. "I hope you have dollar bills. I'm a stripper with standards. No free shows."

"Aren't you supposed to wear a g-string?" She sported a less than innocent smile and a goddamned gorgeous body, all sprawling and relaxed like she understood she belonged in his bed. A cat claiming her territory. "I can't wait to see how you hold those dollars."

"Shooting down my bright ideas with your accountant logic?" He launched himself at the bed. Every angle calculated for a safe landing. "Must be consequences for that." He laid out flat on top of her and kissed her nose. "Big, hard ramifications."

"I like these outcomes." Squirming, she wrapped her legs around the backs of his thighs and squeezed. "How do I get more?"

"Keep doing that and you'll find out." Soon, he hoped. Of course, the longer his dick took to stand up again, the more time he had to tease and explore his woman. "I might be persuaded to let you run a tab." For the rest of their lives.

"Could be dangerous." She rolled her hips, ocean swells fit to drown in. "I'm feeling like a big spender."

"I know you're good for it." He filled his lungs with the sweet musk of her arousal. His inhalation flattened the roundness of her tits to his chest. He hadn't dined on a mouthful of them yet. Fix that in a minute, sure enough. "And I'll cut you a deal."

"A markdown?" She gripped his shoulders and stroked his arms. "Don't undervalue yourself, Rob. You've got great selling points."

"So do you." He waited for her to still, her eyes dark and confident. "I'll respect my value if you'll respect yours. Deal?"

"I don't think that's gonna be a problem anymore." Smile spreading across her face, she wiggled her hips. "What does this deal get me?"

Natural curiosity. Eager interest. No backing down, no shaming herself for sharing herself with him. She'd dropped the weight of her ex-husband's expectations. They'd cracked open the defective code, however deep the fuckwit's spiteful words and selfish desires had invaded, and yanked out the virus that had overrun her system for so long.

"Let me show you all the features." His cock pushed toward half-mast, sluggish but responding to signals again. He'd have more stamina for a second go. Stay inside her longer, take his time, look her in the eyes while she rolled through her orgasm with him buried deep. "I think you'll wanna spring for the top of the line model."

Lifetime warranty included.

"I think I will, too."

* * * *

Nora jerked awake in darkness, fragments of a half-remembered dream fading with each blink. A weight across her collarbone pinned her to the soft bed at her back. Heat warmed her in uneven measure, greater to her left and absent on her right.

Rob. He lay beside her because this bed belonged to him and she hadn't left it yet. He slept on his side, his face bared to her and his arm draped over her. Years since she'd fallen asleep so close to a man, back when she and David were newlyweds. The distance between them had grown every year since.

Keeping this closeness demanded a commitment from two. One alone would never be enough. Reaching for something always beyond their fingers. For some*one* who raced a few steps ahead, who commanded her to follow like a dog. Not so now. She'd done as she pleased and the world hadn't ended.

The dating police weren't barreling down the drive with lights flashing and sirens blaring to brand her a slut. Rob hadn't laughed at her or berated her. He hadn't stopped to "correct" her position or her speed or any of the dozens of faults David had found with her.

Desires she'd shut down and shied away from, afraid to chance raising the subject with David, floated around her in a slow-moving dance. She could trust Rob. She could talk to Rob. She could try things with Rob she'd never let herself imagine before. Terrifying and liberating, all at once.

She inched to her right. His palm, heavy and warm, rolled across her breasts as she slipped free of his hold. Their clothes littered the bedroom floor. Rob curled his fingers into the space she'd left behind.

Beautiful man. The comforter lay unused beneath his nudity. The August heat made their bodies enough. Odd, how he revealed power and vulnerability in the same skin. His broad chest and thick thighs delighted whether as a sturdy platform to ride or a shield to rest under. Draped on his thigh, his cock hung soft and smaller than when he'd helped her roll the condom down his shaft. When he'd laid her back on the bed, risen above her, and entered her with patient strength.

Stepping around the clothes, she tiptoed out of the bedroom and down the hall to the bathroom. She flipped the switch, and invasive light plastered her eyes shut on instinct. Well, the light and the colors.

His bathroom brought to life a pink-drenched nightmare with stately black trim. Somebody'd rebooted this room in the 1950s. Even the toilet and the pedestal sink resembled Pepto-Bismol piggies. At least both worked fine.

The mirror didn't. Couldn't. It reflected an unrecognizable woman. One who stood tall. One whose gaze flicked past the dwindling curls, half matted and flat, without a wince. One who smiled with pride and remembered pleasure at the purpling ovals dotting her neck and breasts. A woman wide-awake at two in the morning and reveling in the thrill of tiptoeing naked around her lover's house.

He'd invited her to make herself at home. "Stay with me, Nora." Lying drowsy and sated after making love the second time, he'd kissed her forehead and cuddled her close. "What's mine is yours."

Her panties hugged the floor at the base of the stairs beside her shoes. She trailed her fingers along the wall. First stop on her house tour. Maybe he'd repeat that stop in the morning as part of a complete breakfast.

The kitchen stood at the back of the house, beyond a dining room set up like a home office. Rob didn't do a lot of entertaining. Or if he did, he served up meals at the homey trestle table in the kitchen. He owned a well-stocked fridge for a bachelor. The glass-front upper cabinets made finding a glass for her orange juice easy.

The window above the sink overlooked a neatly maintained yard with close-cropped grass giving way to wild prairie. Posts supported an empty laundry line. A lone oak's leafy arms waved. A yard for children. Waiting for a swing set and a back porch with a heap of bikes and sports gear.

Condensation dripped from her glass to her chest. Chilly. No wandering bare-breasted in a home full of kids. Enticingly decadent for now, though.

"To everything, there is a season."

If Rob felt the same, they'd see them all together.

* * * *

She hadn't come back.

He'd noticed the minute she left the bed. Impossible to sleep through his woman slipping out of his arms. The creak of the bathroom door, the flush of the toilet, and the sink running alerted him to her purpose. But she had yet to return.

God forbid she gave in to doubts and fears. His Nora, standing in the bathroom, regretting their night together. Crying or worrying how she'd leave without her car here.

He rolled to his feet at the speed of the adrenaline coursing through him. Panic subsided in a puddle of blue silk. He fell back on training. Assessed the environment for what the clues told him.

His Nora, comfortable wandering naked in his house. Staking her claim. Starting her tour without him.

Palming a condom from the nightstand, he began his hunt. Past the empty bathroom, avoiding creaky boards with the ease of long practice, he hugged the wall down the stairs. Her panties greeted him at the bottom. Definitely naked.

No blood left for panic, what with the full volume converging on his cock. He slipped through the living and dining rooms. Stopped.

Moonlight streaming in the kitchen window washed her nude beauty in ghostly white. He'd stood on the same spot the night they'd met. Speckled that window with his own brand of whitewash. Then he'd had his hand

and his imagination. Tonight, she stood before him, a vision of soft, warm flesh, the woman he loved tender and needy or wild and greedy.

Crossing the floor, he hummed so as not to startle her. She tipped her head but didn't turn from the window. He settled behind her, relaxation and arousal mingling when she allowed him to wrap his arms across her shoulders and chest. Pinned her in tight. His woman.

She gripped his forearms. Her man. A silent agreement taking him to full hardness. The corners of the condom packet dug into his palm.

"Thinking good thoughts?" He kept his voice low in a fervent hope for truth.

She bumped his chin with her nod. "You've got a strong oak out there." Her fingers fluttered against his arm. "It should have a tree house."

Thank God for bringing this woman to him. Thank him for her ex's stupidity and Lucas's inability to hold his drink. For all his years of searching and not settling for less than perfection.

He kissed the side of her head. "House like that needs children to play in it."

"Three or four, I think," she whispered, sweet and wistful.

"I think so too. They say practice makes perfect." He dotted her neck with kisses, light and playful, circling the tiny bruises his mouth had left earlier. Those made his cock twitch. *Mine.*

"Mm-hmm. We'll get the most benefit—"

She gasped and shivered. Sensitive spot half an inch below her right ear.

"—from two-a-days."

Three or four, I think.

He pressed into her, aching relief as the soft skin of her backside caressed his cock. "Whatever the lady wants."

"Upstairs?" A touch of uncertainty. A hint of disappointment, maybe.

"You said you wanted to try other rooms." He unfurled his fingers and presented the condom packet.

"I did say that." She plucked the wrapper free and tore the corner. "And I've never…"

"Not in the kitchen?" Taking the latex circle from her fingers, he nipped her ear. "That's a shame, Nora." An ain't-he-a-lucky-bastard shame. A make-her-first-time-memorable shame. "We'll fix that right now."

He rolled on the condom and roused her with stroking fingers and wandering kisses. Teased his tip inside and groaned at her suction. Pressed her hands to the counter and entwined their fingers.

They'd fix the rest day by day. All the time in the world.

Epilogue

Rain dogged them the whole way south, flying in sheets under the old truck's tires. Steam rose from cattle clustered in the muddy fields more akin to spring than December twenty-third. Temps hovered in the upper 40s, but the news folk warned a cold snap was like to swoop down from Canada any day now.

Though the truck heater kept the damp at bay, Nora snuggled alongside him on the bench seat anyhow. Inched outta her seat in the first hour and never gone back. Her head rested light on his shoulder. They sat denim to denim.

Rob dropped his hand off the wheel and squeezed her knee. Driving home for Christmas alone didn't hold a quarter the joy of her at his side. Their five-and-a-half-hour drive crested seven with the bad weather, the holiday traffic, and the tractor-trailers throwing up road tsunamis. The hours slipped by to the tune of the radio's Christmas music marathon under an unbroken dome of dull gray clouds.

He swung through his hometown to show her the main street all gussied up in holiday finery. The garlands and wreaths slung under the store awnings stayed safe and festive even if the bright red bows on the streetlights hung limp and waterlogged. A left at Carson's Crafts and Collectibles—boasting eBay services in the front window now—would take them out past the high school. Near dark going on five o'clock, though. Mama would have supper waiting on them if he towed Nora all over the county and back of beyond just to show her his childhood haunts.

He'd have a next time, a whole stretch of years, to share his memories with her. The game when he'd hit the home run clear across the outfield and busted a bus window in the parking lot. The Nesleys' sledding hill the year they'd gotten the whopper of a storm. Hell, he and Marcus hauled Daddy's old smooth-bottomed toboggan again and again while Jilly and Sara clapped and cheered, 'til all their fingers froze in their mittens. They piled through the front door, stomping snow off their boots, and Mama appeared with mugs of hot cocoa and fresh-baked gingerbread men.

Pressing her legs together, Nora grew squirmy as an inchworm in the seat. "How much further?"

"Ain't but ten minutes now." He hung a right, the turnoff one he'd made a hundred times before, but never with his woman at his side. "You want me to stop in town, or you wanna hold it?"

"Huh?" She blinked twice, pure deer-in-headlights, and shook her head. "I don't need a bathroom break."

"You sure?" Hell if she didn't. Her knee jounced as if the truck bumped along washboard ruts instead of smooth pavement.

"Mm-hmm. No pee-jitters. Just the ordinary kind." She spread her fingers in front of the heat vent. Pale fingers, slim and bare, they offered no hint a wedding band had ever circled one. "What did your parents say when you told them you were bringing me to Christmas?"

"That they can't wait to meet you." A reassurance he'd repeated half a dozen times in the last two weeks. Not strong enough, seemed like. He eased onto the shoulder, threw the truck in park, and unsnapped her seatbelt.

"Rob, what—"

He hauled her into his lap and kissed her. Tight fit, his arm wedged between her back and the steering wheel, but Christ she belonged just so. "You planning to call my daddy a hayseed hack who can't plow a straight line to save his life? Tell my mama she's fat and ugly and her cooking tastes like the back end of a cow?"

"Good God, no, of course I'm not." An adorable divot perched between her eyebrows.

He kissed her frown line for good measure. "Then here's what's gonna happen."

A familiar red truck coming from the other direction slowed, the driver's window dropping, and Rob punched the button to lower his own.

The vehicle rolled to a stop alongside his, a lane-width away. "You folks all right?" A man's hand emerged from the window. The driver gripped the roofline in the growing dusk and peered out from under an old-school plaid hunter's cap, earflaps and all. "Outta gas? Got a flat?"

"All good, Mr. Nesley." He leaned into the drizzle and raised his voice. His folks' oldest neighbor had to be nearing eighty these days. "It's Rob, Rob Vanderhoff."

"Oh, Rick's younger boy, sure enough. You've grown some. Not so big as your brother, mind. The wife's sending me to the store." With arthritic fingers thick and curving, Mr. Nesley patted his chest. "Got my marching orders tucked away. You in town for the holidays, son?"

"Yessir. Taking my girl here"—he tipped her backward, and Nora obliged with a wave out the window—"home for Christmas, and she's caught a touch of nerves." Her light slap at his shoulder came expected and went undodged. "'Preciate you stopping, though."

"Ah, yeah, that'll do ya. First time my girl and my mother got in the same room, hoo boy, fireworks flew. Singed me something good. Sixty-one, no, sixty-two years now, and those burns still smart." He smacked the roof twice. "Give 'em hell, girlie. Rob, you thank your mama for the cookies she sent over. All that bending and stooping at the oven's gotten to be too much for my Louise. Merry Christmas!"

"Merry Christmas, Mr. Nesley." He tossed the words over the rising crank window. Same truck the Nesleys'd had since his boyhood, well cared-for and purring quiet and steady as a cat on the hearth. The red truck slipped away just as smoothly. "Now where was I?"

Nora nestled against his shoulder and wormed her arms around his back. "Calmly reassuring your anxious girlfriend her fears are a pyramid scheme cooked up by her overactive imagination."

He sent his own window skyward, cutting the chill and the mist swirling in. "Right—so Daddy'll yank you into a hug and tell you to keep me in line, and Mama'll drag you straight to the kitchen and shove a stirring spoon in your hand and a cookie in your mouth. You watch."

Lifting her chin, she sent a honey-brown wave of hair tumbling across his arm. "Is that where you get your habit of shoveling food in my mouth?"

He swiped his thumb across her lower lip, soft and full and a tad reddened from his kiss. "Best hope not. I don't want my mama knowing the thoughts I think when you open your mouth for me."

"I like your thoughts." She captured his thumb and sucked hard, teasing with her tongue. "They all seem to end with me relaxed and sleepy."

Merciful Christ. "Only when I'm getting 'em right, honey girl."

He slipped her off his lap in an attempt to stop his cock from gaining more altitude against her warm, cozy backside. Too late to prevent takeoff. He buckled her in and rejoined the sparse traffic headed northwest.

Little subdivisions, clusters of five to ten houses, squatted across the road from family farms now, creeping deeper into the rolling hills and prairie grass. Thick as deer mice. His faming neighbors up in Iowa probably thought the same of him. Five years he'd had his modest acreage, and he'd yet to plant a thing. A big kitchen garden would start things off nicely come spring if he had a pair of feminine hands to play in the dirt with.

Once her ex had backed off his threats over the house, and her boss—good man—had refused to play ball with the asshole's harassing complaints about her moral suitability for bank work, Nora'd talked some about selling her place. In the spring, when the market rebounded. When new growth started.

She spent half her nights in his bed already. But damn if he didn't need her the other half, too. A good night text held little appeal compared to her cuddled up alongside him with her soft skin, her sweet scent, and her round curves. Space to be independent though. She needed some, and railroading her along wouldn't gain him any ground. He'd had eighteen years of adult bachelorhood. She'd had a fair bit less, and her boldness grew with every discovery, every step toward being the woman her first marriage had stunted.

Coming up on six months, their relationship. They'd done Thanksgiving at his place with Brian and a handful of other buddies from work, a real casual friends affair. But Christmas, Christmas called for family, and not once had he considered Nora anything less. The proof lay snug in a tiny satin bag in his pocket. The slim circle of white gold alternated channel-set garnets and diamonds for their birth months.

Thirty-four days he'd carried the darn thing, since the week before Thanksgiving, and he hadn't worked up the gumption to ask her. Not the nerves so much as the how. Every fool with a notion in his head and a ring in his pocket these days laid out some elaborate scheme and recorded the whole shebang, posted his bragging cleverness online for the world to praise. Not his style.

But Nora deserved praise. If a fancy proposal showed a woman her worth, a man ought to slap on his thinking cap and get the job done right.

"It's so green here." Nora leaned to and fro, spilling her hungry blue-gray gaze through the windows as evenly as the sky covered the fields. "I thought it'd be all broken gold."

"Winter wheat. You're used to corn stubble." He pointed across his grip on the wheel. "Those up there are ours." The south field ran thick with rows of short, splotchy green wheat spreading tendrils. The day's soaking would do them good if the rain hadn't come too fast and hard and driven off the nutrients in the soil. "Must be staying too warm to go dormant yet—ask my daddy about his wheat, and he'll talk your ear off."

Daddy would love her forever, because once Nora asked, she'd dig herself right into the conversation of percentages and yields and temperatures and rainfall. A hatful of numbers made for a common language even with this being her first visit to a working farm.

He took the turnoff for the house and headed up the slope into the last rays of sunlight. The rain registered little more than the odd sprinkle now, but he pulled up alongside the front porch anyhow. The tieback curtains framed the Christmas tree in the parlor window. Same curtains, fresh tree. Mama insisted on the real thing, and Daddy obliged her on all house matters.

A step or two'd have Nora under the roofline with no cause to worry about impersonating a bedraggled mouse fleeing an unexpected flood. He cut the engine, and the low pings of raindrops played a scattershot medley. Their seatbelts, unsnapping, added a deeper click-and-zip. "Ready?"

Turned toward the house and fumbling behind herself, Nora squeezed his thigh. "Nope. Not even close." She scooted across the seat and out, leaving the door hanging wide. His bold girl took the porch stair in two quick hops.

The screen door whined open as if it'd been waiting all day on the chance.

"Come in, come in"—Mama shooed her in the house—"you must be Nora. Robin sends such nice photos in the email. Of course the printer won't do them right, I—"

The screen door snapped shut, and him still warming the driver's seat with his lazy ass. His mama, alone with Nora, already talking photos. The family albums sat in the dining room hutch on a direct line between the front door and the kitchen where it'd be only proper to offer a guest a drink.

Baby bathtimes. Childhood Halloween costumes. That school play—Christ.

He hustled around the truck and snatched the bags from under the slate gray tonneau cover on the bed. One for him, one for Nora, since his folks were like to bunk them in odd corners of the house unsuitable for sharing. His siblings and their spouses got the doubles. He beat feet through the front door.

"Robin, don't you forget"—Mama hollered from the kitchen before the closing snap—"to leave your shoes on the rug."

He rocked at the edge. A raindrop made the wise decision to slide off his boot and onto the braided oval instead of the hardwood.

"I'm finished cleaning the floors"—well of course, wasn't nothing Mama couldn't get done early and perfect the first time—"and you'll have the mop handle in your grip quicker than a hawk scoops a mouse if you track mud all over. God bless this awful rain. Take your bags on upstairs, please."

"Where to?" Stooping with the bags slung over his back, he wrestled his shoes clear of his feet and promptly stepped, sock-footed, in a wet spot. *Yech.* "You putting Nora in the front on the right?"

Too small to be a true bedroom, Mama's sewing room got good eastern light and served fine as a guest room in a pinch. The cozy corner chair unfolded into a narrow twin.

"Don't be silly, Robin. You'll share your old room."

His foot skidded off the first step. His shin banged the riser. *Sonuva—*

"Beef stew's waiting on you. You haven't fed this girl since Des Moines? I'm surprised her stomach isn't rumbling a hole clear through on both sides."

"She's a survivor, Mama, strong and resilient. I'm lucky enough she's"—not blind, nothing hidden from his honey girl except the ring in his pocket, and she'd have it soon as he settled on the best damn way to show her his love—"kind to my faults."

He attacked the steps with more care, Nora's easy laughter from the kitchen a welcome balm. If his shin bruised, she might offer a kiss or two to speed the healing along.

The first room on the left at the top of the stairs had changed. The bunk beds he and Marcus had shared for more than a decade, long after the novelty had worn off and the irritating lack of privacy for teen-hormone-fueled masturbation had begun to grate, no longer stood against the far wall. A double bed had taken up residence. Odd as hell pairing for the old dressers cluttered with athletic trophies whose owners had moved out. Though Marcus hadn't gone far, just up the road a ways. Maybe his big brother dropped by nightly to kiss his old awards for luck.

He lowered the bags whisper-quiet beside the foot of the bed. The. One. A parent-provided bed blessing his relationship with Nora. And Mama hadn't said a word, sly woman.

"Not how you left it?" Daddy leaned on the doorframe. "Wrestled that up here not two days after you asked your mama about bringing your young lady down for Christmas. 'It's time,' says she."

They exchanged a backslapping hug, the proud post-game clinch, and the heat of his folks' approval chased away the last of the damp clinging to his thoughts. "Well and past time. I didn't figure I'd ever get the bedroom back. Thought you'd put Nora in the sewing room and me in a sleeping bag guarding the tree from Santa-peepers."

"Corralling the rugrats up here makes getting the presents under the tree easier, but we'll manage with them camping down in the family room. Shut the parlor while they nod off."

Eight little ones, from two years on up to twelve. Getting that bunch to sleep before midnight would take luck and skill both. A few years down the road, they'd have new cousins to keep the Santa magic alive for. Three or four babies he and Nora'd be making in beds like the solid double in front of him with its curving headboard and heap of pillows.

"You feeling all right, son?" Daddy elbowed his ribs with a solid poke. "Drive getting too long for your old bones?"

"Wasn't expecting that"—he waved at the extra quilt folded across the foot, sure to be hiding sheets pulled neater and tighter than any barracks inspection ever turned up—"is all."

Daddy grunted. "You've been dating this girl of yours for months. That picture you sent your mama of her in the batting helmet, all bright eyes and dusty face, has been staring at me from the fridge since August. Not once in the eighteen years since you moved outta this room have you ever suggested bringing a girl for Christmas. Your mama and I aren't so old we imagine you're sleeping apart."

Nora's picture on the fridge. Part of the family, her accomplishments and her beauty out for anyone to see, and for sure a topic of discussion when Mama's friends came over for coffee. "Can't get anything by you."

"Just so." His father wagged a stern finger under his nose. "You using protection?"

"I'm thirty-six, Daddy. I think I got it handled." Or Nora did, more like. Her handling kept him ready at a moment's notice.

"You gonna—"

A creak and hustle sounded from the hall, and his dad fell silent. The rich brown of Nora's hair rose like a fawn from the tall grass as she climbed the stairs light and quick.

"—hide up here with me?" Daddy carried on as if he hadn't paused or redirected his attention. "The kitchen's been covered in cookie sheets for days, and I've had my knuckles rapped enough times, thank you. I ask you, can a man ignore the rich, spicy call of fresh-baked cookies when the aroma crawls right up his nose? No, he cannot."

Nora peeked around the doorframe. "Rob? Your mom told me to tell you to wash up, because supper's on in three minutes."

Grinning, Daddy rattled him by the shoulder. "She say he'd be sitting on the stool in the corner watching the rest of us eat until he showed the proper respect and clean hands her table deserved?"

Nora's answering smile set his father to nodding. "You, too, Mr. Vanderhoff. Connie says she's going to charge you with theft if she sees a speck of ginger on your hands."

"Uh-huh. Rob best watch himself if you're learning his mama's tricks already." His daddy beckoned her into the bedroom. "C'mon now, don't be shy, this room's yours for the week, so you show it who's boss."

Daddy operated in two modes—the quiet, solemn listener and the gregarious showman. Not hard to guess which he figured would put Nora at ease fastest. Seemed effective. She'd been nervous as hell a few minutes ago, but she strode forward without a shake.

"I'll do my best, sir." She scanned the room as if she meant to build a mathematical model, the bed of less interest to her than the doodads tucked around. Be a hoot to quiz her on which she thought his and which his brother's.

"Diederik Vanderhoff, Lil' Miss Nora, though most call me Rick. It's nice to see the boy hasn't been funning us with all his talk of the young lady in his life. Lord knows what he can do with a computer." Daddy spread his arms wide. "How's about a hug, make sure you're real?"

Nora wrapped her arms around his barrel chest. Daddy patted her back with the gentle fondness he showed any creature in his care. His level stare over the top of her head, though, and the short nod, those were for Rob. *You take care of this one, boy.*

He heard the message sure as if Daddy had spoken the words. In truth, he spouted off a pseudo-grumble about manicures and excused himself to wash up.

"So this is your room, huh?" Nora ran her finger across his name on an old MVP trophy from his baseball days. No dust, not in Mama's house. "And you were so worried about us having to sleep apart the whole week."

"Usually my nephews'd be stacked five deep in here." His worry had been more for Nora's emotional balance—dealing with a huge pack of new faces, over the whipsaw joys and sorrows of holidays, and him not there to cradle and reassure at the end of each day. Texting between floors would've denied them both the comfort of closeness. He bumped her hip. "We're in uncharted territory."

"You sure?" She pressed her face to his shoulder and breathed deep. "I think you've charted the territory pretty well. Climbed the peaks, explored the valleys."

He nipped her ear and found his reward in her gasp. "If I had, I'd definitely have to wash up for supper, and not just my hands."

"Fifty-nine seconds, Robin," Mama shouted up the stairs.

Nora giggled and pulled away. "I better not make you late, or you'll have to sit in the corner."

"You, too, honey girl." He reached after her but only managed to swipe a few floaty hairs and air.

"Oh no, not me." She twisted and darted backward through the door. "Your mom likes me."

He chased her down the stairs and washed up at the kitchen sink, play fighting over having to share the space with her and a sack of potatoes waiting to get cut up for tomorrow's potato salad.

Mama pitched a drying towel on his head. "You can scrub, peel, and cube those for me after dinner, Robin, while I catch up with Nora."

* * * *

Seven hours of driving, a full supper, and a few rounds of rummy while Mama peppered them with every question on God's green earth ought to have left him drowsy as hell. But by the time he and Nora took their turns in the bathroom and she pulled her PJs from her bag, a newfound friskiness started his cock wagging. Down to his undershorts, he made an obvious statement of interest. Or would, soon as she turned around and caught him.

She wriggled clear of her sweater. Static lifted her hair. Unzipped, her jeans hung off her hips. Three slim, sexy lines divided her back. Her pale blue bra didn't come near to matching the depths of her blue eyes.

He snugged his cock against her ass and hugged her close. "You need those pajamas just yet?"

"This is your parents' house." Whisper aside, she rolled her hips in welcome. The honeyed scent of midsummer rose from her skin. "They're right down the hall."

"They had four of us kids." Her bra came loose with ease, and he spanned her back, smoothing the dangling straps toward her arms. "I'm inclined to think they know what goes on in a bed and don't oppose it."

"Under their roof, though?" Her shimmy lowered her jeans and raised his cock.

He dipped his fingers into her panties. A little drift, a little tease. "The truck's outside, and the bench seat's ample." Her wider stance invited investigation. He slid south and cupped her. Perfect fit for his palm, her lips soft and spreading. "How cold you figure it is outside just now? We can fog the windows if you like."

She turned in his arms, presenting him with a handful of squeezable ass. He sneaked his other hand into her panties to fix the imbalance. Couldn't leave her half unsqueezed.

His bold-eyed woman invaded his shorts and gripped his cock. "Too cold to keep this up."

He hissed through his teeth. "You know someplace warmer?"

Sweet agony, her touch. For all the slow seduction of their teasing games, though, she'd never leave him hanging. Her appetite had grown with her confidence. Christ, they'd had fun building her up. Her promise to initiate, his rock-solid promise not to turn her down once. Whatever she asked for, whenever she asked, had gotten his enthusiastic yes for three straight weeks in September.

She captured his mouth in a deep kiss. "Condom?"

"My bag." He stripped his shorts as she shed hers. "Side pocket."

They'd talked some about Nora going on the pill, but he'd let the issue lie soon as she'd walked a halting path through explaining.

A time or two of forgetting to take hers, and she'd received a barrage of lectures on responsibility—with the end result being her husband had dispensed her birth control pill and supervised her while she swallowed one every damn morning for six years. She'd offered to get a new prescription and start them up again.

"I got a better idea." He'd piled a stack of cock coats in her palms. "We'll stick to these. You put them on me anytime you like, and I won't have a thing to complain about."

Fingers curled tight, she'd clutched the square packets. "You're sure? I don't want—" She'd pinched her lips, and a flicker-twitch had darted across her face. "I don't want to be demanding. Controlling, as if I'm the only one whose feelings matter. I want us to make the important decisions together."

"Whole world of difference, honey girl," he'd told her. "You putting your hands on me is encouraging. And you in control's sexy as hell."

Still true. He lay back on the bed, and her intense focus as she worked the thin shield down his shaft riled up all the little swimmers in his balls. Her squeeze and tug, Christ. Fingers tonight, but she'd used her mouth a time or two, and he'd almost gone off early when she unrolled the latex with her lips and tongue.

Work done, she straddled him. Hell yes. He'd settle back and let her ride, his cock disappearing inside her, her breasts swaying to her rhythm—except she twisted instead of lifting up and taking him in. She gripped his thighs tight between her bent legs, though, and her anchoring her balance on him got him hot more often than not. Possession and trust. She didn't hesitate to lean on him now.

Her twists and turns rubbed her belly against his cock. Her lips slid, slick and inviting, across his balls. She meant to tease him to death without even trying.

"Got it." Her whisper swept over him in the same second she did, the quilts gathered in her fingers and over her shoulders like a cape. She flung the covers high, past their heads, and hot breaths and rustling limbs filled the darkness underneath. "Okay. Now you can love me, Rob."

"Isn't a minute goes by that I don't." He pitched his voice low and set his hands to roaming.

Thank God, the rest of his family lived closer and wouldn't be showing up until morning. Bedcovers wouldn't be enough to help Nora shut out the idea of folk hearing her tomorrow night when feet tromped on the stairs and the bathroom beside their room became grand central.

He loved her tender, their hips dancing to a song of hushed whispers and giggles and sighs. At her peak, she poured out a moan muffled against his throat. The new bed held up well under their finishing thrusts, with nary a squeak or a creak to betray what five'd give you twenty his parents already assumed they were doing in here.

She nudged the blankets down to their shoulders. The air thinned her rich honey musk. Hot enough under the covers they'd both gained a sweaty coating despite the slow pace.

He rid himself of the condom and sucked salt off her neck.

"Don't you mark me with a hickey, Robin Vanderhoff." Snuggling in closer, she resettled breast and hip and thigh in a glorious ripple all down his side. "I didn't pack a turtleneck."

"Gotta mark you somehow." Like with the ring tucked safe in the jeans draped over his duffel. The urge pulled hardest in these moments, when she lay flushed and happy and his, her joy a treasure for his eyes and ears and fingers and nose and tongue. Every sense attuned to Nora please-God-someday-Vanderhoff Howard. "Wouldn't want anyone stealing you away."

"Somehow," she murmured. "You'll think of something." In fumble-fingered bliss, she patted his chest. "My shirtless gentleman never fails."

Her steady breathing and the warm weight of her draped half atop him as she slept inspired a dozen further attempts at composition. Each silent recitation ended with the same question—Will you marry me?—but none approached the grand, memorable event she deserved.

The clock on the nightstand ticked over. Thirty-five days, now. The asking weighed more than the ring.

* * * *

Christmas Eve dawned bright and cold, and the hours slipped by fast as a whirlwind. Marcus showed up with his brood in time to polish off the last of Mama's fancy oven French toast.

Big brother blitzed through the kitchen crowd like the defensive lineman he'd been in school and punched his shoulder in greeting. He would've returned the favor, but Mama handed him fresh plates for the kids.

"Marcus Vanderhoff." He leaned beside Nora at the sink. "The good-looking brother." He waggled his left hand, flashing the titanium wedding band he'd worn for a dozen years. "Sadly, I'm already taken, but Robbiekins might make a passable husband someday."

Nora flicked soapy water from her hands. "I dunno about that."

The floor teetered underfoot, and not from the slam-welcome his four-year-old nephew'd delivered to his knees. The noise level dropped.

"Oh." Marcus shifted his weight and shot him a grimace. "Sorry, I assumed."

Glancing over her shoulder, Nora blushed red enough to pull Santa's sleigh. "No, I was joking, I mean—" She shook her head. "I mean I couldn't pass him up."

The family roared, the littlest laughing with no idea why.

Sara's crew hit mid-morning, and the pack of kids grew to six. Jilly arrived late as always. Soon as she and hers walked through the door, the whole family descended on the kitchen for lunch, scarfing everything in sight. Supper wouldn't come until after the evening service, Marcus's three being in the children's pageant.

Not one moment belonged to him and Nora alone. Mama carted her off to the kitchen, the sewing room, the dining room with its photo albums. His sisters cornered her in the family room, overseeing the chaos eight youngsters caused, and the laughter coming from their nook had to be the scariest sound in the house. By two o'clock, the men had been dumped unceremoniously outside with the rowdiest of the bunch and ordered to spend at least two hours tiring them out.

Christmas finery went on afterward, and they trooped out and loaded up the vehicles to get good seats in the pews for the stunning transformation from nephews and niece to shepherd and sheep. Closest he came to alone time was sitting beside Nora in church. Hardly counted. He couldn't very well interrupt the pastor's sermon to ask how his girlfriend was holding up in the face of an extra sixteen Vanderhoffs in her daily routine.

He clasped her hand between his with the excuse of warming her chilled skin. Her ring would sit just there, add a new texture to memorize when he touched her. He had to abandon his hold all too soon in favor of his two-year-old niece begging "up" with her chubby hands waving. Not for his lap—for Nora's. She snuggled the toddler close and played quiet games of naming and pointing and making faces. Tiny white shoes with gold buckles smacked his leg with every bouncy kick. Down the pew, Jilly whipped her phone out, snapping pictures and flashing him a thumbs-up.

Mama set out the fancy china for formal Christmas dinner in the dining room, the dishes ones she and Daddy'd gotten for their wedding forty-odd years back, after he'd come home from the service. Two tours in Vietnam, Army, maintenance corps, and on his first day back in Kansas he'd walked right into the grocers where Mama worked as a checkout girl and proposed. Down on one knee in front of God and everybody. Columnist even wrote it up for the local paper. For some anti-hippie screed about the importance of old-fashioned family values, sure, but every household in the county knew about Daddy's dedication and the torch he'd carried day in and day out the three years he'd been gone.

Well past nine before they got the dining room squared away, the church clothes traded for comfortable lounging gear, and the younger generation bedded down with a movie marathon in the family room. Closing the panel doors cut off their view of the parlor and the fireplace. The sooty bootprints from the hearth to the tree would be one of the last tasks of the night. Mama hauled out the stocking stuffer box, and Nora helped her load up the socks. More than fit across the mantel. A quilt stand got pressed into service for the runoff.

He planted himself in a seat and followed the proceedings from outside the flow. The mound of presents under the tree grew while the beer dwindled and the wine bottles emptied. Last-minute wrapping jobs went to Mama, and pristine presents came off the assembly line. Red-cheeked and laughing, his Nora, welcomed into the fold like a native. If he'd worked out the damn proposal plans faster, he could've been introducing her tonight at church as his wife-to-be. But every idea crowding his head came with a nagging suspicion attached. Not good enough. Not perfect. Not *Nora*.

She cocked her head toward him, and her wide smile dimmed beneath drawn brows. "What's wrong?" she mouthed.

Shit, now he'd gone and worried her.

Daddy wedged a hand under his arm and heaved him to his feet. "C'mon. Outside. Getting so's a man can't breathe in here without knocking somewhat over."

The cold air blasted his lungs. He stepped up to the porch rail. Stars winked through fuzzy halos of thin clouds.

Daddy smacked his hands down on the wood beside him and leaned out. “You gonna marry this girl, Robin?”

He slipped his hand in his pocket and brought out the ring pinched between his index and middle. “I aim to.”

Daddy’s low whistle cut a crisp note in the stillness. “Got that handled, too. Good man.”

“Not that good.” He folded his fingers tight, cupped the ring safe in his palm, and bounced his fist on the porch post. “I wanna ask her right. Unfurl a banner off the side of the barn. Fill the lobby at her work with balloons.” The first idea nixed—his luck, one of her coworkers would hit the panic button and he’d end up proposing from a jail cell while he explained about not being a bank robber. “Rent out the whole bowling alley for a fake company party and program the scoreboards to flash the question and nothing else.”

Daddy snorted. “Twenty years since the last time I gave you the talk on this porch. You swung outta that truck all scowls and grousing, and my heart thundered loud as the furnace kicking on. One chance, I told myself, to get the message through a mess of hormones and foolheadedness. Your mama wanted gentlemen for sons, and I wasn’t about to have any less in my house. S’pose you might’ve forgotten the finer points.”

“What?” The talk stuck in his head with the permanence of acid-etched metal. “I remember—her conversation, her laugh, her scent. Nora’s the one. I just need to get my head wrapped around this proposal, give her the proper scale. Something grand she’ll remember, so she’ll never wonder how much I love her.”

“Robin. Ain’t one big thing does that, son.” His voice gruff, hoarse from the cold, maybe, Daddy rubbed his wedding band. “It’s a lifetime of little ones. You show her every day, and she won’t forget. Take it from a man married forty-one years.”

The towering non-right-ness toppled. His nagging suspicions hadn’t let him settle on any one scheme because none would do. Elaborate plans wouldn’t make Nora any more or less his wife. She’d hate the secrecy. Other folks knowing before her, and he’d have to keep details from her. Go behind her back.

No.

Not even for a good cause. Sneaky behavior would put her on edge for no reason, and they’d worked hard together to create the security she needed. Trust and honesty trumped impressing her with flash and polish. Trust and honesty, every day of their lives.

"Thanks, Daddy."

"Mm-hmm." A hard squeeze and two pats graced his shoulders. "Time to get some sleep. Kids'll be up early clamoring to unwrap all those boxes."

Santa's cookies and milk had been half-consumed and the soot trail laid. The presents engulfed the base of the tree. His siblings and their spouses ambled up the stairs with Mama shooing them along.

Nora raised her cocoa mug and quirked a smile at him. "I should rinse this out. I'll just be a minute."

"I'll do it." He cupped his hands around hers and kissed her cheek. "Wait for me?"

"As long as you need me to," she whispered. "Same promise you made to me."

Christ. This woman. He took her mug and tiptoed into the kitchen. Chocolate residue rinsed clear, the mug claimed a spot on the drain board with the rest. Silence settled over the house, not even a rustle from the pile of sleeping children on the floor in the family room.

He threaded his way back through the dining room, circling the broad table with its extra leaves for fitting the whole family around. The arch framed Nora in the parlor between the brick fireplace and the red-and-gold bows and baubles on the tree. Back turned, she traced the letters on the newest stocking hanging from the mantel. The quilted green and white base matched his own, hanging alongside, but the bright red embroidery spelled out *Nora* in Mama's neat stitching.

Not a moment to themselves all day, not since the gentle alarm-clock kiss he'd given her eighteen hours gone. He dug in his pocket. The right moment, precious and perfect, and theirs alone. A lifetime of small gestures. Ring clutched in a thumb-and-forefinger grip, he stepped through the arch.

She smiled as she turned. "Did you get lost—" Her gaze dropped, and her voice trembled. "Rob."

"Nora." His lungs flat-out refused to suck in enough air. "Nora."

Words failed. All the pretty speeches blanked. He'd never choked so hard in a crisis, as time slowed and stopped and the whole world filled up with her. Honey brown hair fell in waves around her face. Head tilted, lips parting, eyes gleaming, she stood surrounded by the soft glow of white lights on the Christmas tree.

"Marry me." He raised the ring in offering, his arm operating on brilliant instinct instead of waiting for his head to catch up. His heart and soul would have to do. "I want to wake up beside you every morning and thank God for trusting me with such an amazing woman. I want to be a worthy partner to you. I want to be a man you can rely on, a man whose love you can believe in. Marry me, Nora Howard, and I promise you I will be faithful, and true, and yours, every day of my life."

She pressed her fingers to her mouth, her hands shaking, and tears streamed down her cheeks. But she bobbed her head in an unbroken cascade of nods, and his heartbeat started up again.

"Yes." Voice thick and sniffly, she reached out for him. "Yes, yes, you could ask me a thousand times, Robin Vanderhoff, and the answer for you will always be yes."

He swept her up toward the ceiling with a shout, swung her down, and kissed her. She tasted of peppermint and chocolate from the candy cane swizzle stick in her cocoa. The ring slipped onto her finger with a gentle nudge.

A thundering herd of little stocking feet thudded and slid through the house. "It's Santa! Santa's here!"

"That's not Santa." Hair sticking up every which way, Sara's nine-year-old made a gagging face, complete with sound effects. "That's just Uncle Rob kissing Aunt Nora."

"But he was here—look, presents! And the stockings are full, and the cookies are gone."

"Why's Aunt Nora crying? Didn't Santa bring her anything?"

"Footprints! Uncle Rob, did you see Santa come down the chimney? Did he say what he brought? Did you tell him I was an extra good boy this year?"

The children swarmed around them to reach the tree. He set Nora back on her feet with care and pressed their foreheads together. "Sorry, honey girl. I wanted to make this memorable."

"It is." She kissed his cheek. "You did." She smoothed the button flap at the top of his Henley. "How could I forget the night you kept your shirt on?"

Their laughter melted together beneath the din of excitable kids.

The hall lights snapped on above the stairs. "What in the devil is all the ruckus?" Daddy descended in a blue pajama set and slippers. "It's not even two in the morning. You kids get on back to bed."

Rob buried his face in her shoulder. "Lord, my siblings'll love this. How long you think I'll be making apologies?"

"*We'll* be making, you mean," she whispered. "Probably only the next sixty years."

Hell, he could live with that.

The rest of the family crowded downstairs in their Christmas pajamas. Big yawns and owlish glances made the top fashion statements.

"Sorry, everyone, it's my fault." Nora beat him to the apology by half a second. "I didn't know my way around the house, and I bumped into Santa by accident. He said he'd let me off with a warning, since I wasn't snooping and I'd been a good girl otherwise, and he gave me this ring." She held out her hand, red and white shimmering in the slender circle that called her his.

The congratulations came in a flurry of hugs and the occasional evil eye from sleep-deprived parents.

"I'll put the coffee on." Mama bundled her robe tighter and stepped around a wandering child. "We'll all have a nice nap after breakfast."

Someone tugged on his left hand, dragging him backward with determined, if minuscule, force. He squatted to niece-level.

"How come Santa didn't bring a ring for you, Uncle Rob?"

"He brought me your Aunt Nora." The sweet woman who fretted about making a good impression on his family. The sexy temptress who told him what she wanted and took her pleasure from him. The beautiful angel who shed tears as she promised to love him forever. "He just delivered her early, is all, 'cause I've been waiting a long time for her."

Jilly's oldest clamped her lips together and wriggled around, staring at the Christmas tree. "I waited a long time, too."

He gave her a gentle push toward the tree. If Jilly didn't want hers opening gifts yet, she could steer the munchkins away. He had Uncle Rob duties to uphold. "Santa told me your presents have polar bears on the tags. How 'bout you go find a good one?"

She scampered off, her beaming smile bearing a gap at the bottom where she'd lost her first tooth.

He unkinked his legs and leaned on Nora. Those naps couldn't come soon enough. "You sure you want to enlist in this motley outfit?"

She laid her hand on his shoulder. The light caught the ring's jeweled depths. "Santa brought one gift for the both of us this year. Do you think it's too greedy to ask for next year's?"

"Anything you want." Hell, she'd said yes. She could have a decade's worth of gifts if she liked.

"I want a shared gift next year, too." She cupped his jaw and turned him toward the tree, her ring smooth and cool on his skin. "Give me one of those, Rob."

Clustered in a loose half-circle, his nieces and nephews passed presents. Boxes rattled and shook as the chorus of pleas grew louder. His siblings pulled up chairs and slumped in them with half-lidded eyes.

Nora linked her hand in his and slipped them between their bodies. Her flat stomach rested under his palm. "Give me one of ours."

His Christmas wish granted, his Nora and the promise of a family of their own. The proposal couldn't have gone better. The chaos of Christmas morning surrounded them. Christ, he couldn't wait to see what the next year held.

"Whatever the lady wants." He hugged her close. "My calendar's full up with Nora Howard Vanderhoff."

Meet the Author

M.Q. Barber fell prey to Rob's infectious charm and old-fashioned manners a mite faster than Nora did, but he already had his sights set on his honey girl. Thankfully, the two of them let her tag along with good humor.

In *Her Shirtless Gentleman*, M.Q. aimed to recapture the giddy joy of young love for a pair worried they'd outgrown it. She hopes every nervous, insecure Nora finds the right Rob to tell her how amazing she is every day.

Keep in touch with the author on Goodreads, Facebook and Twitter by searching for M.Q. Barber. For monthly updates, sneak peeks, and exclusive short fiction, sign up for her author newsletter at http://www.mqbarber.com.

If you had fun playing with Rob and Nora, please take a minute and post a review online at Amazon, Goodreads, or wherever else you swap book recommendations. Nora could use the encouragement, and Rob loves anyone who puts a smile on her face.

Don't miss M. Q. Barber's compelling *USA Today* bestselling debut!

PLAYING THE GAME

Book #1, Neighborly Affection

She expects dinner with neighbors, but gets sex with a side of safewords.

Mechanical engineer Alice still drools over her sexy neighbors a year after she's moved in. She can't decide whether they're roommates or partners, but either way, they spark a wanton desire in her that has her imagination—and vibrator—working overtime.

Henry, director of everything around him, studies human nature and applies philosophies to his paintings as well as his relationships. Quirky, polite to a fault, and formal, he follows his own code of honor even when it means denying himself.

Flirtatious and playful, Jay needs stability, guidance, and to please others. His antics counterbalance Henry's stuffy ways while he brings a level of vulnerability and fun to everything the trio does.

BDSM play with the enigmatic artist and flirtatious joker across the hall allows Alice to put aside the linear thought processes that have kept her unsatisfied and distant with other lovers. She must dismiss her preconception of love, sacrificing her independence, if she's to find a permanent place in their beds and hearts.

CONTENT WARNING: Explicit sex, graphic language, BDSM, bondage, spanking, M/M/F ménage.

82,000 Words

Chapter 1

Three flights separated Alice's apartment from the ground floor, but she didn't notice a single step Friday morning. She raced the daylight, as if getting to work sooner would make it end sooner, too. Warp time to deposit her at the dinner with friends she'd anticipated for days. With Henry at the helm, dinner couldn't be less than divine.

She emerged from the stairwell with a growing grin for the man crossing the lobby with sketchbook in hand. A suit and tie, sans coat, though it wasn't eight yet and he didn't have an office to go to. Did he not own jeans?

"Morning, Henry."

"And a good morning to you, Alice. What a beautiful vision for the end of my walk."

She shook her head. He could charm a thief out of robbing him and call it common courtesy. "Out people-watching?"

"Yes, the sunrise first—the sky offered up lovely hues this morning—and then the early morning joggers. Exercise for them, and an exercise in the movement of light and shadow for me. Now it's time to see if Jay has slept through his alarm. Are you off to work, my dear?"

"Got it in one. What gave me away, the basic black pantsuit or the overloaded satchel?" She twirled, knowing he wouldn't take her flirtation as an invitation. Henry had whatever he had with Jay. *The safest sexy guys I know.*

"Simply the time of day and knowledge of your schedule," Henry demurred, his gaze flicking over her form. "Though you do look quite striking in basic black. Have you any plans for the evening?"

He managed to look innocent asking. As if he hadn't left a note on her door a week ago asking for the pleasure of her company.

She lowered her voice to a faux-secretive whisper. "Yeah, with my crazy neighbors. Can you believe this guy? He not only remembers the first anniversary of my move-in date, but he offers to cook dinner to celebrate."

"He sounds like quite the catch." He waggled his eyebrows. "The sort of gentleman who might also remember you often neglect to eat breakfast."

He held out a brown paper bag with a folded-over top.

"You got me breakfast?" She took the bag and peered inside. Apple fritter. Her mouth watered. "My favorite. Careful, or I'll start thinking you're in love with me."

"Oh? And if I declared my undying devotion?" He clasped his sketchpad against his chest. "Here in the lobby, at this very moment? I suppose I could get down on one knee."

She snorted and adopted an airy tone. "Don't be absurd. I insist you don't wrinkle your trousers for me, good sir. Why, it's entirely undignified." She broke off a piece of fritter and took a bite. *Yum.* "Besides, I dumped the last guy who tried that romance crap on me."

"I suppose that would make declaring my love inadvisable." He released a heavy, mocking sigh. "The fritter, however, is acceptable?"

"Delicious." She reached for another bite. "And real. Love's fake. The convenient excuse people give for making stupid decisions. I have a strict no-love policy."

"Ah. Is that why Jay and I haven't seen beaus knocking at your door in months?"

"It's not like I have a no-sex policy. I just keep things short. Simple. Well defined." She popped the fritter piece in her mouth. Chewed. Swallowed. "A couple of months, max. After that, you have to worry about moving in together. Awkward proposals about moving across the country to stay together. Pretty soon, you've been married for years and forgotten how to be your own person."

She wasn't going to end up in that situation and call it love. The word was a four-letter excuse, a chemical reaction tricking the brain into thinking it wanted something it didn't. The way Mom thought she wanted to watch Dad pop pills and forget they'd ever been a happy family. The way her college boyfriend had thought she'd finish her degree at a different school once he graduated.

"Not me," she said. "I avoid love altogether. Thanks for the pastry, though. That, I'm happy to accept."

"You're quite welcome, Alice. Have a lovely day. We'll see you at dinner."

"Seven sharp. I'll be there." She darted outside, waving over her shoulder.

Henry was a nice guy. A good friend. Definitely fuckable. So was his roommate. Boyfriend. Whatever Jay was. She sighed.

That chest. Mmm. Thank God for finding this apartment.

* * * *

Her old place had screamed slum in a shithole neighborhood waiting on urban revival. The charming atmosphere had kept her tense every night from subway stop to front door. She'd split the rent with three near strangers and squirreled money away.

Leases lurched from August to August in a college town like Boston, and moving day meant a mad scramble for scarce resources. Her roommate's quasi boyfriend coughed up his van with conditions. Fuck if she'd pay the blowjob fee for failing to get the van back on time and undamaged.

The hungry parking meter, though, sucked down quarter after quarter. The faster she got everything upstairs, the less money she'd spend. A few cars puttered past at school-zone speeds, and even fewer pedestrians meandered by on Saturday strolls.

A guy on a bike turned the corner down the block. He rode slow, lazy maybe, or cooling down after a workout.

She pulled open the van, its innards packed to the roof, and hoisted a box in both arms.

"Soonest started, soonest finished," she muttered, hustling toward her new home from the closest parking spot she'd found, about three buildings down.

The grinding *whirr* of backpedaling heralded the cyclist on the far side of the parked cars lining the street. She looked away, passed four more cars and glanced left. The cyclist had kept pace as she approached her door.

"Something I can help you with?"

"Looks the other way around to me." He hopped off the bike, hefted it over one arm and joined her on the sidewalk. "Moving in?"

She wasn't above ogling bike boy's tight shorts and the sweat-wicking shirt hugging his biceps. Telling a strange man where she lived and inviting him up, however, contradicted common sense no matter how much his body reminded her she hadn't gotten laid in months.

She yanked open the outer door and resettled the box as it rocked in her arms. Stepping into the mailbox vestibule, she fumbled for the keychain dangling from her belt loop.

"Here, let me."

Alice stepped back against the bank of mailboxes, about to go off on this arrogant ass who thought he'd follow her in and charm his way into feeling her up. Until he produced his own key and unlocked the inner door.

"We can prop that open, you know, so moving won't be such a hassle."

She envied his athletic grace as he balanced the bike over one shoulder and held the door.

"Thanks. That's, umm, I'll do that."

He nodded. She stared.

"Ladies first."

Oops. He'd been waiting on her.

"I mean, I can hold the door all day. I don't have any plans, and my muscles are totally up to it. I don't want you to doubt that, but eventually somebody's gonna need to open their mailbox."

"Sorry, I was…yeah. How about I go in now?" She hurried past, catching a whiff of clean male sweat. How far had he ridden this morning?

The stairs beckoned, back and to the right.

The door clicked closed, and footsteps on the stairs echoed her own. They followed her down the hallway toward her studio, where she'd left the door cracked. She pinned bike boy with an over-the-shoulder stare.

"I'm giving off stalker vibe, right? Sorry. I'm across the hall. Jay. I'd offer to shake hands, but, well, bike." He jostled the bike on his right shoulder. "And you've got—" He gestured at her with the other hand. "Whatever's in the box, so…"

"Alice," she said. "Ignore me, I'm paranoid. But I should get going. I have to finish moving before the van's owner decides I owe him an overage charge." She repressed a shudder. No way in hell was she paying the on-your-knees fees. "Nice meeting you, though."

"Of course." He grinned and winked. "It's always nice meeting me. People tell me that all the time."

He slipped past her toward the door on the other side of the hall and disappeared inside.

She used the box to push the door open wide. Cute guy, but full of himself. She wasn't looking right now anyway. No harm in *looking*, though, right?

She set the box in the center of the tiny space. One down, two dozen to go. Plus the furniture, though hers consisted of a futon, a battered trunk, and a floor lamp.

Leaving the door open, she tromped downstairs, pacing herself so she wouldn't run out of steam. At least moving out hadn't required navigating stairs. A search of the lobby floor turned up a cracked brick to prop the inner door.

Her stomach growled as she scooped another box from the van and made for the door. She bobbled the box against her left arm, stretching out her right hand. She hadn't found the handle yet when the door opened.

"Okay there, Alice? I thought we were gonna prop this puppy open." Jay, bikeless, still wore riding clothes.

Wait, we? He wanted to help? Either he was hard up or she looked like the most pathetic, desperate girl in town. Even friends demanded bribes to tote boxes. This guy had known her all of five minutes.

"Yeah, I haven't grabbed anything for this door yet. But you don't—I mean, I'm fine. I've got everything handled."

"Okay. Sure." He nodded. "You should get out of the sun. That fair skin's already pinking up."

She slid past him, her leg brushing his, her shoulder grazing his chest. They'd be neighbors for the next year at the least. Would this Jay be a nice guy or a creep? She crossed her fingers and hoped for the former.

"Thanks for holding the door."

He shrugged. "I was on my way out."

"Oh! Okay." God, she'd assumed he was offering to help. Fuck it. He hadn't seemed offended, and worrying would be a waste of time. "See you around."

"Yep, I'm sure you will. I'm hard to miss."

She shook her head, trying not to encourage his egotistical comedy antics, and climbed the stairs once more. The place mimicked a free gym with all the stair-mastering she could handle and then some.

She set the second box beside the first, two brown cubes in a bare white room. The August heat made the room stuffy. She unsnapped the latches on the windows and raised the lower panes. The view showcased the alley where a handful of residents paid exorbitant fees for unmetered parking, but the breeze satisfied.

A knock came from behind her, three firm raps, and an unfamiliar male voice followed.

"Alice?"

A man stood in her doorway. Mid-thirties, maybe a little older, neatly trimmed light brown hair, smartly dressed in dark gray slacks and a pale blue button-down shirt. Oddly out-of-place sandals.

"Can I help you?"

"My apologies. You must, of course, be Alice, quite as Jay described you. I'm Henry. I share the apartment across the hall with Jay. I thought I might introduce myself and invite you over for a snack. Lunch, if you'd prefer. Moving is draining work. I try to avoid it myself."

"What, moving or work?" *Wonder if this Henry knows he's living with a serial flirt.*

He raised an eyebrow. "Touche. Both, in fact. But you won't tempt me into a doorway discussion, neighbor. I insist we get acquainted properly over a meal."

He was without a doubt the most formal man she'd ever met. He wasn't even crossing the line of the door. Weird, but sweet. Timid? Courteous? Fuck. She didn't want a bad start with her neighbors.

"I'd love to, but I'm in the middle of the whole moving thing, and I need to get it done first. I have to return the van today."

"Oh? I don't see how that's a problem. Have you run into Jay? He was supposed to—"

"Stand aside, coming through!" Jay's voice rang through the hallway at full volume.

Henry stepped back.

"Really, Jay?" Henry wore a small smile as he shook his head.

Jay came through the door with two boxes piled in his arms and set them beside the others.

"You're not wearing a shirt," she blurted, too busy ogling his chest to censor herself.

He was well muscled, for sure. Firm. Lean and very, very firm. Willpower alone kept her eyes, but not her thoughts, above his waist.

"Yes, Jay, by all means, explain how you lost your shirt between here and the curb. I'm dying to know, and I'd wager our new neighbor is as well."

Henry returned to the doorway, standing with ridiculously perfect posture. Would asking if he'd taken ballet be rude?

Jay flashed her a smile. "Wadded up as a doorstop." He turned toward Henry. "We had one stop for two doors, so—you know how much I love math. Back in a minute with more. Shouldn't you be putting lunch on the table? I'm absolutely killing this move. Forty-five minutes, an hour, tops."

He disappeared before Alice wrapped her head around the idea.

She scurried to the door and popped her head out. No dice.

"Wait, he's—I should—I can move my stuff myself."

"Of course you can."

Wow. She gripped the doorframe as Henry spoke inches from her ear. His smooth voice made her want to drink it in.

"You appear quite fit. But you'll remove a source of ridiculous male pride if you don't allow Jay to complete the lion's share of the task. Did you pack the vehicle yourself?"

She laughed, stepping back to put space between them.

"If you knew my old roommates, you wouldn't have to ask. I woke up at eight to load the van, and at that hour, on a Saturday? They have three states: asleep, hungover or still drunk. Today I had two sleepers and one angry hangover victim telling me to can the noise."

"Not one lifted a finger?"

She shook her head. After two years with her roommates, she'd probably interacted with them less than she had with her new neighbors in the first twenty minutes.

"Well, then, you see? You've already accomplished more than half of the work. Jay will simply do the rest."

"He doesn't even know me. I should—"

"Nonsense." Henry gestured her into the hall. "You've worked all morning. You ought to sit down and have a drink. Water? Lemonade? Iced tea?"

She glanced toward the staircase and then in the other direction, past his welcoming arm. She didn't know this guy, not either of these guys, and she was going to saunter into their apartment like some horror-movie idiot opening the basement door?

"I can bring the food to you, if you prefer. I would hate for our new neighbor to feel herself a fly walking into my parlor."

"Why, are you a spider?" She winced at the unintentional flirtation in her tone.

"I wouldn't think so, no, but then wouldn't I tell you the same thing if I were?" He raised an eyebrow. His lips twitched.

"You've got the charming part down well enough."

It *was* nearly lunchtime. She didn't want to carry boxes all afternoon. Was it too damsel-in-distress to give the job to a cute neighbor? It wasn't as if she'd coerced him. She hadn't been in distress or pretended to be. Jay was thoughtful, or something.

She narrowed her eyes at Henry. "I guess I'll have to trust this isn't a trap and you guys don't kill undesirable neighbors on their first day in the building."

"Oh, no, not the first day. We prefer to let them settle in first. Today, you're perfectly safe. Though whoever called you undesirable was quite mistaken." He frowned and waved a hand. "I apologize for how such a statement could be misconstrued. It appears Jay's habits are rubbing off on me."

Considering her ex-roommates' habits, neighbors with a predilection for charm held incomparable appeal. Especially if they were single.

"He does seem to be a flirt," she agreed.

"When he wants to be," Henry said. "But now we've been standing in the doorway entirely too long, and I haven't—"

"Seriously?" Jay's voice boomed from the stairs. "I'm back with two more boxes—told you I was killing it—and you haven't gotten Alice a drink? You're slipping, Henry. She might die of thirst."

Alice stepped into the hall, following Henry out of Jay's way. "I'm not dying of thirst. But if you're determined to show off your macho skills, I'll go have that lemonade. I've never played Southern belle before. I think I need a veranda and a fan."

"An excellent suggestion." Henry's arm moved as though he intended to sweep it against her back and carry her along with him, but stopped short.

She itched with the desire to lean back and find out how his touch felt.

"Jay, when you've finished, join us for lunch on the roof deck."

"Aye-aye, Cap'n." Jay winked at Alice, lowering his voice to a faux-whisper as he approached her door. "Consider it payment for moving the boxes. Keep Henry company while he waxes melodic about lettuce or something. Please. You'll be doing me a favor."

She glanced at Henry's expression, a sort of resigned fondness, as though Jay had said something expected. Hiding her smile, she matched Jay's tone. "What an astonishing coincidence. He said the same thing about you when he asked me to please find enough boxes to occupy you all afternoon."

Jay's face blanked for a moment before he laughed. He kept laughing, deposited the boxes beside the others and bent over with his hands on his knees, whooping for breath.

"It wasn't that funny," Alice muttered, but Henry, too, seemed to struggle not to chuckle.

Jay straightened. "Five minutes and she's got your number, Henry. You better watch out, or she'll have all of your secrets out of you before lunch is served."

She smiled the small, cautious smile of the unsure. She'd definitely missed the joke here.

Henry spoke up beside her, "Mmm. I see the two of you will be dangerous together. Jay, to the boxes. Alice, this way, please."

CPSIA information can be obtained
at www.ICGtesting.com
Printed in the USA
LVOW12s1503070916
503614LV00001B/164/P

9 781601 835468